PARTNERS

GERRI HILL

Bella
BOOKS
2008

About the Author

Gerri Hill has thirteen published works, including 2007 GCLS winners *Behind the Pine Curtain* and *The Killing Room*, as well as GCLS finalist *Hunter's Way* and Lambda finalist *In the Name of the Father*. She began writing lesbian romance as a way to amuse herself while snowed in one winter in the mountains of Colorado, and hasn't looked back. Her first published work came in 2000 with *One Summer Night*. Hill's love of nature and of being outdoors usually makes its way into her stories, as her characters often find themselves in beautiful natural settings. When she isn't writing, Hill and her longtime partner, Diane, can be found at their home in East Texas, where their vegetable garden, orchard and five acres of woods keep them busy. They share their lives with two Australian shepherds, and an assortment of furry felines. For more, see her Web site: www.gerrihill.com

Dedication

To Diane...who reminds me daily of the true meaning of the word *partner*. "Thank you" can't possibly express my heartfelt gratitude for your patience and understanding while I peck away at the keyboard, day after day. I love you dearly...

Acknowledgement

Many thanks to Judy Underwood for her encouragement to continue the story of these wonderful characters. As always, I appreciate your help. Also, to the many, many fans of Tori and Sam, and now Casey O'Connor, thank you for embracing them and letting me know they're your all-time favorites! I hope you enjoy *Partners* as much as *Hunter's Way* and the go-between, *In the Name of the Father*. It will be hard to say good-bye to these ladies…

Chapter One

"O'Connor, back here."

Casey followed the sound of Tori Hunter's voice, nodding at one of the new crime lab technicians who was dusting for prints near the phone. Whereas the apartment was neat and orderly, the bedroom was in shambles. She stopped in the doorway, finding Tori squatting beside the bed, listening to Mac describe the scene. The bed was a bloody mess.

"*Jesus*."

Tori looked up, then motioned Casey closer. "Spencer already took the body."

"Hell of a lot of blood."

"Her throat was cut." Tori stood, pointing. "She was tied to the bed. Rita didn't think there was sexual trauma."

"But we found semen on the sheets and on the legs of the victim," Mac said. "I've already sent it back to the lab. Spencer will do a rape kit, but it kinda looks like our guy just left a deposit on the body."

"Who is she?" Casey asked. She was used to working with live victims, not dead. She still wasn't comfortable referring to the victim as a *body*.

"Sikes is with the apartment manager now, but the ID in her purse is Dana Burrows. College student. UT Dallas."

"There didn't appear to be forced entry," Casey stated.

"Boyfriend?"

Tori shrugged. "Always possible. I sent a couple of the uniforms around to the neighbors to see if anyone knew her. But it's nearly ten. I suppose most have already headed to work."

"Who found her?"

"The manager. He said he got a call from a friend of hers. She was supposed to meet for a study session last night and didn't show. After not being able to reach her on her cell or by e-mail, she called the manager. He only remembers her name as Julie. He didn't get a last name."

"Okay. Well, I'll start at the university. Want me to take Sikes along?"

"No. I need John here. We'll need to locate the family. I'll have him interview them."

Casey nodded. She'd learned it was something Tori was not comfortable with, notifying families. Sikes, on the other hand, was good at it. His good looks and charm helped portray genuine regret and compassion, and most believed him when he said the police department would have the killer behind bars sooner rather than later.

Tori went back into the living room with Casey, motioning with her hand. "Nothing looks disturbed in here," she said.

"Maybe he had a key and came inside while she was asleep," Casey suggested.

"Possible. And if it was a boyfriend, having a key is probable."

"Well, let me go see what I can dig up at the university. I'll be in touch."

Tori stopped her. "Come by for dinner?"

Casey raised her eyebrows.

"Judging by what was on the counter this morning, Sam is making chicken spaghetti."

Casey grinned. "My favorite. I'll bring the wine."

Chapter Two

"Look, I understand the privacy rules. Really, I do. I just need some information."

"Detective O'Connor, I can't give you anything other than published directory information," the registrar said for the fourth time.

"We can subpoena the information," Casey threatened, watching as the older woman's eyebrows shot up over her black-rimmed glasses.

"Then please do so. It would make it so much easier on me."

Casey leaned forward. "This girl was brutally murdered. A student of yours. All I'm asking for is a little help. If I could find someone who knew her, someone who took a class with her, that's all I need." She gave what she hoped was a charming smile, one the registrar couldn't resist.

Finally, she saw a crack in the professional mask. "Listen, why don't you wait in the hallway? I'll ask around. Maybe I can find someone who knew her."

"I appreciate this, Mrs. Wheat. Thank you."

"Don't thank me yet, Detective. I haven't given you anything."

Casey nodded, then left with only a slight bow in her direction. She hated begging for information. And they would most likely subpoena the girl's records anyway, but leads ran cold if left too long.

She sat down on one of the hard-backed chairs and folded one leg over the other, resting it on her knee as she watched students walk by. They all looked so young, making her feel much older than her thirty-three years. She wondered if any of these students may have known Dana, may have passed her on the way to class, may have even sat beside her in class. She wondered if the word had spread yet that one of their own had been killed—ruthlessly murdered.

It had only been a few months since she'd transferred to Homicide from Special Victims, and she still wasn't used to it. But as Tori had told her, you never get used to it. And she hoped she didn't. She never wanted to become accustomed to murder. But it was the main reason she'd left Special Victims. She'd become nearly immune to rape, to sexual assault. To the tears. And it had become exhausting trying to convince her victims to testify in court, to face their attackers, when all they wanted was to forget. So when Lieutenant Malone had offered her a spot on the team, she'd accepted after only a little prodding from Tori. After the St. Mary's fiasco and Father Michael's murder, they'd remained in touch, with Tori and Sam inviting her often to dinner or out to the boat for a weekend of fishing. They'd become close. In fact, so close, she'd call Tori her best friend.

The soft buzzing of her cell phone put an end to her thoughts and she opened it, seeing *Hunter* displayed in bold.

"O'Connor," she answered.

"We have the name of the boyfriend. He's a student there. Night classes. Are you having any luck?"

She shook her head. "None. The registrar doesn't want to break FERPA."

"What the hell is FERPA?"

"Privacy act that governs higher education. I tried to sweet-talk her. I'm waiting while she sees if there is something she *can* give me."

"Okay. Don't waste too much time. We're on our way to pick up the boyfriend."

"You got in touch with the family?"

"Yeah. Sikes did. They live in Arlington. And the boyfriend is practically a part of their family. They said no way could he have done this."

"They always say that."

"We also found out who the Julie was who called the manager. Julie Watts, her best friend. She's not answering her cell. Since you're there, maybe you could try to get in touch with her. She lives on campus."

"Yeah, okay." Casey jotted down the number Tori gave her then folded her phone and slipped it into the leather pouch clipped to her belt. She felt eyes on her as students passed by and she consciously moved her holster to the back and out of sight. Fall, winter, even spring, she could wear a jacket to hide her weapon. But summer? There wasn't a lot you could do, and she—like Tori—refused to wear a sports jacket with her jeans when it was a hundred degrees out.

"Detective O'Connor?"

She turned, nodding at a young girl who approached.

"Mrs. Wheat asked me to give you this," she said quietly, handing over a piece of paper.

"Thank you. Tell her I appreciate it."

She turned away and unfolded the paper. *The Debate Club.* Under that was written a name and room number. She walked down the hallway, stopping the first student who looked her way.

"Excuse me. Can you tell me where I can find Dr. Arness? She's with the debate club."

"She's in the business building."

Casey was about to ask where she could find that building when the student hurried off. The campus wasn't that big. Surely she could find it.

"Next block," Sikes said, then held on as Tori sped around a corner. "I swear, it's a miracle you haven't killed us yet with the way you drive."

"I get us there, don't I?"

"Oh, yeah. You've just taken years off my life, that's all."

Tori grinned as she slammed on her brakes, tossing Sikes forward.

"Jesus Christ, Hunter!"

"The light was yellow."

"You barely stop at red lights, much less yellow."

"Cops aren't above the law." She glanced in the rearview mirror, thankful they didn't get hit. No one stopped at yellow lights. As soon as it turned green, she sped through the intersection, tossing John back against the seat.

"You're such a guy," he muttered as he adjusted his seatbelt. "A *teenage* guy."

"Glass Sporting Goods, there it is."

"You think the family already called him?"

"You asked them not to, right?"

"Doesn't mean they didn't."

"And most likely they did."

There were only a few customers inside, but at one of the registers, a group was gathered, all wearing nametags. She looked at Sikes. "They called him." She walked over to the group, holding up her badge. "We're looking for Brian Helms. This is Detective Sikes, I'm Detective Hunter. Is he around?"

After only a slight hesitation, one of the young girls came forward. "No, he left. Dana's mother called. We just can't believe it. Brian was so distraught."

"Do you know where he went?"

"He went to their house, I guess."

"The parents' house?"

"Yes."

Tori sighed. "Wonderful," she muttered.

Chapter Three

Tori slipped quietly into the apartment, smiling when she heard Sam singing from the kitchen. She sniffed. Chicken spaghetti it was. She stood in the doorway, watching Sam as she poured her concoction into a baking dish.

"I know you're there," Sam murmured without turning around.

"Do you now?"

"Yes. So don't try to be sneaky."

"Need some help?"

"Yes, please."

Tori took the pan, holding it as Sam scooped the last of it into the baking dish. She leaned closer, placing a light kiss on Sam's lips.

Sam smiled, then took the pan from Tori and placed it in the sink before wrapping her arms around Tori's shoulders. "I missed you today."

Tori sighed, letting Sam hold her. "Yeah, me too. It was a rough day."

"I heard, sweetheart."

Tori pulled away slightly. "Feel like a shower?"

"Sure. But we'll need to make it quick."

"How so?"

Sam led Tori into their bedroom. "Because being the good

detective that you are, you knew we were having chicken spaghetti tonight."

"And?"

Sam pulled Tori's shirt off, her hands going to her breasts immediately. "And that means you invited Casey to dinner."

Tori closed her eyes as Sam's mouth closed over her nipple. "Do you mind?"

"Of course not." Sam left her breast, finding her lips instead, smiling against them. "Like I said, we'll just have to be quick." She pulled away, slipping out of her shirt and dropping it on the floor next to Tori's. But she stopped Tori's hands when she reached for her. "Meet you in the shower."

Tori kicked off her boots and jeans, following Sam into the bathroom. The water was already running and she opened the glass door, her breath catching like it always did when she saw Sam this way—naked, her skin glistening from the water, mist much like a halo surrounding her. She closed the door behind her, her eyes sliding shut as Sam moved into her arms.

"I love you," Sam whispered against her mouth.

Tori deepened the kiss, moaning as Sam's tongue found its way inside. She slid her hands lower, cupping Sam, holding her firmly against her. Again, it amazed her, the passion they had for one another. No matter how many times they touched, it was never enough. No matter how many times they made love, each time was more powerful than the one before. So she gave in to that passion, moving Sam against the wall, pressing her thigh between Sam's legs.

Sam's hands moved at will across her body, boldly cupping her breasts, her fingers teasing her nipples into hard peaks.

"I love you," Tori murmured.

Sam met her eyes, nodding slightly before lowering her head and capturing a wet nipple in her mouth. Sam's teeth raked against it, causing Tori to flinch before Sam's lips claimed it, sucking it hard into her mouth.

No, she would never tire of this. She leaned her head back, letting Sam have her way. And she did, turning them, pinning Tori against the wall, her thigh nudging her legs apart. Tori's breath came fast as Sam moved her hand between them, slipping into her wetness. She spread her legs, her eyes closing as Sam thrust into her. She let herself go, her hips moving wildly against Sam's hand, her breast aching as Sam's mouth devoured her, her nipple swelling as Sam suckled it. She jerked as Sam's thumb found her clit, moving in circles as her fingers continued their penetration.

Her orgasm hit then, suddenly, without warning. Her hips bucked, her mind exploding as she screamed out in pleasure, the sound echoing around them. Sam pulled her close, moving them into the water, letting the warm stream wash over them.

"God, I love doing that to you," Sam whispered.

Tori opened her eyes, letting Sam brush the water from her face. She smiled. "How is it we never get around to the soap during our showers?"

Sam took her hand and brought it between her legs. Tori's fingers touched her wetness. "Because something always distracts us," she breathed as Tori's fingers filled her. "Soap can come later."

"I heard a rumor today," Sam said as she filled their wineglasses. "From a good source."

"Rumor about what?" Casey asked.

"About you."

"Me?"

"Leslie Tucker from Assault is transferring to Homicide."

"And?"

Sam grinned. "New partner."

"Partner? For me?"

"About time," Tori said. "I can't believe Malone has let it go this long."

"Man, I hate getting new partners." Casey took her wineglass. "Thanks."

"I hear she's nice," Sam said.

"Why is she transferring?"

9

"She's from Fort Worth. She worked homicide there for six years, I think. She's only been with us for nine months."

Casey looked at Tori. "Did you know?"

"No. Malone hasn't said a word to me. But it'll be good to have your own partner. You won't have to tag around with me and Sikes. Or worse, Donaldson and Walker."

Casey reached for the plate Sam handed her, piled high with chicken spaghetti. "Thanks, Sam."

"I wouldn't worry too much. I've heard good things about her."

"How old is she?"

Sam laughed. "What? You afraid she's older than you and is going to boss you around?"

"Well, it's not like I have a lot of experience in Homicide. And if she's got six years, yeah, she's going to boss me around."

"I think she's our age, so I doubt she's going to be a hard ass."

"Besides, you have seniority," Tori said, taking her own plate from Sam. "She should defer to you."

"Seniority? I've been with you guys for four months." She took a bite of the spaghetti and moaned. "God, Sam, this is so good."

"Thank you."

"And you're right. It will be good to have a partner. Today, for instance, Tori had me running all over campus. And I didn't learn a whole lot in the process."

"And you're sure the boyfriend didn't do it?" Sam asked Tori.

"Yeah. He was beside himself. I don't think anyone is that good of an actor." Tori twisted spaghetti on her fork, then paused. "Besides, he volunteered his DNA."

"It's scary to think it was just random," Casey said. "Because random means no motive."

"And no motive means he could easily do it again," Sam said.

"Maybe we'll get lucky," Tori said. "Mac might get a hit in CODIS."

Chapter Four

"O'Connor? A word," Malone called from his office.

Casey glanced at Tori. "This is it."

"What?" Sikes asked. "You in trouble?"

"Sam heard we're getting a new team member."

Casey stood, shoving her chair back. "I get a partner."

"Ah. Well, I hope he's cool."

"She," Tori corrected.

"She? Well, I hope she's straight," John said with a laugh. "And cute," he added.

"I just hope we like her," Casey murmured as she went into Lieutenant Malone's office. "Yes, sir, you need to see me?"

"Sit, Casey," he said, motioning to his guest chairs.

"Is everything all right, Lieutenant?"

He rubbed his bald head, and she could see perspiration glistening on his skin. She sat opposite him, waiting.

"Fine, O'Connor. In fact, I have some good news."

"Really?"

"Yes. You finally get your own team."

She raised her eyebrows but said nothing.

"You're getting a new partner," he said. He opened a file on his desk, reading. "Leslie Tucker. She's transferring in from Assault."

"I see. You know, I worked in Assault for a few years before

Special Victims. I don't recognize the name."

"She's been there less than a year. Comes from Fort Worth Homicide. Has an impeccable record. I think you'll like her."

Casey tapped her fingers nervously on her jeans, then stood. "You know, I've never had a female partner before. Are you sure? I mean, if we're doing partners, me and Tori, we get along really well," she said. "Maybe you could give the new partner to Sikes."

Malone laughed. "No way. Sikes can't handle working with a pretty face. Besides, I like Sam too much."

"What does Sam have to do with it?"

"Well, you and Tori," Malone said, shifting uncomfortably in his chair. "You're together all the time, both...well, you know. Anything could happen."

Casey laughed. "Are you suggesting Hunter and I might become involved?"

"It's a possibility."

"No, no. Definitely not." She sat down again. "It's like, you know, every relationship needs a yin and yang, you know what I mean? And Tori and I, well, we're both pretty much yangs, if you get my drift."

Malone blushed and looked away. "Well, yang or not, I'm not pairing you two. In case you're not aware, Hunter's history with partners is legendary. And we've finally got one big happy family. Well, ever since Sam came aboard. So when Tori's happy, the squad is happy. And she and Sikes, as surprising as it is, are working out, so I don't want to upset the applecart. You get the new partner, O'Connor."

"What if I don't like her?"

"She seems nice, about your age. She put her time in. Why wouldn't you like her?"

Casey shrugged. "Why'd she leave Fort Worth?"

"Her fiancé works in Dallas and they live here. She got tired of the commute."

Fiancé? Great. We'll get to plan a wedding, she thought with dismay. "When is she coming on board?" she asked instead.

"Today."

"Didn't want to give me much advance warning, huh?"

"You'll be fine, O'Connor. Like I said, she seemed real nice."

Casey nodded. "Okay. So you got something new for us? Or you want us to work with Tori and Sikes on their college student?"

"Work with Hunter and Sikes. You've started with it. Donaldson and Walker just wrapped up their case so I gave them the grandmother who was found this morning."

"What grandmother?"

"Found in her car. Shot once in the head."

"Damn."

"Yeah. Crazy times we live in." He looked out the windows in his office, nodding. "Perfect timing."

She followed his gaze, an eyebrow arching in surprise. *This* was her new partner? Dark hair, nicely layered, reaching nearly to her shoulders framed a tanned, smooth face with only a hint of makeup. Oh, damn. If she was being paired with a straight woman, at least she could have been a dog. Not this…this *beauty* walking through their squad room. How fair was that?

But Malone was standing, moving to his doorway. "Detective Tucker? In here." He stepped aside, motioning for her to enter.

Casey stood, offering her hand politely. "I'm Casey O'Connor. The lieutenant was just filling me in."

"Leslie Tucker, nice to meet you." She slipped an errant strand of hair behind her ears, her smile confident, showing no hint of nervousness. "I hope you don't mind, but I asked around about you. You still have friends over at Assault."

"I don't mind as long as they lied to you," Casey said with a grin, noting the amused expression in the woman's dark eyes.

"They had very nice things to say about you. Were they lying?"

"Well, since we'll be working together, I guess you'll find out sooner or later."

Malone was the one who gave a nervous laugh as he looked from one to the other. "I'm sure you'll—"

"Hey, sorry to interrupt," Tori said as she stuck her head in the door. "Mac called. They've got results. He had a hit in CODIS."

"A name?" Casey asked.

"He didn't go into it. We were about to walk over. You want to come?" Then she glanced at Malone. "Sorry, Lieutenant. I'm assuming she's still working the case with us."

"Yeah. And this is Detective Tucker."

"Leslie," she said, offering her hand to Tori.

"Tori Hunter. Welcome aboard." Tori stepped back out of the doorway. "Let's walk over. Have you met Mac and his team before?"

"I know who he is, yes. One of his guys, Emerson, was the one who worked with Assault the most."

Casey followed Leslie Tucker out of Malone's office, then stopped and turned back with a grin. "Dang, Lieutenant, couldn't find someone old and frumpy I guess?"

"I was about to warn Sikes to keep his hands and eyes off her. Do I need to warn you as well?"

"No, no. I learned a long time ago never to mess with straight women. Don't worry. I won't pull a Tori and Sam on you."

Leslie sat around the small table with the others, her gaze moving over them one by one. John Sikes, ladies' man and resident pretty boy. She'd been warned about getting too friendly with him. He was always looking for a date, they said. And Tori Hunter, she'd heard all the horror stories from pushing her partner out a two story window to punching out a lieutenant. But she seemed pleasant enough. Of course, she'd heard those other rumors too, about her affair with Samantha Kennedy. Samantha, like Casey O'Connor, had started out in Assault. The guys there had been only too happy to share what they knew about both women. She let her eyes drift to Casey, her new partner. She was tall and thin, her dark blond hair an unruly mess, as if the wind had blown it dry this morning. Everyone she asked had practically the same thing to say about her. She was a good person who genuinely cared about her job. She was friendly and likable and very popular on the force. All-around good gal, to which Leslie was thankful. She'd never been partnered with another woman. How hard would it be if it ended up being someone like Tori Hunter? She was still staring when Casey turned, catching her eye. She smiled, then looked away as Mac came into the room.

"Sorry to keep you waiting. I wanted to pull the post Jackson did on this previous victim."

"What previous victim?" Tori asked.

"The DNA hit matches a crime scene about three months ago." He looked at his notes. "Donaldson and Walker had the case. The girl was found in her apartment. Cause of death was strangulation. Her throat was cut postmortem."

"Raped?" Casey asked.

"No. Just like your vic, tied to the bed. Semen was found on the sheets and on the victim's legs. That's it."

"And Donaldson and Walker had the case?" Tori stood, pacing behind their chairs. "Goddamn."

"Don't overreact, Hunter," Sikes said. "Read the file first."

Leslie watched them, wondering if she was about to get a Tori Hunter moment. She looked across the table at O'Connor with eyebrows raised, but Casey only gave her a *tell you later* look.

"We're running all the prints now," Mac continued. "No hits in AFIS from the first crime scene, but we might be able to match prints from both scenes. Not that it's going to help you much with IDing our guy."

"Okay. Did Spencer find anything on her post of our vic?"

"Tox is not back. COD was a severed carotid artery." He looked up from his notes. "Of course, we already knew that. No trace. There was an unusual fiber that didn't appear to match anything in the bedroom. My guys are trying to find the origin on that."

Leslie listened, curious about the case she was being thrust into. She'd hoped to start fresh, not in the middle. Of course, it would help if she'd at least had the opportunity to read the file. As it was, she had no clue as to what case they were working.

15

"You want me and Tucker to pull Donaldson's file and go over it?"

Leslie was surprised when Tori flashed a smile at Casey. "What? You afraid for me to do it?"

"No sense in someone getting shot, that's all."

She was even more surprised when Tori Hunter laughed.

"Yeah, that's probably a good idea, O'Connor. Besides, she needs to get up to speed on our case," Tori said, tossing a glance her way. "Fill Malone in. Don't just pull the file."

Casey stood and grinned. "Why? You'd just pull it."

"Yeah, but I don't have any qualms about shooting Donaldson. You might."

"Okay. We'll meet you back there." Casey looked at her and motioned to the door. "I'll fill you in on the way over."

Leslie stood, not sure what to say, so she said nothing, and just followed O'Connor out the door. Despite what she'd heard about Tori Hunter having mellowed in the last couple years, she never heard anything about her having a sense of humor.

"Our victim is Dana Burrows," Casey said when they walked outside. "She was found in her apartment. No forced entry."

"Wait." Leslie stopped Casey with a light touch on her arm. "Why was Hunter upset about Donaldson?"

"Bad blood between them. A few years ago, there was a serial killer. Turns out the first victim was a case Donaldson and his partner had. Transvestite. They hardly worked the case, turned up no leads and let it go as a cold case. When Tori found the link between that case and her serial killer, she went ballistic. She refuses to work with him. She doesn't trust him."

"What about you? Is he a good cop?"

"From what I hear, yeah. He was fairly new at the time, paired with an old guy who couldn't get past the transvestite thing. And well, there was some personal stuff, but I don't think Donaldson had a whole lot of say on the case."

They continued walking and Leslie was surprised at how close the new crime lab was to their squad room. Much more convenient than driving downtown to the old building. "Okay, how do you normally do this? I've never worked a case where there were four detectives on it. I'm assuming Hunter is the lead?"

"We don't normally have four, no. But I've been here less than six months and haven't had a partner, so Malone has had me tagging along with Hunter and Sikes, learning the ropes."

"You were Special Victims, right?"

"Yeah."

"How was that?"

"Sucked. I used to think it was better than Homicide because at least my victims were still alive. But it takes a lot out of you, seeing the despair in their faces, listening to their agony, knowing some of them wished they weren't still alive."

"How'd you end up here?"

"I worked a case with Hunter. Father Michael from St. Mary's. They were going back and forth as to whether he was a victim of sexual assault or just plain murder."

"Yeah, I remember that one."

"Well, we hit it off. Stayed friends. She and Sam are great." Casey paused. "Samantha Kennedy. She's with CIU now."

"I've heard of her. She was with Assault before."

"That's right. I suppose you would have heard her name. Anyway, Malone had a spot open so I requested the transfer after a bit of prodding from Hunter." She smiled. "It just took a little while to get a partner."

"Well, I'm happy to be here. Not that Assault was bad or anything, but after six years in Homicide, Assault seems a little tame."

"Yes, I'm finding that out." Casey held the door open and Leslie preceded her inside.

"What will you tell Malone about Donaldson's case?"

"You mean, what will *we* tell him?"

"Throwing me to the wolves right away, are you?"

"No. But I've never had to do this before. If it was me and another detective was going over my case, I'd be pissed as hell. But I've learned that Malone is easy to talk to. He doesn't play

17

games. Everything is out in the open."

They walked into the squad room, finding it empty. Casey went purposefully to Malone's office, motioning for her to follow.

"You didn't get to meet Donaldson and Walker, right?"

"No. But their desks are over there, right?" she asked, pointing to the far wall. "I saw them."

"Yeah." Casey tapped on the doorframe with her knuckles. "Lieutenant? Got a minute?"

"Sure, O'Connor. What's up?" He looked past Casey and smiled at her. "Need to break up the partnership already?"

Leslie shook her head, then looked at Casey, hoping she would take the lead. She did.

"Got some news from Mac. The DNA hit on the semen matches a case from about three months ago."

"That's great, O'Connor. But why the long face?"

"Cold case," she said.

"I wouldn't call a three-month-old case a cold case."

"Donaldson and Walker had the case. No leads."

"Jesus," he muttered. "And I guess Hunter flipped out over that one."

"Yes, sir."

"And you want to pull the file and take a look?"

"If we can, yes."

"May I ask why Hunter is not the one in here demanding the file?"

Casey grinned. "I was afraid she might shoot Donaldson."

He laughed and Leslie was surprised at the amount of levity in the group. First Hunter teasing with O'Connor, now the lieutenant. This was something she wasn't used to. Not at Assault and certainly not in Fort Worth.

"Okay, pull the file. Do what you need to do. I'll let Donaldson know what's going on."

"Thank you, Lieutenant." Casey took her arm and led her back into the squad room. "That wasn't so hard, was it?"

Chapter Five

Leslie unlocked the door to their apartment and went inside, hearing the TV blaring a baseball game. She sighed. Just once she'd like to come home without there being a game on, without ESPN on, or without one of Michael's buddies over competing in a video game. Just once.

"I'm home," she called as she walked into the empty living room and on to their bedroom. She paused at the door to the spare room, knocking loudly. "I'm home," she said again.

The volume was muted and a door flung open as Michael rushed out into the hallway and gave her a bear hug, picking her up and twirling her around.

"And how was your first day on the job?"

She laughed. "Please put me down." He did. "It was fine. I came aboard in the middle of a case, so I'm kinda lost." She leaned closer for a kiss. "And the neighbors hate you. You can practically hear the TV in the parking lot."

"Sorry. Got carried away." He turned to go back to his game, then stopped. "Plans for dinner?" he asked.

"No."

"Good. Jeff has invited us up for pizza. We've got a friendly wager on the Rangers game. You know what a big Yankees fan he is."

"Pizza, huh? Well, you know what, why don't you go without

19

me? I've got a case file to read through."

"You don't mind?"

"No, of course not."

A part of her knew she *should* mind, of course. Jeff was his best friend. He also lived one floor above them. And on the third floor lived Miles and Russell. The four of them had been buddies since college. The problem was, they all thought they were *still* in college. At least Jeff dated occasionally. Miles and Russell never dated. But they had season tickets to every professional sports team in the Metroplex. And more times than not, Jeff and Michael were their dates.

She kept thinking it would change. When they started dating seriously, she thought Michael would stop spending so much time with them. Then, when they moved in together, she assumed he would stay home more. She now knew even if they got married, it wouldn't change. Not unless they moved into a house in a remote neighborhood. And so far Michael had balked at that suggestion.

And she, in turn, balked at setting a wedding date.

Casey sat on her deck overlooking White Rock Lake. She'd traded her water bottle for a glass of wine, which had turned into two. It was the deck. She found she could sit out here for hours, just staring at the water, her mind drifting. Even though it was nearly September and the days were still as hot as mid-summer, the evenings turned cooler, chasing the humidity away, hinting at what fall would feel like.

She'd only lived here six months, but it felt like home. The lake was small and surrounded by the city, but it was as peaceful as you could get within the city limits. And it was convenient. Tori and Sam lived just on the other side of the lake, making it hard for her to say no when Sam invited her for dinner. Which was often.

She smiled and sipped her wine, thinking how much her life had changed since she'd met Tori. As she'd told Tori once, she had a lot of friends, a lot of buddies on the force who she could grab a beer with or a quick dinner. But she didn't have a really close friend, and she certainly didn't have a lover to come home to every night. Well, one of those things had changed. Tori had become that close friend she'd craved. They escaped often for a beer after work, just to talk, just to share things. Sam didn't mind their friendship. In fact, she encouraged it. And Tori had finally told her about her family and their murders. Casey had wept with her as Tori recounted that night all those years ago. And Casey had finally told Tori about how her brother had forbidden her to see his kids, forbid her to contact them. She leaned her head back, looking into the sky, remembering that day so well. Her niece was a tomboy, just like Aunt Casey. Her niece wanted to be a cop, just like Aunt Casey. And her niece never wanted to get married, just like Aunt Casey. That had been the breaking point. Casey was a bad influence, so her brother had a *talk* with her. Don't come around anymore, he'd said. Don't call. *You're not needed here.*

Damn, that had hurt. Her niece was all of twelve years old. She didn't understand. Hell, Casey didn't understand. So she reached out to her grandfather, hoping he could talk some sense into her brother. No. He'd agreed with him. None of them wanted Erica to turn out like Casey. They all had big plans for Erica. Doctor or lawyer, anything but a lowly cop. Anything but a *lesbian* cop. And so she'd faded away from the family. Even her mother, she lost touch with too. Of course, her mother had been ostracized from the family years before. A bitter divorce will do that. Her father's death hadn't helped ease the strain between her mother and her brother.

That was seven years ago. Her grandfather's death and funeral had come and gone, all without Casey. Oh, she'd tried. But her brother had said a firm no, she was not wanted there. And her niece's high school graduation had just come and gone. For that, she had made no attempt to go, to contact Erica. It had been too many years.

So she made up for her lack of a family by being a friend to everyone and surrounding herself with lots of people. And for the most part, she was happy. She dated some. Not a lot. Dating took time. But she wasn't lonely. Not really. All she had to do was pick up the phone. Which she'd been doing less and less of lately. As much as she enjoyed being around Tori and Sam, it made her realize how superficial the relationships in her life were. What Tori and Sam had was something Casey longed to emulate. That special someone, that one person who loved you without doubt, without cause. That's what she wanted in her life. And so she'd stopped most of the meaningless one-night stands. If she were simply craving a physical release, she could get that all by herself. The last time she'd slept with someone without worrying about tomorrow had been when Marissa Goddard had buzzed in and out of town in a week's time. And while the sex had been good—great, in fact—it was still just a meaningless act once it was all said and done.

So for now, she was content sitting on her deck, watching the water and the twinkling of lights that surrounded the lake. For now, she had her career. And she had two really good friends in Tori and Sam. For now, that was enough.

Chapter Six

Leslie sat quietly at her desk watching Casey watch Tori. Tori was reading through Donaldson's file. She and Casey had gone over it yesterday, seeing nothing out of the ordinary. Every lead was followed up on. Interviews were documented. All possible angles were covered. And as Casey had warned her then, Tori was going to be pissed.

She flinched as Tori slammed the file closed. "Goddamn."

Casey flicked her gaze to Leslie, then back to Tori. "Told you. It's clean."

"Okay. So I jumped to the wrong conclusion. No harm, no foul."

"No, no. You owe him an apology."

Tori's eyes narrowed. "The hell I do."

"You know you do. You might as well get it over with."

"Kiss my ass, O'Connor."

Casey laughed, glancing quickly at Leslie and winking. And she couldn't help it. She found herself grinning back, not really knowing what was so amusing. She apparently had a lot to learn about her new team.

"Just having a little fun, Hunter." She pointed at Leslie. "Tell Tori what you found, Les."

Tori looked at her expectantly. Leslie pulled up the screen where she'd put her notes, her mind still reeling from Casey's shortening of her name. She hadn't been called Les since college. "I went back to the first murder, just to crosscheck the apartment to see if any nine-one-one calls were made from there. Not her apartment, no. But the complex, yes. Two days before the murder, a call came in reporting a Peeping Tom. So I widened the search. In the three weeks before the murder, nine Peeping Tom calls came in from a four-block radius. After the murder, none." She paused, seeing the thoughtful expression on Tori's face. "Then I checked our current victim. Same thing. Two calls from her complex came in for Peeping Toms. In all, seven calls in three weeks in a four-block radius. Again, none since." She shrugged. "Of course, it's only been three days."

Tori nodded. "Good work, Tucker." She turned in her chair, looking at Casey. "What do you think?"

"Our guy gets off watching them. And that's enough for awhile. Then he wants to get closer. By now, he knows who lives alone, knows their routine."

"But neither place had forced entry," Tori reminded her.

"Maybe it's someone they were familiar with. A delivery guy," Leslie suggested. "Pizza, for example."

"Or he could pretend to be a delivery guy," Casey said. "What better way to get them to open up?" She knocked on an imaginary door. "Pizza," she called. "The girl says I didn't order a pizza. He says, I don't know about that, but I've got two larges for this address. You want them or not?" Casey stands, pacing. "So, without thinking, she opens the door just to see what he has. Boom, he's in. No forced entry."

"Wouldn't she scream? Surely someone would hear," Leslie said.

"But he's ready. She's not expecting it. She opens the door, he grabs her, covering her mouth to prevent her from screaming."

"At some point, if you're not gagged, you're going to scream," Tori said. "And tox on the first victim was clean, so he didn't drug her. How does he keep them from screaming?"

"Maybe there's an accomplice. Someone holding a gun to her head. Or a knife, in this case." Leslie felt Casey walk behind her and tensed as Casey's arm locked around her throat. "Scream and I'll kill you," she said menacingly. She released her, moving away. "If you're scared enough, if you believe him, you keep quiet."

"And if she's not actually being raped, she may not scream, thinking if she's quiet he won't hurt her," Tori said.

Leslie tilted her head, thinking. "Or maybe he kills her right away. Maybe he ties her to the bed afterward."

"And maybe he leaves his semen deposit afterward too." Casey shrugged. "That's probably more plausible. No one hears them screaming because they're already dead."

"Wonderful," Tori said. "We've solved the mystery. Now who's our murderer?"

Leslie turned as Casey walked behind her again, pointing to her monitor. "Pull up a map. How far apart are these two apartment complexes?"

"Oh, not far at all. The four-block radius I used overlapped." She pointed to the map, moving her finger across the screen. "Seven blocks apart."

"And how many apartment complexes are in this area?"

Leslie grinned. "If I were on TV, I could click a few times and have that information for you. But we're not. Gonna take a little time."

"There were a few complexes that I remember," Tori said. "But there were residences there too. Not all apartments."

"I can research it," Leslie said. "Some of the nine-one-one calls may have come from a private residence near the apartments."

Casey squeezed her shoulder as she moved back to her own desk. "You're doing great. I hate those things."

Leslie frowned. "What? Computers?"

"Call me old-fashioned."

Leslie laughed. "My fiancé would cringe to hear you say that. He's a geek. Computers are our friends, Leslie," she mimicked him.

"Ah, so you're not crazy about the damn things either."

"They serve their purpose. I just don't see the point of eating, sleeping and drinking with them."

"Fiancé, huh? When's the wedding?"

Leslie fingered her wireless mouse, glancing at Tori who appeared to be absorbed in reading through files. "We haven't set a date yet."

"Really? You just got engaged then?"

Leslie hated this question. "No. A year or so." She saw the surprised look cross Casey's face.

"So, you want to be absolutely sure before you say I do? Good plan."

Leslie flashed a quick smile, recognizing the teasing tone of Casey's words. She pulled up her notes again, rereading them before she started her research on the apartments in the area. She'd only been here two days, but she felt more relaxed with this group than she ever had in Fort Worth. There, it was all business, all the time. And there were very few discussions about the case without their lieutenant being present. Here, while Malone appeared to be in control, she noticed he kept to the background, allowing his detectives free rein. It was a practice she would have to get used to.

"So, you going to like her okay?" Tori asked as they walked to the deli for sandwiches.

"Tucker? Yeah, she seems nice. It would help if she wasn't so damn gorgeous. I mean, middle-aged and portly would be better."

"Portly?"

"Frumpy, portly. You know what I mean. She's too pretty to be a cop. Like Sam, you know. They just don't look like cops."

"You mean like us?"

"Yeah. You and me, a couple of dykes, we fit the description perfectly," she said with a laugh. "But she seems pretty sharp."

"Yeah. I liked the way she just jumped in. She wasn't afraid to give her opinion."

"And she didn't seem intimidated by you at all, Hunter. Maybe this new reputation you have is starting to get around.

The mellow, *nice* Tori Hunter."

Casey stumbled as Tori playfully bumped her shoulder.

"Don't say that too loud."

"Nothing wrong with being nice, Tori. It's a lot less exhausting than being a bitch all the time."

Tori laughed. "How would you know? I doubt anyone's ever called you a bitch."

"Yeah, you're right." Casey held the door open, motioning Tori inside. "Age before beauty."

They waited in line, neither needing to look at the menu boards. They were creatures of habit and always got the same thing. Casey nudged Tori with her elbow. "So, what do you think of her idea of surveillance?"

"Seems like a shot in the dark, but what else do we have?"

"Yeah. And if it holds to form, the Peeping Tom reports were all between eight and eleven. Not too long for us to cruise around."

"The only problem, they seemed to escalate right before the murders. Three months apart. We can't sit here and twiddle our goddamn thumbs for a couple of months."

"If there are no leads, there are no leads, Tori." Casey stepped up to the counter. "Turkey on wheat, no onions." She turned back around. "And Sikes, with his charming self, has interviewed everyone in the family and most of her friends, and they all say the same thing—she had no enemies. What else is there for us to do?"

"Roast beef on rye. Spicy mustard." Tori fished out some crumpled bills from her pockets, then looked at Casey. "Got a couple of bucks?"

"Oh, hell, Hunter, put that away. Lunch is on me."

"Thanks. And I don't like sitting on a case and doing nothing."

"I know that. But we can't invent suspects."

"You saw the family. They want answers."

"Of course they want answers. So do we." Casey took her sandwich basket and tea, then found an empty table.

"We need to come earlier. It's getting too damn crowded," Tori complained as she was bumped from behind. "Attorneys. They think they own the place."

Tori sat down, but Casey motioned with her head. "There's one staring at you. You know him?"

Tori turned to look. "Great," she murmured.

"Who is he?"

"Robert."

"Robert who?"

"Sam's ex."

"Oh, my. The guy she was seeing when—"

"Well, well, if it isn't Tori Hunter."

Casey watched as Tori slowly turned, a bored expression on her face. "Robert."

He looked at Casey, then back to Tori. "And Samantha made me think it was true love with you two. I guess that didn't work out so well, huh?"

"It's worked out great, thanks. This is Detective O'Connor, a colleague. I'll be sure to give Sam your best," Tori said with just a hint of sarcasm.

"Yes, do that. Tell her I'll give her a call. She still owes me dinner."

Tori scowled as he walked away and Casey leaned closer. "What the hell was that all about?"

"He left town. Went down to Houston I think. Apparently, he's back."

"Sam owes him dinner?"

"No. Sam does *not* owe him dinner. He's just being Robert."

"Defense attorney?"

Tori took a bite of her sandwich and nodded. "He's a jerk."

"Well, who could blame him? He's dating a beautiful girl like Sam and she leaves him for *you*." Casey laughed. "It would make anyone bitter."

"Very funny."

"Oh, just kidding. You know you're cute as pie, gorgeous." She had the pleasure of seeing her friend blush.

Chapter Seven

Leslie sat in silence as her future mother-in-law rambled on about plans for their honeymoon. So far, Michael was receptive to Cancun, St. Thomas, or a seven-day cruise to the Bahamas. She put her fork down—her dinner largely uneaten—and reached for her wine instead. She hated these occasions when Rebecca joined them for dinner. The conversation always centered on their impending wedding and, like now, the honeymoon.

"I don't know why you won't just set a date so we don't have to keep speculating on the season."

Leslie looked up. "What?"

"A date? A Christmas wedding, a spring wedding?"

Leslie glanced at Michael. "We haven't set a date yet."

"Yes, dear, I know. That's my point. You've been engaged for nearly two years. I can't contain my excitement any longer."

She put her wineglass down, choosing her words carefully. "You know, I can't just plan vacations and expect everything to fall into place. I mean, if we're in the middle of a murder investigation, I can't just leave for two weeks and go on a honeymoon. It just doesn't work that way."

"Another reason to change careers," Rebecca said. "Michael can get you on with his company, can't you, sweetheart?"

"Yeah, we always have receptionist jobs open."

Leslie stared, dumbfounded. "Receptionist?"

"Nice eight to five job," Rebecca said with a smile, as if this would entice her.

"Rebecca, Michael, no offense, but I chose my career long before I met you. I've worked hard to get where I am. And I feel very lucky I was able to transfer to Homicide here in Dallas after only being with the department such a short time. So no, I won't be changing careers to that of *receptionist* at your company." She stood with a curt nod. "If you'll excuse me."

"Leslie, I didn't mean to upset you, dear," Rebecca said quickly. "It's just—"

"You haven't upset me. But I have some work to do."

She closed the door to their bedroom, then leaned against it, staring at the far wall. A part of her just wanted to get it over with, even if it meant a quick wedding in front of a judge. But another part of her couldn't shake the nagging feeling that she was making a mistake. Was she really happy? Was this what she wanted for the rest of her life? A mother-in-law who interfered in everything? A husband who was more interested in his games than in her?

Is that what she wanted out of life?

Chapter Eight

"So, they're ready for you to set a date, huh?" Casey drove slowly down the street, her black SUV blending in well. Like Tori, she preferred to drive her own vehicle. The fleet of cars that were at their disposal were fine in a pinch, but they were dirty and smelled of takeout food and coffee.

Leslie rolled her head against the seat, watching her. "They've been ready. Or at least Rebecca has. Michael hasn't pushed too much."

Casey stopped along the curb, their view of the grassy area behind the apartment impeded only by passing cars. "Why aren't you ready?"

"Honestly, I don't know. We've dated for years, have been engaged for almost two, have lived together for one." Leslie adjusted her seatbelt, pulling it away from her chest. "It was one of those situations where you don't know why you're dating, but you are. And before long, a year has passed and it's become familiar, so you ignore the fact that you don't really have anything in common and you continue dating. And after several years, it's only natural to take the next step."

"He's a computer guy?"

She nodded. "He's a gamer. The company he works for does the graphics and special effects on computer games, video games. That's what he does. They design it, then play it, then tinker with

31

it, then play it again."

"So he's like a programmer?"

"Yeah. I guess." She hesitated. "He likes to play. Our spare bedroom is his game room. The TV is a huge monster. Not only for his video games but for sports. His buddies live in the same complex. They're sports fanatics. They live and breathe for the next game. Michael is as addicted as the rest of them." She laughed. "And I'm making him out to be a big ogre. He's not really. It's just sometimes I feel like I'm an afterthought to him. If someone offered him tickets to a game, I'm convinced he'd forget all about whatever plans we had." She shifted in her seat. "What about you? You've not mentioned a single thing about your personal life."

Casey shrugged. "Don't really have one to mention."

"You're not dating anyone? In a relationship with someone?" Casey hesitated and was surprised when Leslie reached over and touched her arm briefly. "I know you're gay. You don't have to avoid that subject with me."

"You do, huh?"

"It's common knowledge."

"Yes, I suppose it is."

"So?"

Casey laughed. "So there's still nothing to tell. I date some. Not as much as I used to when I was younger, that's for sure."

"Someone broke your heart?"

"No, nothing like that. Just haven't met the right one yet. I had kinda given up hope, but being around Tori and Sam made me realize it's still a possibility."

"I've heard stories about them. Rumors, really. She was dating an attorney when they met, right?"

"Yeah. I just met him for the first time the other day. He didn't take the breakup very well, apparently. Still quite bitter. But you should see Tori and Sam together. They're so much in love. You just look at them and you know." Casey glanced at Leslie. "I've never had that with anybody. That *I'm so in love I can't stand it* feeling, you know. They've got it. Tori turns into a big mush ball when she's around Sam." She laughed. "And don't you dare tell Tori I said that."

They sat quietly, both watching the apartment in silence. There were a few people milling about but none that looked suspicious. Casey started up the engine again. "Let's try another." Two blocks away, they pulled into the parking lot of another complex, driving slowly. The common area was dark, quiet. Casey parked and killed the lights. "It would be easy to watch someone from here," she said. "Lots of shadows to hide in."

"Like looking for a needle in a haystack though."

"Yeah, it is." Casey leaned back, trying to curb her curiosity, but it got the better of her. Like Tori said, she always had to ask a hundred questions when she met someone new. "You mention Michael's mother, but not your own. Does she not live here?"

Leslie turned, smiling. "I'd heard that about you, you know."

"Heard what?"

Leslie laughed. "That you talk too much and you're full of questions."

"Oh, I see. Markie had to fill you in, didn't he?"

"Yeah, he did. He also said no matter what people tried to hide from you, you could dig it out. I'm pretty sure that was a compliment."

"I haven't seen Markie in a while. I swear, talking to him was like talking to a rock."

"Maybe that's why he thought you talked too much. He doesn't talk at all."

"I'm inquisitive."

"So I see."

"Yeah. And is your mother pushing you to get married like Michael's mother is?"

"Oh, same question, different wording. Do you always do that?"

"Do what?"

"Keep asking until you get an answer."

Casey shrugged. "I'm a detective."

"A curious one at that."

33

Casey waited what she thought was an appropriate amount of time, then turned. "Your mother doesn't like Michael, does she?"

Laughing, Leslie held up her hands. "Okay, you win. I'll talk."

"Mother?"

"She doesn't know I'm engaged."

"Why the hell not?"

"We're not close."

"That's not an excuse. Half of every mother-daughter relationship could be explained the same way. Try again."

Leslie leaned her head back with a sigh. "My mother is...well, she's different. When I was in high school, my father took up with his secretary. He left us. And my mother went off the deep end. After their divorce, she started dating younger men. Much younger. Parties, drugs, she did it all, as if she was reliving college or something. She's been married four times since then. Currently, she's living with a guy six years younger than me. So we don't really have a relationship anymore." She turned in her seat. "And Michael's mother is just the opposite. She was widowed at an early age, yet never remarried. She still wears her wedding ring. She's very conservative and reserved. A *normal* mother. I would be embarrassed for the two of them to meet."

"And your dad?"

"It's strained. Always has been. He's still with the same woman though, I'll give him that."

"But you're not close with him either?"

"Not really, no. I mean, I see him more than my mother, but it's just very forced. And he still calls me on my birthday, things like that." She paused. "He has two kids with this woman, so I think he just calls me out of obligation, you know."

"Does he know you're getting married?"

"He knows I'm engaged, yes."

"So he's—"

"Enough." Leslie turned in her seat, tucking her dark hair behind her ears in a gesture Casey noticed she did before speaking. "My turn."

"Your turn?" Casey tapped her leg nervously. She'd always been curious about other people and their lives. She'd always been full of questions. But when others wanted to reciprocate, she clammed up. She didn't have a happy childhood, she didn't have memorable teenage years, she never had the typical American family. Dysfunctional was even too mild a word to use to describe her family. And as she'd grown into adulthood, not a lot had changed.

"You said you're not dating anyone, so let's back up. Mother?"

Casey nodded. "Yes."

"Yes? That's all I get?"

"She's in California now. I don't see her."

"Okay. Father?"

Casey shook her head. "No. Deceased."

"I'm sorry."

"No, no. He wasn't a part of my life. They divorced when I was a child. Nasty divorce. And anyway, he died years ago."

"Okay, so siblings?"

"Not really."

"That's more of a yes or no question. Either you do or you don't."

Casey smiled. "Okay, I'll go with no then."

Leslie stared at her. "I just told you about my crazy mother. I doubt you can top that."

"No. But it's…it's painful. I don't think about it much. I talk about it even less," she admitted.

"Okay, I'm sorry. That's fair enough. And it's not like we really know each other well enough to share those kinds of things."

Casey laughed quietly. "She says after she's already told about her crazy mother."

Leslie laughed too. "I didn't mean it that way. Really. I was being sincere. Some things you just don't tell to strangers."

"Unless that stranger happens to be great at asking questions?"

"Yes. But I've learned my lesson with you."

Casey shifted in her seat, turning to face Leslie. "I do believe in getting to know my partners, though. I think it makes for a much stronger relationship. I know there are those where it is just work between them. They don't want to know about spouses and kids. I think that's crazy."

"I agree. You spend so much time together, your relationship has to be about more than the job. You have to *care* about the other person. And if you know nothing about them or their life, it's hard to care."

"Hard to care, yes. But it's just a defense mechanism. Especially in our line of work. If I don't get to know you as a person, if I don't know your husband and kids, then we're not really friends. So if you should get injured, or shot and killed, then I've only lost someone from the job. I've not lost a friend."

Leslie smiled and touched her arm again. "You're speaking hypothetically, I know, but please don't mention *me* and shot and killed in the same sentence."

"Sorry. And I've never lost a partner, so you should be safe."

Leslie squeezed her arm, then released it. "Tell me why you're not dating anyone."

"Ah, safer subject?"

"Perhaps."

Casey rolled her shoulders, loosening them. She hated sitting this long. "Nothing's happening here. Want to move on?"

"Is that your way of avoiding the dating subject?"

"No. I don't mind talking about my lack of a love life," Casey said with a grin, but she started the engine anyway. "What's next on the list? Twin Peaks?"

Leslie laughed. "Twin Gables. Next block."

"It's nearly ten. What's Michael doing that he didn't mind you being on a stakeout?"

"He went to a Rangers game. Miles and Russell, two of his buddies, have season tickets. They usually invite Michael and Jeff as their dates."

"These are the buddies who live in the same apartment

complex as you?"

"That's them."

"So do their girlfriends and you all pal around together?"

Leslie laughed. "What girlfriends? Miles and Russell don't date. Ever. In fact, I think they would make for a wonderful beer commercial. Jeff dates some, not much. I think the girls take one look at his game room and run." Her smile faded. "Unlike me, who stuck around."

Casey drove through the parking lot, but the common area was hidden from view. She parked and cut the engine. "Feel like a walk?"

"Sure."

They closed their doors quietly and moved into the shadows between the buildings. The common area was mostly grassy, with a few mature trees. Four picnic tables and charcoal grills were positioned at each corner. In the middle was a volleyball net, the grass worn bare around it.

Casey saw the man across the way as he, too, moved in the shadows. She grabbed Leslie's arm and pulled her closer, hiding them from his view.

"I see him," Leslie whispered.

They watched him as he moved quickly from shrub to shrub, hiding. He was making his way around the complex, heading in their direction. Suddenly he stopped and crouched low.

"What's he doing?"

Casey shook her head. "Don't know." Then they saw—and heard—a group of people heading to the volleyball court.

"At this hour? I'd be pissed if I lived here," Leslie said.

"Look at our guy."

He stood, walking back the way he'd come, his hands shoved nonchalantly into his pockets as if he were just out on a stroll. He reached the sidewalk and disappeared behind the building.

"Should we try to follow him?"

"No. Let's drive around to that side. Maybe we can find him in his car and run the plates."

But all was quiet when they reached the other side of the

complex. No one walking about, no cars driving through, no lights on.

"Of course, what are the chances he was even our guy to begin with?"

"Slim," Casey said. "Like you said, needle in a haystack." Casey glanced at the clock. "Ready to call it a night?"

"Yeah."

Casey pulled out of the parking lot and onto the street, the traffic light at this hour. "Where do you live?"

"Nearly in Irving. Michael's office is just two blocks away."

"That was the reason you transferred here? Malone said something about the commute to Fort Worth."

"Yeah. We used to live in Arlington, but Michael's company relocated."

"And he hated the drive?" Casey guessed.

"Yes. And I know what you're thinking. His argument was that we'd see each other more if we lived in the same complex as his buddies because it would save him drive time."

Casey groaned. "And you bought that?"

"No. But I got tired of arguing about it. So I did the commute for five months, then applied at Dallas P.D."

"And how does he feel about your job?"

"What do you mean?"

"Well, some guys are either intimidated that their spouse is a cop, or they feel it's too dangerous a job for a female. Very few wholeheartedly accept it."

"I'm not sure where he stands on it. I think to him, it's just what I do. I mean, I was a cop when we met. I think he's totally indifferent to it. Now his mother, she hates it. And I'm not sure if it's because she thinks it's dangerous, or because I use it as an excuse not to set a wedding date."

"That's the excuse you're using?" Casey stopped at a light and turned to look at her. "Why do you need an excuse?"

"It's not really an excuse. I mean, say I had a date set for this week and we were in the middle of a murder investigation. How thrilled would you be if I just took off for two weeks on a honeymoon?"

"Well, not thrilled, yeah. But it's a fact of life. Other people get married all the time. We just have to make exceptions."

"Okay, so maybe it's just a convenient excuse then."

The light turned green and Casey drove on. "So back to my question, why do you need an excuse?"

"Because it's a little late to say I'm not sure if I'm ready. I mean, I accepted his ring."

Casey laughed. "So many gays and lesbians want the right to marry, but we've got it easy, I think."

"Don't you wish you could get married?"

"Oh, I don't know. It's not that important to me."

"Maybe because you're not in a relationship."

"Probably so. I mean, I look at Tori and Sam. I could see them getting married. Well, I could see Sam." She laughed, trying to picture Tori in a tux reciting her vows while people looked on. No, she could probably see them out on their boat, anchored in a favorite cove, both in shorts and swimsuits.

"So tell me again why you're not dating anyone."

"God, back to that question? Talk about not giving up."

"I have told you practically my life story tonight. You need to give me some back."

"And I just haven't met the right woman is not good enough?"

"You're only going to meet her if you date, and you said you don't date."

"I said I don't date much," Casey corrected with a sigh. "When I was younger, I didn't think so much about having that one person, you know. It was all fun and games and sex," she said, glancing quickly at Leslie. "And I was focused on my career. It was enough. I had lots of friends, it wasn't like I was alone. And I went through this phase where I thought it was time to settle down, so I tried it. I thought maybe she could have been the one. But she couldn't understand the job. She wanted me to get out. We lived together about a year and a half. The only time I've lived with a lover," Casey admitted. "But toward the end, it got pretty bad. That was when I decided I wouldn't live with anyone again until I was certain it was the real thing."

"That still doesn't explain why you don't date."

Casey turned to look at her. "I got tired of one-night stands. It became a chore. Meeting someone, making conversation, wondering if they expected you to sleep with them on the first date," she said with a laugh. "Or worse, thinking they did only to find out they didn't." She turned into their parking lot, pulling up beside Leslie's car. "That's not to say I don't want a relationship. I do. I'd like to fall in love. I'd like to have someone to come home to. I'd like to have that feeling where you look across a crowded room and can find her eyes on you and there be nothing but love there. And I'd like to know there was someone I was going to grow old with." She cut the engine, turning to look at Leslie. "I just haven't met her. And I don't think I'm going to meet her on a blind date or out at a bar. Those kinds of things are just so forced."

Leslie smiled slightly. "I met Michael on a blind date. A friend of mine thought we would hit it off because we had so much in common. I remember thinking at the time we had *nothing* in common." Her smile disappeared. "Turned out to be true."

"Then maybe it's a good idea you keep making excuses not to set a date."

Leslie turned away, staring out the window. "I just realized what a predicament I'm in."

"What do you mean?"

"I'm engaged to be married to a man I don't want to marry."

Casey said nothing, just sat there quietly. They'd known each other a few days, yet she suspected Leslie had shared more of her feelings tonight than she had in a very long time. Perhaps that's why it was such a revelation to her. She hadn't really said the words out loud before.

Chapter Nine

"God, that feels good," Tori groaned. "Harder."

Sam laughed. "Why is it I never get the backrubs?"

"Because you always try to turn it into more. I, on the other hand, *love* backrubs and don't associate them with sex."

"But turning it into sex is a *bad* thing?"

"No, not as long as I get my backrub first."

Sam's hands squeezed harder and Tori bit her lip, her eyes rolling back in her head in pleasure. Sam had the *best* hands. She smiled into the pillow. Yeah, the best hands.

"What are you smiling about?"

"How do you know I'm smiling?"

"I can tell."

"Just smiling with pleasure, isn't that okay?"

Sam squeezed harder. "You never said how Casey liked her new partner."

"Okay. She seems nice. Cute as hell."

"Cute? Oh, no. Poor Casey."

"Yeah, poor Casey," Tori said with a laugh. "She was hoping she'd be portly or something."

"She's straight?"

"Yeah. Engaged."

"So you guys get to go through a wedding?"

"I suppose. *Ouch.*"

"You said harder."

"I didn't mean to bruise me."

"Sorry. Let me kiss it."

Tori felt Sam's lips caress her neck and she closed her eyes. The backrub was over. She rolled, taking Sam with her, covering her with her weight. "I love you, you know."

"Mmm."

"Your turn."

Sam smiled against her mouth. "It won't take long."

Chapter Ten

Leslie paused at the door to their apartment, wondering—again—whether she should have a talk with Michael, wondering if she should discuss her uncertainties with him. After last night, after she'd admitted to Casey—a perfect stranger—that she didn't want to get married, guilt had set in. She had tossed aside her questions, her doubts and her fears, and had crawled into bed beside Michael, had wrapped her arms around him and pulled him close, trying to conjure up some feelings that resembled what Casey had called the *I'm so in love I can't stand it* feeling.

Those feelings never came and Michael never woke, so she slipped away from him, rolling to her side and staring at the wall, wondering what she was going to do.

And now, after a hectic day of interviewing those who had called in Peeping Tom reports from the two murders, hoping to get a description, she and Casey had called off their impromptu stakeout of the apartments. One reason being they had no concrete description of their guy. In fact, three had even insisted it was a girl. So they'd decided to compile all of their interviews tomorrow and see if they could come up with something, calling it an early day. And so on the drive home, she'd fought with herself over what she should and should not talk to Michael about. For one thing, she couldn't just say she was having second thoughts. He would never understand that. If you're having second thoughts, you don't accept a wedding proposal, you don't move in together.

She slipped the key in, unlocking the door, and paused again. And why was she just now having second thoughts? She tilted her head, trying to recall what had prompted those feelings. Was it simply Casey asking direct questions and she answering them truthfully? It dawned on her then that that could very well be the truth. She had no close girlfriends in her life. She had no one she talked to about her *feelings*. There was her job and there was Michael. And when Michael was off with his friends, she didn't fill the time with another person—a best friend—she filled it by being alone. But now, another woman had asked her direct relationship questions and she'd answered just as directly. And the doubts had crept in.

She took a deep breath, shoving the door open. She was tired and her thoughts were a jumbled mess. Now was not the time to have a talk.

"I'm home," she called, surprised there was no TV blaring. Instead, enticing smells were coming from the kitchen.

"In here."

She poked her head in, seeing Michael hovering over the stove. "What in the world are you doing?"

"What does it look like? I'm cooking."

"That's just it. You don't cook."

"Meatloaf."

Leslie's eyebrows shot up. "Meatloaf? You made meatloaf?"

"Well, my mother made meatloaf. She just brought it over for me to bake. I've got green beans here," he said, pointing to the pot on the stove. "And a salad in the fridge."

"So, Rebecca's coming over for dinner?"

"Oh, no. She just brought this by." He turned and grinned. "I think she's hinting that we need to cook more instead of eating out."

"Great. It could be a new hobby for you. It smells wonderful," she added as she walked away.

And minutes later, instead of having to decide between takeout, fast food or a sit-down meal in a restaurant, they were sitting at their own table having dinner. Which struck her as funny. The only time they used the table was when his mother was over. And that involved ordering take-out and hurrying home to set the table before she got there. Now, here they were, feasting on a meal Rebecca had cooked, sitting properly at the table sipping wine instead of on the couch watching TV or surfing the net on their laptops, or Michael eating in the spare room while he watched a game. No, here they were, practically like normal people. Normal *married* people.

But she wondered if conversation was this sparse between *married* people. Surely, they had something they could talk about. And Michael was the one who surprised her by starting the conversation.

"You haven't said a whole lot about your new job. Are you liking it okay?"

"Yes, it's fine. Why do you ask?"

"Well, when you were in Fort Worth, you mostly complained about how they treated you. And when you first transferred over here to Assault, you talked about how different it was, then about how bored you were. Now, you finally get to where you want, but you haven't said much about it."

She frowned, not realizing it, but it was true. She had said very little. Which was surprising, considering how at ease she felt with her new team. "I like it here a lot," she said. "They're very nice. It's a relaxed atmosphere. And there aren't any good old boys there. Not even Lieutenant Malone."

"What about your new partner? I know how important it is to you that you click."

Leslie smiled. "Yeah. And Casey is great. She's from Special Victims. She's only been in Homicide a few months."

"She? I thought it was a guy. You've never been paired with another woman before. Is that safe?"

"Safe?" Leslie put her fork down. "Like, because she's a woman she's not a good cop?"

"I didn't mean it like that. It's just…you know, if something

45

came up and you had to use a gun or something, it'd probably be better if at least one of you was a guy."

Leslie laughed, although it was totally devoid of humor. "Oh, my God. I can't believe you just said that. I *do* know how to use my weapon, you know. It's required, whether you're male *or* female."

"You're getting defensive because you're taking my statement wrong. I in no way meant that you were an inferior cop because you're a woman. I was simply being a man," he said with a smile. "And men are the protectors."

Leslie's smile faded. "If you think you're smoothing things over with that last statement, forget it. You're digging your hole deeper."

"Oh, come on. This isn't Cagney and Lacey. There aren't any women's issues you have to fight with me. I know you're a good cop," he said. "But how do we know if this Casey person is?" Leslie stared at him, feeling a frown cross her face but unable to stop it. How did he know she was a good cop? Because she had a handful of commendations? Because she was still alive? Because why? He wasn't really involved in her job. He rarely made it a point to get to know her partners or her team. He didn't attend any of the functions. How did he know she was a good cop?

"What?"

She blinked several times, clearing her mind. "Hmm?"

"You were staring like I'd said something wrong again."

She shook her head. "Nothing."

"Well then?"

Although her appetite had fled, she picked up her fork again, pushing the meatloaf around on her plate. "I'm sure Casey and I will be fine together. In fact, I feel honored that they paired us, considering she has so little experience. That means they were impressed with my Fort Worth record."

"In other words, I shouldn't be concerned with it."

"Exactly."

And so their dinner ended, with Michael going into the spare room and shutting the door firmly, the TV soon ripe with the sounds of a video game while she cleaned up the kitchen and put away the leftover meatloaf.

She escaped into the bathroom, filling the tub with hot water and bubbles, wondering why her life suddenly seemed so empty. The man she planned to marry was in the next room, spending his time with a game and most likely a chat on his cell with Jeff. She wondered what he would choose if she invited him to join her in a bubble bath. She smiled wryly. Most likely the game.

Didn't matter. She preferred to be alone. She stripped where she stood, then stepped into the warm water, sinking down to her neck as bubbles surrounded her.

"Heaven," she murmured as her eyes closed. She pushed her thoughts away, choosing instead to lose herself as the warm water enveloped her.

Chapter Eleven

Casey juggled four cups of coffee as she hurried into the squad room, stopping up short at Sikes's vacant desk.

"I finally stop for coffee and he's not here?" She handed Tori her cup, accepting her smile as a thank you. "Les, since I didn't know your favorite, I took a chance on mocha. I mean, everyone likes mocha, right?"

"Good job, O'Connor. That actually *is* my favorite."

"Cool, I scored points." She turned on her computer before sitting down, then glanced at Tori. "Anything new?"

"There was a Peeping Tom report last night."

"No kidding. Where?"

"Twin Gables."

Casey looked at Leslie and winked. "Twin Peaks."

"Anyway, by the time patrol got there, our guy was gone. Sikes is interviewing the woman who called it in."

"So maybe it's time we do surveillance for real. I mean, that's how it started before. We can concentrate on that area. Beef up patrol maybe," she suggested.

Leslie shook her head. "But if we have patrol units cruise by more, that might scare off our guy. He may move somewhere else and lessen our chance to nab him while his offense is only peeping."

Tori nodded. "I agree. And let's see if Sikes can get a good description. Because what you guys got yesterday sucked."

"I swear, three people said it was a woman," Casey said.

"Try convincing Mac that a woman left semen behind."

Casey looked at Leslie and grinned. "She's in good humor this morning. Did you have a real nice evening, Hunter?"

"Probably better than yours, O'Connor."

"Oh, now you're just being mean."

"Yeah, that was low. And Sam's coming by after work. She's in the mood for Mexican food. She said to invite you."

"Okay, sure. You know me and margaritas." Casey turned to Leslie. "I'd invite you to come with us, but I guess Michael would be at home waiting."

"Actually, he's out with his buddies tonight."

"Great. Then why don't you join us?" Casey arched an eyebrow at Tori.

"Yes, join us. Sam would love to meet you."

Leslie looked from one to the other, then nodded. "Okay, thanks. I'd love to."

"Good." Casey motioned to her monitor. "Why don't you pull up that map thing you did? Isn't this the first call from Twin Gables?"

"I think so."

Casey stood behind her, waiting. "It's obviously in our target area since we were cruising by it the other night."

"So, taking into account both murder scenes and the Peeping Tom calls, we have an eight-block radius?" Tori asked.

"Yes. And what I find odd," Leslie said, "is that he's targeting apartments so close to the downtown area, where it's more congested. Why not apartments on a major highway where you have more escape routes?"

"That's true. I mean we saw the other night, parking is limited. Where does he stash his car? How far does he walk to get to his target?"

"Both murders were at conventional apartments, with ground floor windows."

"And outside entry," Casey said. "Most of the refurbished

apartments in downtown have a central entry. The newer ones have gated entry. That would be harder for our guy to get in."

"But the apartments that he's targeting, he has more choices," Tori said. "And it's right at the edge of Deep Ellum. Maybe he doesn't use a car. Maybe it's all on foot."

"And easy to disappear in Deep Ellum."

"I've only been to Deep Ellum a handful of times," Leslie said. "But during the week, there's not a lot of street traffic, is there?"

"Certainly not like on weekends, no. And even then, it's tamed a bit. A lot of the clubs and restaurants have closed down in the last several years. But there's still enough people walking the streets, going from bar to bar, for him to blend in with," Tori explained.

"Okay. So what's the plan?" Leslie asked.

Casey squeezed her shoulder as she walked behind her, then pointed to the monitor again. "Since you're so good with that thing, how about a spreadsheet or something of all the apartments in that eight-block radius? Then we can set some guidelines. Which ones have outside entry? How many floors are there? Which ones have those tiny patios? Ground floor windows? Things like that." She went to her desk but stopped when fingers wrapped around her arm.

"I'll do the spreadsheet, but let's drive the area later. It'll be much easier to log all this information in the daylight instead of trying to figure it out at night while we cruise by."

Casey was conscious of the fingers still clinging to her arm, and she was conscious of Tori watching them. For some reason, the touch on her arm made her shiver. She nodded, trying to find her voice. "Sounds good to me." The hand finally slipped away and she moved again, glancing briefly at Tori who still stared.

Casey splashed water on her face, then looked up as the door to the ladies' room opened and Tori stuck her head in. Their eyes met in the mirror.

"What's up?"

Tori grinned. "Been a week, huh?"

"A week?"

"With your new partner."

"Oh." Casey reached for the towels and pulled two out, drying her face. "Yeah. A week."

"Watching you two out there, it reminded me of Sam."

"What do you mean?"

"When Sam first got here, it used to drive me crazy. She would always touch me when she talked to me." Tori laughed slightly. "But you're different than me. You touch too."

Casey frowned. "I do not."

"You probably don't even realize it." Tori walked past and into one of the stalls. "It's kinda cute."

Casey met her own eyes in the mirror. "It would help if she was frumpy, you know."

"Yeah. Frumpy. And what was the other word you used?"

Casey smiled at her reflection. "Portly."

Chapter Twelve

"Trust me, Casey is the margarita expert," Sam said with a laugh.

"I have sampled my share of margaritas, yes. And the Rios Rita is the very best."

"Well, then I'll have to try one," Leslie said, looking at her menu. "What's the specialty here?"

"Chicken enchiladas," they said in unison and Leslie laughed.

"I see you come here quite often."

"Casey refuses to eat Mexican food anywhere else," Tori said.

"Yeah, but with you, I hardly get margaritas anymore." Casey turned to Leslie. "Tori doesn't drink much, and when she does, it's beer. And on a hot summer day when we're out on the boat fishing, that's fine, but even now when we go out for a drink after work, she's got me ordering beer. So tonight, I get to indulge."

"Who's got a boat?"

"Sam and I do," Tori said. "It's a cabin cruiser we keep out on Eagle Mountain Lake."

"They let me tag along sometimes," Casey said. "There's nothing better than pulling into a cove and fishing all day, then spending the night on the water." She laughed. "Of course, that's if we can talk Sam into cooking for us."

"Well, I think it's great that you guys do stuff outside of work.

I've never had that in all my years on the force. In Fort Worth, well, I was the only woman and I think the guys either wanted to protect me because I reminded them of their daughters, or they thought I was there to make sure the coffeepot was always full."

"There are a few old-timers who think that way," Sam said. "But for the most part, we don't have that stigma. It's all very gender fair." She touched Tori's arm. "Not that Tori hasn't had her share of run-ins."

Leslie nodded. "I've heard some of the stories."

"Don't believe everything you hear," Tori said.

"Yeah. Only about ninety percent of it is true," Casey said with a laugh, then turned at a touch on her arm. "Fran," she said, standing to greet the older woman.

"If it isn't my favorite police detective." She smiled warmly at them. "And I see you bring your good friends. Hello, Tori and Sam."

"Hi, Francesca."

"You are crammed in a tiny booth, Casey? Why didn't you come get me? I could have found a table for you."

"Tori and Sam like the booth. See how close they can sit?"

Leslie couldn't help but smile as a blush crossed Tori's face, but Sam simply leaned closer to her, completely at ease.

Casey stepped back. "And this is Leslie Tucker."

"Oh, yes. How do you do, Leslie Tucker? I am always so happy when Casey brings a lady friend around. You are very lovely," she said, taking Leslie's hand. "Casey can be a handful. Don't let her scare you off." She winked. "She is a good catch, they say."

Leslie raised an eyebrow, then smiled as Casey's face turned a cute red. For two tough cops, Casey and Tori sure embarrassed easily. "I'll try to keep her in check."

"Drinks are on the house." She turned, clapping her hands, and a waiter appeared. "Keep my friends happy, Carlos." She bowed in their direction. "Enjoy your meal, ladies. Tori and Sam, good to see you again. And, Leslie, make sure Casey brings you back soon."

"I'm so sorry," Casey whispered as she slid back in beside

53

her.

"No problem."

"You should have just shown her your ring."

Leslie glanced at the diamond on her finger. It was obscenely large, in her opinion. She'd never been one for jewelry and stones. Even her earrings were simple diamond studs, nothing flashy. She remembered when Michael had given the ring to her. She'd been speechless. He'd assumed it was from delight—and awe—of the size. No. It was from the realization that she'd have to *wear* the thing. She'd gotten used to it and hardly gave it a thought anymore, but for some reason, it seemed to mock her this evening, so she slipped her hand under the table and out of sight.

"What can I get you to drink, ladies?"

"Three Rios Ritas," Casey said. "And a beer for Tori."

"A Corona," Tori said.

"Excellent. Chips and salsa will be right out."

"I hope Fran didn't make you uncomfortable," Sam said. "She's always playing matchmaker with Casey."

"No, it's okay."

"I understand you're engaged." Sam smiled. "I don't know how it is with you, but when I was dating Robert, he thought being a female cop had to be *the* most dangerous job on the planet."

"You know, it's funny. Michael really has never had much to say about my job in the years I've known him. Not until the other night when he found out my partner was another woman. Then he started on the *shouldn't at least one of you be a guy in case you need to shoot somebody* argument," she said.

"You're kidding?" Tori shook her head. "Men," she murmured, which drew laughs from around the table.

Casey nudged her with her elbow, then wiggled her eyebrows teasingly. "I'll be the guy."

Leslie laughed. "Only if you beat me to it."

They all reached for chips at the same time when their waiter placed the basket within reach.

"Mmm, excellent salsa," Leslie said as she sampled from both

54

the red and green bowls. "There's this little dive in Fort Worth—El Lugar—and they serve only wrapped burritos. I think eight different varieties. Anyway, their green salsa is to die for." She glanced at Casey. "Their margaritas aren't so hot though."

"Well, then what's the point?"

"Do you like Dallas? I mean, compared to Fort Worth," Sam asked before biting into a chip.

"You wouldn't think the attitudes of two cities could be so different, would you? I was in Homicide there six years, with pretty much the same guys the whole time. I think I did a good job, despite the limitations. To the public, equality was the word. But in my squad, I was the woman, period. They politely held doors open for me, and were quick to pass me their empty coffee cup for a refill."

"How did you stand it?" Tori asked. "I would have shot someone."

She laughed. "The thought did cross my mind. But after six or eight broken coffee mugs, they learned to get their own, so I didn't have to pull my weapon."

"Ladies, here we go. Three Rios Ritas and a...beer," he said, eliciting a dour look from Hunter. "Have you decided on dinner?"

Casey turned to her, eyebrows raised, and Leslie nodded. "Yes, I'll try the famous chicken enchiladas."

"Us too," Sam said.

"All the way around," Casey said. "Thanks."

"You were right. This is fabulous," Leslie said, sipping from her drink.

"Mmm, we don't come here enough," Sam said.

"Not for lack of my trying," Casey said.

Sam grabbed another chip and loaded it with salsa, but paused before eating. "By the way, what do you think about us buying a house?"

Casey's eyebrows shot up and she stared at Tori. "What?"

Sam also glanced at Tori. "You didn't tell her?"

"No. And this is why."

Casey looked from one to the other. "You guys want to move? Like away from me?"

"Not far, Casey."

"But still."

Sam reached across the table and squeezed Casey's hand. "Not far, I promise." She looked at Leslie. "We live on White Rock Lake, as does Casey. But we're in an apartment and Casey is in this cute little house."

"Little being the key word," Casey said.

"Aren't homes around there expensive?" Leslie asked.

"Well, there's the good side of the lake and the bad side."

"Currently, we're on the cheap side," Casey said.

Sam leaned forward and smiled at Casey. "How does the country club sound to you?"

"Oh, my God! You're not serious?" She stared at Tori. "The country club, Hunter? What the hell?"

"I told Sam as long as we were still near work and still near the lake, I didn't care."

"Yeah, but the *country club*?" She lowered her voice. "Do they allow lesbians there?"

Leslie laughed, enjoying the conversation.

"We found a house that's somewhat reasonable," Sam said. "And compared to the prices of those new homes they're building on the north side, this is like a bargain."

"But the country club. That's just not *right*." She tapped the table with her fingers. "So like, we have to take up golf now?"

"I doubt they'd let you and me out on the course, O'Connor."

Casey grinned. "Yeah, but we could ride around in a golf cart, drink a beer or two, and check out the ladies. You know, drive by the pool, things like that."

Sam grabbed Tori's arm and laughed. "You will not."

Leslie found herself laughing along with them, then was surprised to find her shoulder pressing playfully against Casey. "Sounds like you're a troublemaker," she teased.

"Me?" Casey grinned. "Not at all."

"Don't believe her," Sam said. "Get the two of them together and they're quite a handful."

Leslie sipped from her drink, thoroughly enjoying the evening and the company. They made her feel at ease and never once excluded her from the conversation, always making it a point to explain to her what they were talking about. By the time dinner was served, they were all chatting like old friends. And she remembered what Casey had told her about Tori and Sam. All you had to do was take one look at them and know they were deeply in love. Sam's hand was never far from Tori, touching her frequently when she talked. And Tori, well Casey was right. She turned into a big mush ball around Sam. It was obvious how much they cared for each other.

She let her eyes drift to Casey, again wondering why she was alone. She was delightful to be around, charming and funny, talkative. Why hadn't she found someone to love?

Casey turned then, meeting her eyes. Leslie was surprised by the gentle gaze. She returned her smile, then motioned to the stack of hot tortillas with her head. "May I?"

"You may, Detective Tucker," Casey said with a grin, grabbing one and handing it to her. "Okay?"

"Excellent."

Chapter Thirteen

"I can't believe you hung out here over the weekend," Leslie said.

"Why not? I'm the only one without a life," Casey said as she pulled into a parking space.

"It's not like I was doing anything exciting. You could have called me."

"No sense in both of us driving around until midnight. Besides, I didn't see anything out of the ordinary."

"And there were no Peeping Tom calls from this area."

"So there you go. A wasted weekend stakeout." Casey stretched her legs out and tried to get comfortable. It would be a long three hours. That was the plan, anyway. She and Leslie would take Monday, Wednesday, Friday. Hunter and Sikes would take Tuesday and Thursday. They would decide weekends later, but Casey wouldn't mind volunteering. Like she'd said, she was the only one without a life, even though it was boring as hell over the weekend by herself.

Leslie unfolded the spreadsheet she'd brought along, then pointed her small penlight at it. "Did you do Brookhaven?" she asked.

"Yeah, but it requires walking. The parking lot is away from the building. But the interior common area opens up to all the ground floor units."

"Sliding door patios?"

"Yeah. Brookhaven is one of the most accessible. We can go there next."

"We thought Creekside would be tough," she reminded her. "Did you check it out?"

"Yeah. Ground floor units, but they all have tiny privacy fences around the patios, so you can't see in. And all the front doors face the opposite building. I don't think our guy is going to target Creekside."

"And I'm sure you did Twin *Peaks*," she said with a smile.

"I did. And I don't think our guy will choose a Friday or Saturday night for his business. There's just way too much activity. He would have a hard time sneaking around. Not to mention, most people are out on Friday and Saturday nights."

"The first murder was on a Monday night, the second on a Sunday."

"Yes, the two quietest nights. Yet most of our Peeping Tom calls have been on Wednesdays and Thursdays."

Leslie folded up the spreadsheet and put it aside. "Maybe that's when he's doing his surveillance. And it's just going to be a matter if we luck upon him."

"Afraid so."

They were quiet and Casey let her eyes slip closed for a second. She was tired. She'd been out until midnight the last two nights cruising around the apartments. By the time she'd gotten home and taken time to unwind, it'd been nearly two before she crawled into bed. Unfortunately, her internal clock had her wide awake by five thirty, the normal time she got up.

"I really enjoyed dinner with you guys the other night," Leslie said after a while.

Casey opened her eyes and rolled her head along the seat. "Yeah? Good."

Their eyes met for a moment. "You're exhausted."

Casey nodded. She was too tired to lie. "Yeah, not a lot of sleep this weekend."

"You surely didn't patrol around here all night, did you?"

"No. Just until about midnight." She sighed. "I've got the habit of…well, to unwind, I sit out on my deck in the dark and watch the lake, and just enjoy the quiet and all." She closed her eyes again. "And maybe a couple of glasses of wine."

"That's your ritual? Before bed, you sit outside in the dark?" She leaned back against the seat. "I think that sounds wonderful."

Casey smiled. "Yeah. Being on the lake reminds me of happier times," she said quietly. "My grandfather had a place out on Lake Fork. When I was younger, we used to go out there."

"But to hear you tell it, you have no family. I think you chose the *no* option on siblings."

"Is this your subtle way of fishing for information?"

"Is it working?"

Casey straightened up in her seat and rubbed her face. "I guess we should talk or I might fall asleep on you." She cleared her throat. "What do you want to know?"

"You already told me your mother is in California and you're not close, but you drew the line when I mentioned siblings."

"I did, didn't I?" She tapped the steering wheel absently, her mind flashing back over the years, snippets of events and conversations running by at lightning speed. She'd told Tori and Sam about her life. Before that, she hadn't really told anyone, not the whole story anyway. It was still a painful memory, but not talking about it wouldn't make it go away. She felt warm fingers caress her forearm before squeezing. She glanced over at Leslie, wondering why her touch caused her heart to quicken its pace.

"I don't want to pry, Casey. If it's something you'd rather not talk about, then tell me to mind my own business and we'll move on to lighter topics."

She met Leslie's eyes in the shadows, surprised by the gentle concern she saw there. She waited, feeling an odd sense of loss as Leslie's fingers slipped away from her. "I have a brother," she said. She sighed again, feeling how heavy it was. "He's ten years older than I am." She swallowed, trying to get the lump out of her throat. "And we were very close at one time." She reached for the binoculars, watching a man walking his dog. She lowered them again and smiled. "I saw that guy last night too." She drummed her fingers on her leg, wondering where to start with her story. "I had a pretty crappy childhood," she finally said. "My parents hated each other. They fought constantly. Hitting, screaming, fighting. All the time." She glanced at Leslie. "I thought that was what married life was all about, you know. I just thought *everybody's* parents did that."

"Your brother was still home?"

"Until I was eight. He and three buddies got an apartment when they went to college. He just went up to Denton, so close enough to home. Anyway, it got worse when Ryan left. He was a big guy. He was a buffer."

"Why did they stay together?"

"Oh, they split up once, when Ryan was young. But they got back together." She pointed at herself. "I'm the result of that wild night. I'm pretty sure that's the last time they slept together," she said with a laugh. "It was all so weird, you know. During the week, it was holy hell with them, but every Sunday morning we'd get all dressed up and head to Mass. And Sundays were always the best days. It was like they called a truce on Sundays. But that ended too. And the divorce was nasty. Restraining orders and accusations and more fighting. And in the end, the judge awarded custody to my mother and my father was not allowed visitation because of the alleged abuse."

"I'm so sorry," Leslie said. "When you said painful, I had no idea."

"I'm not even at the painful part, Les. That happened as an adult."

"I don't understand."

"My father never hit me. He hit my mother a few times, but the way they would go at it, I can't really blame him. I mean, she used to beat the hell out of him."

"Would you have rather gone with your father?"

Casey shook her head. "I loved and loathed them both equally. That wasn't really an issue. And anyway, Ryan would come get me on the weekends—most weekends—and take me to Lake

Fork and we'd stay with my grandfather. That was the only time I felt normal, you know. There wasn't any fighting. There were no conflicts. I was just hanging out with my big brother. And even when he got married, he still came and got me. I was fourteen then, I think. Anyway, he had a couple of kids and I was Aunt Casey, and even that was normal. And he helped me get into college, helped me out with money, let me stay with them some. By this time, my mother had moved. She moved that summer right after I graduated high school, so it was really just us. His family and me."

"But you had a falling out," Leslie guessed.

"I guess you could call it that." Casey gripped the steering wheel, flexing her fists as she squeezed. "Their daughter, Erica, she just thought I hung the moon. She wanted to hang with me, no matter what. And when I became a cop, she thought that was so cool," Casey said with a quiet laugh. "Yeah." She wasn't surprised this time when Leslie's hand found her arm and gave a comforting squeeze. Leslie was affectionate. She liked that about her. "Erica was such a little tomboy. And she wanted to be just like Aunt Casey. She wanted to be a cop, just like Aunt Casey. And that's when my brother freaked. Because being just like Aunt Casey meant being gay. And even though both he and his wife were always accepting of me, apparently they drew the line at their daughter." Casey turned, glancing at Leslie who sat quietly watching her. "He very politely, but firmly, forbid me to come around anymore."

"You have got to be kidding?"

"Erica was twelve. I was twenty-seven." Casey tilted her head. "I was devastated."

"I take it your father was already gone?"

"Yeah. He died only a few years after they split. Dropped dead of a heart attack one day. But yeah, it was just me and my brother. So I went to see my grandfather. I mean, he was getting on in years, but I thought we were close, I thought he could maybe talk some sense into Ryan." She took a deep breath. "No. He agreed with Ryan. Erica had potential, he said. They didn't want me bringing her down."

"God, I am so sorry, Casey."

"So when you ask me if I have family, if I have any siblings, that's why my answer is no."

"And you just never saw them again?"

"My grandfather died, oh, three or four years ago now, I guess. I tried to get in touch, I wanted to go to the funeral. But my brother said…he said no." She took her hands off the steering wheel and rubbed them together, noting the dampness. She tilted her head back, then squared her shoulders, feeling them pop. "So there's my horrible little story," she said, trying to smile. "In a nutshell."

"After all that, I am totally amazed by you."

"What do you mean?"

"You're such a happy person. You always have a smile on your face, you're always in a good mood. I can't believe you're not bitter and just pissed off at the world."

"No, that's my mother," Casey said. "She always told me she got screwed at life. She said she got dealt a bad hand." Casey shook her head. "I didn't want to be like her. If you get dealt a bad hand, fold and ask for new cards. There's no sense in hanging on to it for years, hoping things will change."

"So that's the real reason you've not settled down, isn't it? You're afraid you're going to end up like your parents did?"

Casey ran her fingers through her hair a couple of times, finally nodding. "Yeah. I guess. I mean, the one time I tried it, it wasn't good. Toward the end, there was a lot of arguing, bickering. Not fighting, really. But like I said, she wasn't the one. And I refused to force things to make her the one. Because I think that's what my parents did. They tried to force the other into being something—someone—they weren't."

They were quiet for a moment, both looking out the windshield, watching the handful of people walking about the complex. After a while, Leslie turned to her.

"No offense, but your brother is an asshole."

Casey laughed quietly, but said nothing. Yeah, she'd used that word a time or two. She sat up straighter, starting the truck. "Let's try another, huh?"

"Sure. Brookhaven?"

"Yeah, but remember, we'll have to walk it."

"That's fine. Beats sitting still for so long."

"Yeah, at least it's cooler tonight. Can you imagine doing this in the middle of summer?" Leslie's reply was cut short by Casey's cell phone. She unclipped it from her belt without looking. "Yeah, O'Connor," she answered. She flicked her glance to Leslie, listening. "We're about four or five blocks away." She closed the phone, then sped up, turning at the next intersection. "That was Malone. They've got a body in Deep Ellum. Appears to be a homeless man. Homicide."

"Where?"

"In the alley behind Curtain Calls. It's a comedy club."

"I don't know this area at all."

"It'll take time," Casey said, turning again onto Elm Street and heading toward downtown.

There were three patrol cars with lights flashing, and Casey pulled to a stop next to the curb. She held her badge up before one of the officers could detain her. "O'Connor, Homicide. This is Detective Tucker. You got a body for us?"

"Yes, ma'am. Down the alley."

"Thanks." She walked on, then stopped. "Crime lab?" she asked.

"Yes, ma'am, they've been notified. And the ME."

"Okay, thanks." She glanced at Leslie with a half-smile. "I've never done a scene without Hunter or Sikes," she explained. "That's the first thing Hunter always asks."

"We'll be fine."

But as soon as they reached the alley, they stopped, both covering their mouths as the sweet, putrid smell of death hit them. "Jesus," Casey murmured. She looked at one of the patrol officers. "What the hell?"

"Been dead a few days."

"I'll say." Her gaze followed where he pointed, just a lump

beneath a blanket. "Who found him?"

"One of the clubs was taking out trash. Smelled him."

"Is this a hangout?" Leslie asked, looking around. "There are a lot of boxes broken down."

"Yeah. A lot of the homeless sleep here," he said. "They disappear during the day."

"Any of them around?"

"Yeah, they scattered when we showed up, but we talked to a few."

"This guy got a name?" Casey asked as she walked closer, moving the blanket aside with her foot.

"Depending on who you ask, it's either Rudy or Bobby."

She let the blanket fall and stepped back. "Damn, his throat's been cut." She looked at Leslie. "Let's see if we can find anyone who'll talk to us."

"There's a couple of guys standing down at the end."

But when they headed their way, the guys took off.

"Hey, wait up. We just have a some questions," Casey called as she chased after them. They caught up to them on the street. "Hey, man. Just a few questions."

"Don't want no trouble."

"There's no trouble," Casey assured him. She motioned to Leslie with her head, who went after the second guy. "You sleep out here?"

"Sometimes, yeah."

Casey looked him over, guessing his age to be about sixty or so, but knowing the street aged you. His hair and beard, both dirty and matted, were showing gray. His clothes were old and torn, his coat nearly in shreds. "Did you know him?"

The man shrugged.

"Know his name?"

"Rudy."

"Was that his normal spot?"

The man nodded.

Casey tilted her head. "And I don't guess you know who killed him?"

"Don't know nothing."

"How long's he been dead?"

The man closed his eyes and Casey imagined him counting. He opened his eyes again. "Three days."

"Friday night?"

He leaned closer and Casey tried not to back away from his smell. "You don't never know what day it is on the streets."

Casey finally took a step back and the man did the same. "If you knew he was dead, why didn't anyone tell the police?"

"Don't want no trouble."

"Do you think maybe he had something someone wanted? Money? Booze?"

The man shook his head. "If you score, you don't come back here until it's gone."

"Where do you eat?"

"At the shelter."

"Did Rudy go there?"

"Most days."

"Did he have a fight with someone? Was someone harassing him?"

The man took another step back. "Don't know nothing."

Casey leaned closer. "Who are you afraid of?" she asked quietly.

The man looked around them quickly, then shook his head. "Don't know nothing."

He turned to go and Casey let him. Whatever he did know, he wasn't telling. She looked down the street, finding Leslie. She was still talking to her guy and Casey took the opportunity to watch her unobserved. Tall, she was dressed similarly in jeans and lightweight boots, her dark hair windblown and unruly. Casey nodded. She fit in. The first couple of days, she'd worn pressed slacks and fancy loafers. But now, she'd taken her cue from her and Tori, dressing for the streets, not the office. As she stared, Leslie turned, catching her. Their eyes met for a quick moment, then Leslie jotted down something on her notepad before heading her way.

66

Casey waited, finally raising her eyebrows when Leslie got closer.

"Bobby."

Casey smiled. "Mine said Rudy."

Leslie shrugged. "Okay, so Rudy Bobby it is." She glanced at her notes. "He'd been around here the better part of a year. No fights with anyone, no enemies. Kept to himself. He's been dead a couple of days."

"Yeah, about what I got." Casey looked around the street, seeing several people watching them. "So, what does your gut tell you?"

"That he knows who did it and he's scared to tell."

Casey stared at her, again meeting her eyes head on. "Funny, that's what my gut says too."

"Another homeless man? Someone they see every day?"

"Most likely." She took a deep breath. "But we'll never get them to talk. They don't trust cops. If the killer was some stranger off the street, they'd come forward. They would have reported the murder. But not this. Not when it's one of their own."

"They'll just move on?"

"Yeah. Those who know what happened, they'll find another place to sleep. They don't want any trouble." Casey headed back down the alley. "Let's go to the shelter. Maybe someone there will talk to us. If there was some kind of turf war going on, they'd know about it."

But even there, they seemed nervous, unwilling to talk. Casey finally lost her temper after the fourth person told them he didn't know anything.

"Look, cut the crap, okay," she told him. "I'm in no goddamn mood for games. We know he came here to eat, so you know who the hell we're talking about."

But the man still shook his head. "No. There are so many. I don't know him." He glanced around him quickly. "Come back tomorrow. You ask for Maria."

He hurried away from them and Casey shoved her hands into the pockets of her jeans. "Whatever happened to the good old days where a cop could ask a simple question, get a simple answer, and arrest the bad guy?"

Leslie smiled. "TV."

Casey tilted her head, watching Leslie as her fingers threaded through her hair, brushing her bangs out of her eyes. "It's nearly ten thirty. Ready to call it a night?"

Leslie followed her outside, pausing on the street. "Should we follow up with Spencer or Mac?"

"No. They won't work this until tomorrow. Besides, if they find something, they'll call," Casey said as they made their way back to her truck.

The drive back to the squad room was done in silence. Casey glanced a few times at Leslie, who simply stared out the window, a thoughtful expression on her face. Casey started to ask several times what she was thinking about, but she managed to curb her curiosity for once. She pulled up beside Leslie's car and cut the engine. They sat still for a moment, then Leslie turned in her seat, facing her.

"About earlier," she said. "I enjoyed our talk." She looked up, meeting Casey's eyes. "Thank you for telling me about yourself. I hope I didn't pry too much."

Casey shook her head. "No. No, it's okay."

"Good. Because I really want us to be friends. My other partners, they were always men, always older. We never really had a relationship other than work."

Casey shifted in her seat too, turning toward Leslie, whose face was hidden by the shadows. "It's funny. I've always gotten along with my partners, considered them friends, but if I think about it, we were just friends on the surface really. There's not a single one of them I'd ever have told my life story to. I knew them and their families, but I guess they never really knew me."

Leslie surprised her by leaning closer and pulling her near for a quick hug. "Thanks for trusting me."

Casey nodded mutely, staring as Leslie opened the door and got out.

"See you tomorrow, O'Connor."

Casey flashed a quick smile, waiting until Leslie had her car started before pulling away. She took a deep breath and let it out slowly, moving into traffic without thinking, her mind still focused on the quick hug. And the unique smell of Leslie's perfume.

Leslie hit the expressway and eased into traffic, her hands gripping the steering wheel tightly.

Why did you have to hug her? Jesus!

Why indeed?

"I like her."

Yes, Casey was that type of person. Who wouldn't like her? But a hug? *You don't just hug.* People don't just hug anymore.

She wondered what Casey thought of her. First, she pried into her personal life, practically dragging out her painful memories. Then she has to go and hug her.

I like to touch, she reminded herself. A curse, but yes, she'd always been that way. When she felt comfortable with someone, when she felt affection, she touched them when she talked. And for some reason, when she was near Casey, she simply felt drawn to her.

"There's nothing wrong with that."

Chapter Fourteen

Leslie turned, her gaze lingering as Casey bounded into the squad room, her energy level a bit elevated it seemed. She stopped beside Leslie's desk, her eyes twinkling.

"For the beautiful lady, a mocha with extra whipped cream." She winked as she pulled a coffee cup from her bag. "I flirted with the coffee girl, got it for free," she teased.

"Aren't you sweet? Having to flirt with cute teenagers for my whipped cream. Must have been painful," Leslie said with a laugh.

Tori snorted and rolled her eyes.

"She's a freshman in college, thank you very much." She turned, "And for the old sourpuss, cappuccino," she said, handing Tori her cup.

"Thanks, cradle robber."

"Ah, you're just jealous, old lady," Casey shot back. She turned to John. "And for my favorite straight boy," she said, handing him his coffee. She made an exaggerated show of trying to hide it as she slid a pastry across his desk.

"Sweet."

"Oh, no. No, no, no, O'Connor. No fair. You can't bring a pastry for one and not for all. You know the rules," Tori said, glaring first at Casey, then at Sikes as he bit down into the fresh pastry with a groan. "How the hell did Sikes rank a pastry?"

"He's my boy."

"Boy toy, maybe," Tori muttered, causing Casey to laugh.

"Here you go, sweet pea. I got one for everybody, I'm just messing with you." She tossed one to Tori, then placed another in front of Leslie. "I love doing that to her. She gets so riled up."

"Shut up, O'Connor."

"Damn, you're cranky this morning, Hunter. Didn't get any last night or what?"

Leslie nearly spit her coffee out at the glare Tori shot across the desk, which only caused more laughter from Casey and John. Her smile vanished as Tori turned her scowl in her direction.

"Oh, Hunter, don't try to scare the new kid." Casey squeezed her shoulder, then leaned closer, whispering just loud enough for Tori to hear. "She's all bark, no bite." Leslie laughed again as Casey blew an exaggerated kiss to Tori.

"What the hell's wrong with you this morning, O'Connor? You get laid finally?"

"I wish." She moved to her own desk. "No. It's just a beautiful day and I'm happy. Besides, I've had three cups of coffee and I'm just a *little* wired."

"Just a little," Leslie agreed, then turned as Lieutenant Malone walked behind her.

"Tucker? Got a minute?"

Leslie nodded. "Of course." She stood, wondering what was up. She glanced at Casey who simply shrugged.

"Come on in. Sit," Malone said, closing the door behind her. She waited as he sat down behind his desk, her hands clutched together nervously as she tried to think if she'd done something wrong. She took a deep breath. "Is there a problem, Lieutenant?"

"Oh, no. No, no, nothing like that." He smiled and leaned on his desk, his hands folded together on top of a file. "But it's your second week. I just wanted to check on things, see how it's going."

She frowned. "Going?"

"I mean, you know, you and Casey, is that gonna work out

okay?"

"Oh." Leslie relaxed. "Yes, of course. Casey's been great. We get along fine. I don't see a problem, Lieutenant."

"Good, good." He opened his hands, tapping his index fingers together. "It's changed since Casey's been here." He looked out the window. "She keeps things light, always in a good mood. Keeps Tori in line, that's for sure."

"Yes. They seem like good friends. I had heard stories about Hunter, of course. Everyone has. She's nothing like I imagined." She saw the affectionate smile cross Malone's face.

"No, she's changed. Sam did that." He looked at her. "Do you know Kennedy?"

She nodded. "I had dinner with them one night. She's very nice."

"Oh, yeah?"

"Casey invited me to join them."

"I see." He shifted uncomfortably in his chair. "I thought you were…well, engaged."

"I am."

"To a man," he added quickly.

She laughed. "Yes, to a man. Is there a problem?"

"No, of course not. It's just—"

"They were all very nice. I think Casey and Tori were just trying to include me, that's all."

"Good. Times have changed, that's for sure. A few years ago, before Kennedy, there was no socializing among the detectives. I don't think any of them could stand each other's company that long," he said, rubbing his bald head. "Everyone is tight now. Sikes and Tori even. I like that."

"So do I."

He stood up then. "Well, I just wanted to touch base with you, make sure everything was fine." He looked out the window again, then back at her. "We're very open around here. If you have a complaint, a concern, you can come to me." He smiled sincerely. "Okay?"

She nodded, still confused by his questions. When she got

back to her desk, the others were silent, staring at her. She raised her eyebrows questioningly.

"So, Tucker," Casey said in a low voice, mimicking Malone. "Everything going okay with you? You think it's going to work out? I mean, you got to watch O'Connor. She thinks she's a chick magnet. Don't trust her."

Leslie laughed.

"And that Sikes, don't turn your back on him He'll chase anything in a skirt."

John laughed but threw a pen at her. Suddenly, his smile vanished. So did Leslie's as she heard Malone clear his throat. Casey turned several shades of red as she looked at him.

"Christ! Who's supposed to have my back here?"

There was a moment of silence, then Malone chuckled. "You're getting better, O'Connor. That was pretty good."

"Thank you, Lieutenant," she said weakly.

He walked closer. "Now, what about this homeless man?"

Casey ran her hands through her hair twice. "Yeah. Yes, sir. The homeless guy. Well—"

"She's had too much caffeine," Leslie said, coming to her rescue. "We went by the shelter last night, but couldn't find anyone willing to talk. We're going to head back there this morning." She looked to Casey for confirmation, who nodded. "We only have a street name so far."

"What homeless man?" Tori asked.

"Last night while we were out," Casey explained. "He'd been dead a few days. One block off of Elm."

"Deep Ellum?"

"Yeah."

"Natural?"

"Oh, no. Throat was cut."

"Good luck with that. They don't talk to cops."

"Yeah, we found that out," Leslie said. "Even the people working the shelter wouldn't talk."

"That means one of their own is the killer," Tori said. "A homeless kills a homeless, they won't talk."

Leslie and Casey exchanged glances.

"Well, see what the post reveals. Maybe Mac's team found something," Malone said. "Don't just let this one slip through your fingers. A homicide is a homicide."

Casey nodded. "Yes, sir." She watched him go, then turned to the others. "I can't *believe* you let me get busted," she said under her breath.

Tori laughed. "Serves you right, hotshot."

"Maybe I should stick with juice in the morning."

"Maybe you should limit yourself to one cup."

She stood. "All right, Tucker. Time to work."

"I'm ready," she said as she drank the last of her coffee. She'd only eaten half of her pastry. She looked at Casey with raised eyebrows. "Want it?"

"Yeah, bring it. We'll fight over it on the way over."

"Hey, wait a minute," Tori said. "What about last night? The apartments."

"Nothing," Leslie said. "I've got a log set up on the spreadsheet I made. I'll update it this afternoon, then you can take it with you tonight."

"Okay, thanks."

"Catch up with you guys later," Casey said. Leslie was surprised to feel Casey's hand lightly touching the small of her back as they walked away. The hand disappeared quickly and she smiled. Most likely, Casey wasn't even aware she'd been touching her. At the doors, Casey opened them, holding them as Leslie passed through.

"You don't have to always do that, you know."

"Sorry. Habit." Casey laughed. "I'll let you be the guy tomorrow."

"No, no. You're good at it. I don't mind."

Casey paused at the door to her truck. She unlocked it, then pulled out her cell. "Let me check with Mac first. See if they worked it yet."

Leslie got inside, wondering if she should volunteer her car for a change. In Fort Worth, they always took the departmental issued cars, never their own. Even when she worked Assault, it was rare for them to use their own vehicles.

Casey got in and closed the door, starting it quickly and turning on the air. "Sorry, I know it's hot."

"Calendar says September."

"Yeah, the calendar people don't live in Texas, do they?" She backed up, then pulled onto the street. "Mac said they haven't worked it yet. Spencer's scheduled to do the post at two."

"So we'll work on Maria then."

And surprisingly, Maria—who was not much older than them—was more than happy to visit with them. She took them through the kitchen, where no less than fifteen people worked at preparing lunch. The back door, marked with a red NO EXIT sign, was propped open, letting some of the heat escape. Maria pushed the door, holding it as they walked out into the alley. There, amongst the Dumpster and trash, she turned to face them.

"This is the best I can do for privacy," she said.

"No problem," Casey said.

"I've been expecting you, of course. I knew eventually his death would be discovered."

"We have two names. Rudy and Bobby," Leslie said.

"I knew him as Rudy. To some, he was Bobby."

"I don't suppose you know his real name?"

"Most of *them* don't even know their real names."

"Okay. Then I don't suppose you know who killed him?" Casey asked.

She turned, glancing behind her, then pulled them farther away from the door. "He was killed Friday night. He saw something he shouldn't have."

Leslie glanced at Casey, eyebrows raised.

"If you knew he was dead, why didn't you report it?" Leslie asked.

"No. That's not the way it's done on the street, Detective Tucker. I would put myself in danger, and the ones who told me."

75

"So, you *do* know who killed him?"

"I only have a name. They say Patrick."

"But this Patrick doesn't come here?"

"If he does, I don't know him as Patrick. There is no one called Patrick here."

"But it's someone from the street?" Casey asked.

"Yes."

"And they're scared of this Patrick?"

"Oh, yes. And for them to be scared, then he must be younger, have more assets—"

"Assets?"

"Money, booze, clothes, food and apparently a knife."

"So, even on the streets, there's a pecking order."

"Oh, yes. Very much so."

Leslie stepped forward. "Forgive me for being so ignorant about all this, but the shelter, it provides meals, cots, right?"

"Yes. And clothing when we can get it."

"Yet not everyone takes advantage of it."

"Sadly, no. Of course, if they all did, we would run out quickly, I'm afraid. We issue tickets for showers. Two per week. We try to find work for them, those that are able, those that are willing. If we can find them a job, eventually, we can find them low-income housing. We try to get them off the streets. But it's a losing battle."

"Anyone can come in and eat though, right?"

"Yes. And even though we offer cots, only during the coldest days of winter are they filled. They would rather be on the street. That's where they're more comfortable."

Casey pulled out her card and handed it to Maria. "You can reach me day or night. If you have any more information, or you hear something…"

"Of course, Detective."

Casey turned to go, but Leslie grabbed her arm, stopping her. "What is it you think Rudy saw, Maria? What would get him killed?"

She shrugged. "He saw a crime, I would assume."

"What kind of crime?"

"Oh, it could be anything. But obviously it was something this Patrick doesn't want revealed."

"How do you know this?" Casey asked.

"Because he was screaming, 'I won't tell, I won't tell,' before he died."

"Jesus." Casey shook her head. "And the chances of finding this Patrick?"

"They won't give him up. Not even to me."

Chapter Fifteen

Casey pulled into her driveway, shaking her head as Mr. Gunter stood on a ladder, cleaning out his gutters. She stopped the truck and hurried out, easily jumping the short hedges that separated their yards.

"What the hell do you think you're doing?" she said as she grabbed the ladder. "Haven't we had this talk already?"

"Oh, Casey, you worry too much. I'm perfectly fine."

"You're seventy-eight years old. You don't need to be climbing ladders." She looked up. "What the hell are you doing, anyway?"

He had a small spade in his hands and he held it out. "Supposed to rain tomorrow."

"And?"

"The gutters haven't been cleaned all summer."

"Oh, good grief. Come down now."

"I've just gotten started."

"I'll finish," Casey said. "Where's Ruth?"

"She was napping."

"And she'll kill you when I tell her what you were doing. Now come down." She held the ladder steady as he slowly descended, helping him down the last two steps. "Ronnie, you've got to be careful. What's Ruth going to do if something happens to you?"

"I know." He pulled off his gloves and wadded them together.

"It's just, sometimes, I want to *do* something."

"Oh, man, I'm sorry." She hugged him quickly. "I know."

He stared up at the gutter. "Seemed like a good idea."

"Come on. You want a beer?"

He smiled. "That would hit the spot."

"Well, come on over. Let me change into shorts and we'll kill a couple of beers before we tackle the gutters, okay?"

"You're too good to us, Casey."

Casey only smiled. He said those words to her every time she helped them with something around their house. Mowing the lawn, hauling bags of compost for their flower beds, fixing the leaky faucet in the bathroom, and putting their trash out on the curb for them every Tuesday and Friday morning. But it was all stuff she enjoyed doing for them. They had two kids and seven grandchildren, and in the six months Casey had lived there, she'd seen them visiting twice. The house was full of pictures, but she could see the sadness in their eyes when they spoke of their grandchildren. Apparently, no one had time for visits anymore.

Later, after she and Ronnie had finished their beer, they tackled the gutters. Her reward was getting to share dinner with them. Ruth made chicken potpie and Casey, despite her protests, was sent home with the leftovers. It was a favorite meal and Ruth knew it.

Now, as she sat in the dark sipping her wine, the lights were already out next door. It had been a hot day and even now, nearly ten, the humidity was still high. Casey stretched her legs out, resting them along the railing of her deck, swatting at the occasional mosquito. She looked out over the dark water, seeing the twinkling of lights on the distant shore. Across the way was the country club and golf course. She smiled, wondering if Tori and Sam would really go through with it and buy a house there. She wouldn't mind it, really. It'd be better than them moving off somewhere, away from her.

She leaned her head back, watching the stars overhead, letting her mind drift. She wasn't surprised when thoughts of Leslie came to her. As far as partners went, she couldn't complain. They seemed to sense each other's questions, actions. There'd been not even a hint of a problem between them. She liked her. She must. She'd told her practically her life story. And she enjoyed their conversations, even enjoyed the monotonous chore of staking out the apartments. And like Leslie said, it'd be nice if they became friends.

It'd be nicer if she was old and frumpy, though.

She smiled. "Or ugly and portly," she said out loud.

Chapter Sixteen

"Okay, so they report four possible Peeping Toms...what is that?" Leslie asked. "I mean, we didn't even have *one* possible."

She and Casey walked along the sidewalk, the morning coolness already giving way to the afternoon heat. At the door to the lab, Casey paused, letting Leslie go first.

"Thank you, Detective O'Connor."

"My pleasure."

They passed the reception desk with a wave and Leslie noticed the quick smile Casey gave Sarah. And the lingering look Sarah gave Casey. She'd found that Casey was a flirt. A flirt in a subtle, gentle way, which for some reason, made it okay.

"Okay, so their Peeping Toms," she said again.

"Either they're making it into a contest, and okay, let's say they're cheating," Casey said with a smile. "Or we have different descriptions of what constitutes a Peeping Tom. I mean, if we want to report every male who walks in the common area as a *potential*, then we can. I just think it clutters up things."

"I agree. Maybe we need to clarify with them what we're both looking for."

Casey stopped at the door to Mac's office and knocked.

"Come on in."

She opened the door, then stepped aside to allow Leslie to enter first. Leslie brushed her arm as she walked past, giving her a smile. With anyone else, she may have thought it was a condescending act to constantly hold the door open for her. But not with Casey. She'd noticed Casey did it with nearly everyone, including Tori.

"Morning, ladies. Have a seat."

"Hey, Mac. You got something good?" Casey asked.

"I think so." He shoved a piece of paper across his desk. "Take a look."

Casey took it and held it up so Leslie could see too. It was a picture of two pieces of thread or yarn.

"Okay. And?"

"They are identical."

Casey tossed the paper back on his desk. "Wonderful. I'm so happy." She leaned forward. "What the hell does it mean?"

Mac tilted his head. "It's uncanny how much alike you and Hunter are sometimes."

"Please, we are nothing alike," Casey scoffed.

Mac flicked his glance to Leslie. "Right," he said dryly. "The fibers are identical. The first was found at the crime scene of Dana Burrow's."

"The second apartment victim?"

"Yes. Spencer found the fiber in the genital area. It matched nothing in her apartment. We logged it as transfer."

"And the second?" Leslie asked.

"The second is from your homeless man. It's from the blanket he was covered with."

"So, theoretically, that could put our homeless man inside Dana Burrows apartment."

"Theoretically."

Leslie shook her head. "I can't see her opening her door to a stranger, especially someone off the street. I mean, people just don't do that. Especially young women who live alone. You just don't do that."

Casey nodded. "So? Transfer from the killer? That would mean our killer would have been in physical contact with our homeless guy before he killed Dana." She turned to Leslie with raised eyebrows. "Patrick?"

"Who's Patrick?" Mac asked.

"Someone named Patrick killed Rudy Bobby."

Mac frowned. "Who?"

"The homeless guy. Rudy Bobby."

"I didn't think we had a name for him."

"Don't know his legal name, no."

"Any other link?" Leslie asked. "His throat was cut. So was Dana Burrows's. Can we match it?"

Mac nodded. "I've got Emerson going over the photos now. I'll let you know as soon as he's done."

Casey stood. "Okay. Great job, Mac. I'll fill Hunter in."

"Thanks. And I'll e-mail over the report. Spencer's post was plain Jane, nothing jumped out. We'll have tox back tomorrow."

"Thanks."

Back outside, they headed down to their building, keeping to the shaded side of the street. The whole thing didn't make sense to her. She reached out, stopping Casey.

"It seems like too much of a coincidence," she said. She let her hand drop from Casey's arm. "If we theorize that Dana Burrows wouldn't open her door to Rudy Bobby, a homeless man, why would she open it for Patrick, another homeless man?"

"We may never know that. I doubt she knew *who* she was opening it for. I mean, it could be anything. We guessed pizza or delivery guy. How about he found out what her name was, so he simply knocks on her door and calls out her name in a friendly voice. Maybe she thinks it's a neighbor or something and just opens up."

"Scary."

"Yep."

At the door to their building, Casey paused. "Everything's okay with you, right?"

Leslie frowned. "What do you mean?"

"I mean tonight, with Michael."

"Oh. You mean because I'll be with you staking out apartments?"

"Yeah." She held open the door. "I mean, if I was him, I'd want you at home. Civilians don't always understand the job."

"Thanks. But I'm afraid he's not going to miss me. The Rangers are in town. They're all going to the game tonight."

"Good. Then I won't feel bad."

"Why would you feel bad? It's my job."

Casey grinned. "Because if I had some hot woman waiting for me at home, I'd hope you'd feel bad that I was having to go on a stakeout."

"Oh, so you're assuming Michael's hot, is that it?"

"Gross. Let's don't go there."

Leslie laughed and squeezed Casey's arm quickly as they walked inside. Sikes sat alone in the squad room. Tori was nowhere to be seen, and Leslie glanced at the two empty desks that sat by themselves, away from their four. Donaldson and Walker. She'd seen them exactly one time since she'd been here. In fact, she almost forgot they were in the same squad together. But judging by the distance their desks were from the others, they probably didn't feel like they were a part of the team.

"Where's Hunter?"

"She went to pee."

Leslie smiled, still surprised at the lack of formality among them. But Sikes must feel like a brother with a house full of sisters sometimes. And she suspected he liked it.

"Well, Mac found something. We may have caught a break." Casey looked at her. "Of course, we don't know if it's a break of not."

"What kind of break?"

They all turned as Tori came into the room. Casey pointed to her monitor. "Mac was going to e-mail you. But remember the post for Dana Burrows? Spencer found a fiber and they couldn't match it to anything in the apartment."

"Yeah. And?"

"Mac said it was an exact match to the blanket Rudy Bobby was covered with."

"Who the hell is Rudy Bobby?"

"Oh, sorry. That's our homeless guy. We don't really know his name."

"Rudy Bobby?"

"Some called him Rudy, some Bobby," Leslie explained. "Casey and I have just referred to him as Rudy Bobby."

"I see." She opened up her e-mail, scanning the report. "So, transfer?"

"They're checking the knife wounds on both victims, but it's highly likely that whoever killed Dana Burrows also killed our homeless guy."

Tori took a deep breath, then leaned back. "Okay, hotshot, what's your theory?"

Casey grinned. "I'll let Tucker give it to you."

Leslie nodded. "Maria at the shelter said his name is Patrick, or at least that's what she was told. She doesn't know of a Patrick who frequents the shelter. But he is another homeless man, that's why they won't give him up. Based on Rudy Bobby's dying words—"

"*I won't tell, I won't tell*," Casey supplied theatrically.

"We think Rudy Bobby *knew* that Patrick killed Dana Burrows. Whether the fiber is transfer from Rudy Bobby to Patrick and then to Dana, or if Rudy Bobby was actually in the apartment, we would only be guessing at this point."

Tori leaned forward. "How do you know those were his dying words?"

"He was killed Friday night, presumably while in bed, just like the others were who use that alley."

"And that's what they told Maria they heard," Casey added.

Tori nodded. "Okay. So now what?"

"Well, I guess that's kinda the problem. We're still looking for a Peeping Tom."

"Speaking of which," Leslie said. "How is it you had four possibles?"

"We had four suspicious guys lurking," Sikes said.

"Lurking? Lurking where?"

"You know. Around."

"Look, if we're going to start listing every suspicious guy who's *lurking*," Casey said, "then we're wasting our time. This isn't a contest, you know." She raised her eyebrows at Tori. "Or is it?"

"No." She smiled at Sikes. "We were just bored. It made it a little more exciting to have a *possible*."

"So in other words, you really didn't have any."

"No, O'Connor, I guess we didn't," Sikes said. "But Tori made me do it."

"Ah ha," Casey said, tossing her pen at Tori. "The truth comes out."

Tori laughed. "I knew you wouldn't be able to stand it."

"Me? Tucker was the one who said you guys were smoking crack or something. I just said you were cheating."

Malone stuck his head out of his office. "What's going on?"

Tori winked at Casey, then turned to the lieutenant. "Just discussing the case."

He nodded. "I just read Mac's report. It's something, at least."

"Yes, sir," Casey said.

"You two going out tonight?" he asked, pointing at Leslie and Casey.

"Yes, Lieutenant," Leslie said.

"Okay. Well, be careful."

Chapter Seventeen

Casey pulled up beside Leslie's car, surprised she was already here. She was fifteen minutes early. She smiled through the window, watching as Leslie juggled purse, water bottle and a bag of chips while she tried to lock her car.

"Need some help?" Casey asked when she rolled down her window.

"I got it."

Casey leaned across the console and opened the door, then took the bottle that Leslie handed her. "Miss dinner?" she asked, looking at the bag of chips.

"I wasn't in the mood for takeout," she said. "There's only so many fast food places you can go to before you're sick to death of them."

"Ah, don't cook," Casey guessed. "Does Michael?" she asked as she backed up.

"Are you kidding?"

"So you guys eat takeout every night?"

"Not fast food takeout, no. But yes, we eat out. I mean, not necessarily out. You can pick up orders at just about every restaurant nowadays."

"It's not that hard to cook," she said.

"I know. It's not that I can't cook. Well, not gourmet or anything, but I can get by. But it's that I don't cook."

Casey raised her eyebrows.

"At first, I cooked all the time. However, more often than not, I ate alone. Our schedules weren't in sync. So, it's evolved into getting takeout and each can eat when they want."

"I see."

Leslie sighed. "No, you don't. It's an insane arrangement, I know." She turned. "But I wouldn't picture you as a cook."

"Oh, I know my way around a kitchen." She shrugged. "Just, it's hard to cook for one. Steak on the grill, baked potato and a vegetable, I'm good to go. But I eat takeout a lot too." She turned on Live Oak and headed east. "And you know, Sam cooks. They invite me all the time, but I try not to go too much. I don't want to be a pest."

"And did you eat already?"

She laughed. "No. I was hoping we could take a break and grab a burger or something. Or else I'll steal half your chips."

"Good thing I opted for the bigger bag." Leslie tossed it behind them on the backseat, then pulled out the spreadsheet and her penlight. "Let's see. Brookhaven requires walking, and Creekside we think is inaccessible to a stalker. So, want to try Cascades? Or Twin *Peaks*?"

"What all did they hit last night?"

"Since Brookhaven requires walking, I'm assuming that's why they skipped it. Other than that, it looks like they hit them all."

"How would they have time for all of them?"

"Because they probably didn't sit and park like we did."

"No wonder. I should have known. Tori can't sit still this long."

"Let's do Cascades," Leslie suggested. "We never made it by there the other night. My notes say it has outdoor patios on each ground floor unit."

"What block?"

"Turn right on Hall. It's before you get to Gaston."

Casey saw the well-lit entryway—along with the cascading waterfall—well before she saw the sign. She pulled into the parking lot, driving slowly until they saw the opening between the four buildings.

"The view's not great," Leslie said when she parked. "We may need to mark this one as *walking required* too."

Casey cut the engine and opened the windows, letting in what little breeze there was. "Gonna be a warm night."

"Oh, well. I guess we're all used to it by now." Leslie turned toward her. "I picture you as the summer type anyway. All tan and everything, playing at the lake."

"Yeah. I enjoy the summer. Back in my twenties, I was at the lake all the time." She smiled. "I had a lot more energy back then."

"Didn't we all."

"Yeah. More energy, less sense."

Leslie rolled her head along the seat, watching her. Casey finally turned and raised an eyebrow.

"When did you know you were gay?"

Casey smiled. "The standard straight woman's question, huh?"

Leslie shrugged. "Just wondering."

"I knew when I was young, I guess. I always kinda felt different. So I kept to myself. I didn't have a whole lot of friends then. But I think, at the time, I attributed it to my life at home. It wasn't normal, therefore I didn't really feel normal. And it wasn't like I brought friends home or anything. I didn't want to chance that both my parents would be there at the same time. If they were, that usually meant a fight. It was easier to keep my distance with people…boys."

"How old were you when…you know?"

"What? Sex?"

"Yeah. Your first time."

"I was seventeen. She was the sister of a friend." Casey leaned her head back, remembering. "She was a freshman in college. She had the longest legs I've ever seen." She turned quickly, looking at Leslie with a smile. "Every time she saw me, she flirted with me. I never really understood it. Not until that day. It was Thanksgiving. I'd been invited to their house. She took me upstairs to listen to some new music she'd just gotten."

"Where was your friend?"

"Helping in the kitchen."

"She didn't know?"

"No. Of course, neither did I. I mean, I thought we were *really* going to listen to music. We went into her room and before I knew what was happening, she had me on the bed and her hand was down my pants."

"But you *knew*, right?"

"Yeah. I knew. It just wasn't the way I imagined losing my virginity, you know, with a quickie right before Thanksgiving dinner."

Leslie smiled. "Did you see her again?"

"Yeah. At Christmas." Casey turned back, looking out the windshield. "But that was the last time. She came home that summer and she had a boyfriend. She wouldn't even speak to me."

"So she wasn't gay?"

"No, she was gay. But like some, she tried to fight it. It's okay. I didn't blame her for that."

"Did you try to fight it?"

"No. It never really occurred to me to fight it. It was just who I was. Who I am. I didn't see the point of pretending."

"So you've never slept with a guy?"

"No. I try not to think about it." She grinned. "Because that would just be gross."

"Mmm."

"Mmm?"

Leslie shook her head. "Nothing."

"Okay. So now that we're acting like teenagers and talking about sex, when was your first time?"

"I'll give you a hint. I was the oldest virgin at college."

"No way."

"Yes."

"Man, those boys had to be falling all over you. You're gorgeous. How'd you manage?"

"I had this silly idea I'd wait until marriage."

"And I take it you didn't." She stared. "Michael's not your first, is he?"

"No. Of course not. I held out until my senior year. It was torture. Most of the girls knew I was still a virgin. I got teased constantly."

"Hope he was at least cute."

Leslie laughed. "No. It was awful. He was a virgin too."

"Oh, my God!"

"Yeah. Pretty bad."

"Then what?"

"Well, I thought, so what's all the fuss about? Sex is way overrated."

Casey laughed. "I hope your girlfriends didn't know the guy was a virgin."

"Probably. What was worse, we continued to date the rest of that semester."

"Did he get any better in bed?"

"Not one bit."

"Poor girl."

"Yeah."

"So, now—"

"No, no, no. I will *not* discuss my sex life with you."

Casey leaned back and relaxed. "Good. I like you. I try not to think about you and a guy." As soon as the words left her mouth, she cringed. *What the hell?* She closed her eyes, hoping Leslie wouldn't comment. She didn't.

But the truth was, she did like Leslie. And she also realized she tended to forget Leslie was living with a guy and engaged to be married. And probably having heterosexual sex every night. *Gross.* But there was something about the way Leslie carried herself, something about the look in her eyes. Something about the casual way she touched her all the time. There was *something* about her that drew Casey. She liked being near her, like now. Just sitting, not talking. Just being in her physical presence, it *did* something to her.

91

She turned to look out the window. *Jesus, please don't get a crush on your straight partner.* Idiot.

"Kinda quiet around here," Leslie said after a long silence. "Want to head to Brookhaven?"

Casey sat up straight. "Yeah, sure." She started the truck and backed away, then smiled. "You know, there were a couple of guys *lurking* around the pool area. Maybe we should put those down, huh?"

"Yeah, I think I will, just to give Sikes something to comment on."

"Okay, Brookhaven, that's up near Ross, right?"

"Yeah, this side of Ross," she said, looking at her notes.

Casey crossed over Bryan, going through the residential area before nearing Ross. "You'd think I'd know them all by now, but they're starting to run together."

"Brookhaven is right on the edge of our radius. I think if we don't have any hits this week, I'd feel comfortable striking it off the list. That would give us less to monitor."

"Yeah, but I have this fear we're going to be at one apartment while a murder is going on at another."

"I know. I've thought of that too. But we can't possibly be everywhere at once."

"No. But I've been thinking. On nights when Hunter and Sikes are pulling apartment duty, I think I may cruise Deep Ellum. If we really think Patrick our homeless guy is a person of interest, then it wouldn't hurt to look for him where he hangs out."

"But we don't have any idea what he looks like."

"No. But based on what Maria said, he's younger than most and has more *assets*. I'd take that to mean he may not actually look like a homeless person. Maybe his clothes aren't quite as worn and ratty. Maybe he's clean-shaven."

"Okay. I'm game."

Casey shook her head. "No, I didn't mean for you to join me. Three nights a week is plenty. It's just, you know, I've got free time."

"Well, I have two problems with that. One, if it's part of

working the case, whether or not I have free time is not an issue. And two, you shouldn't be out alone without backup. And I'd venture to guess if Malone knew that, he'd have your ass."

Casey found a parking spot on the middle row and cut the engine. "Yeah, he probably would. But I was really just planning on observing, not trying to arrest someone."

"Sorry. You're still not doing it alone."

"We'll talk about it," Casey conceded. But she recognized the look in Leslie's eyes and realized they had already talked about it. Okay, so she wouldn't go out alone. She turned away, allowing a brief smile. It'd been awhile since someone worried about her. "Don't forget to put your cell on vibrate," she said as she got out.

"Already did. I hate cell phones."

"Yeah. A necessary evil."

They blended into the shadows, walking between the buildings and heading to the common area. After nine on a Wednesday night, there weren't very many people milling about, with the exception of the pool. There appeared to be six or eight people still in the water.

"Lots of shrubs and bushes," Leslie noted.

"And short fences around the patios. Not much privacy." She stopped, pointing. "There, for instance. Blinds are open. You can see all the way through the living room and into the kitchen."

"Yeah. Two guys sitting around with their shirts off. They probably do it on purpose."

Casey snorted. "Yeah, that's the way to attract women."

Leslie smiled and touched her arm, holding her. "You want to stop and give them pointers?"

"I mean, my God, he's got hair all over his back." She shuddered. "That's disgusting." She glanced quickly at Leslie. "Should I apologize? I mean, does Michael have—?"

"No. No hairy back." Then she laughed. "And please say you're not picturing Michael naked."

"Of course not." *Not Michael anyway.* She kept walking, feeling Leslie's hand slip away from her arm.

They were quiet as they walked past the pool, moving slowly as if taking an evening stroll. There were picnic tables and benches on the lawn, but they were empty at this hour. They crossed the sidewalk, moving to the other side. The shadows were heavier here, the trees blocking out the light from the security lamps. They both saw him at once and they stopped, instinctively shrinking back against the building.

He walked in quick, short steps, stopping frequently to look around him, then moving on again. Casey felt Leslie tense beside her.

"You think it's him?" she whispered.

Casey wanted to think it was him, but he was too far away to make out his features or his clothes.

"Let's follow."

They moved silently, slowly, staying hidden behind the shrubs. They stopped when he stopped and moved when he moved. Leslie was anxious, Casey could tell. She grabbed her arm, keeping her quiet beside her. The man finally stopped, creeping along the short fence of one of the apartments. The light was on, but the blinds drawn. When he hopped the fence, Casey felt Leslie stir.

"It's gotta be him," she said, moving out of the shadows.

Casey grabbed her, clamping one hand over her mouth and pulling her back against her, holding her still. "Shhh," she whispered in her ear. She felt Leslie tremble against her and the hand at Leslie's waist tightened involuntarily. It was only then she realized their position.

"Shhh."

Leslie wasn't prepared. She had no time to react. She felt her body tremble as Casey's larger frame wrapped around her. Her vision swam as hips molded against her buttocks and two firm breasts pressed into her back. *God, couldn't she have worn a bra?*

"Watch," Casey whispered into her ear as she removed the hand covering her mouth.

But the hand at her waist remained, and Leslie tried to focus

94

on their guy, but all she could think about was the woman who held her so close, and the hand still resting at her waist.

"I don't think he's our guy."

Leslie nodded, blinking several times to clear her head. *Move away*. But she couldn't. She stayed rooted to the spot, safely within the confines of Casey's arms. She relaxed, letting her body rest comfortably against Casey as they watched. The man pressed his face against the glass, as if looking inside. Then, to their surprise, he started knocking lightly. The blinds were pulled apart and a woman's face appeared. She broke into a smile then disappeared. A few seconds later, the back door opened and the two embraced and shared a kiss.

What the hell?

But still, she couldn't concentrate. She felt Casey's grip loosen, but she couldn't move away. She closed her eyes, absorbing her warmth, imagining the breasts that were pressed against her. She bit her lip, containing the tiny moan that threatened to escape. Finally—mercifully—Casey stepped away.

"Sorry," she murmured.

Leslie ignored her comment. If she acknowledged it, then she acknowledged what had just happened. And she knew she couldn't do that. She knew she had to *ignore* what had just happened. "So they know each other?"

"I'd guess."

"An affair?"

Casey shrugged, moving on. "Who knows?"

And so the rest of the night went, with short questions and even shorter answers. They hit five complexes. And nothing noteworthy to report at any of them. When Casey dropped her off at her car later, their good-bye was as brief and abrupt as their conversation had been.

But she didn't dwell on it. She drove home without thinking, conscious of the tight grip she had on the steering wheel. And thankfully, Michael wasn't home yet. She locked the door, went into the kitchen and poured herself a glass of wine. After drinking nearly half, she took the bottle with her, going into the bathroom and locking that door as well, stripping where she stood as the tub filled with hot water.

Only when she sank into bubbles up to her neck—wineglass in one hand—did she acknowledge what had happened tonight. It could be construed as perfectly innocent. It wasn't Casey's fault that her body had responded. But then again, Casey knew, didn't she? Why else would she have been so withdrawn for the rest of the evening? Casey *had* to have known how her body responded.

She took a sip of wine, letting in memories she thought were long buried, long forgotten. But all it had taken was a few short moments of being held in another woman's arms for them to surface.

She'd been nineteen, young and naïve. Her mother was already on her second marriage, this one to a musician twenty years younger. And as far as relationships went, she knew what she *didn't* want. She didn't want a marriage like her parents, one that ended in divorce. And she certainly didn't want what her mother had, one man after another, trying to fill the void left by her divorce. No, she wanted a normal life, a normal marriage, a normal man. And so she'd had a plan. Study hard, graduate with honors, get a good job, marry a nice man and move into a big house in the suburbs. And having a female lover didn't enter into the equation.

Carol Ann.

Leslie let her eyes slip closed, remembering the girl from her past, the one who had stirred such passion within her. Two strangers thrown together because neither had a roommate, they were assigned a room in the dorm. Strangers, yes, but Leslie was drawn to her from the start. Tall and lanky, confident and sure, Carol Ann just exuded sex appeal. The first time Leslie saw her naked, she remembered how her heart skipped a beat. She remembered how dry her mouth got just watching Carol Ann. And to her horror, Carol Ann noticed.

And Carol Ann was thrilled. Because she was a lesbian. The first time they kissed, Leslie was sure she was going to pass out. It was nothing like the kisses she'd had from boys. No, Carol Ann's lips were soft, not bruising. But still, Leslie fought it. She wasn't a lesbian. It didn't fit into her plan.

But she couldn't resist. The chaste kisses turned to more. Each night, Carol Ann would come to her, climbing into the twin bed with her. Leslie tried to fight it. She did. But she simply couldn't turn away. Kissing and make-out sessions eventually led to touching. Each time she stopped it before it went too far. And each time, Carol Ann backed away, never forcing her.

No one ever knew. They didn't hang out together at school. They didn't share any of the same friends or classes. At night, it was just their secret. They would undress and lay naked, touching. And desire would build as Carol Ann's mouth feasted on her small breasts. Yes, she wanted her. But she never let her go all the way, always stopping her before her hand could creep between her legs and into the wetness she'd caused. She was a virgin. She was saving herself for marriage. And eventually, Carol Ann gave up, tiring of their game. The next semester, she moved on and Leslie got a new roommate. And she safely tucked away the memories, shoving them away as if it never happened.

Because it didn't fit in with her plans.

She poured more wine, replacing memories of Carol Ann with a new, fresh vision of Casey. Over the years, she'd been so careful. She didn't have many female friends. Those that she allowed herself to get close to were usually married, usually with kids. They were safe. And when she met Michael, when their dating evolved into them being a couple, she no longer feared being close to a woman. She was over it. It was a one-time thing, she convinced herself. And it was true. She never had those feelings again.

Not until tonight.

Not until Casey pulled her close, wrapping her body innocently around her own. Her hand shook as she brought the wineglass to her lips. Casey's body had been warm, her hand nearly searing as it rested at her waist. And her breasts...

"*God,*" she groaned, remembering how it felt to have them

97

press into her back. *Stop it!* She slammed her eyes shut. It was perfectly innocent. Casey hadn't meant anything. She was simply stopping her, that's all. Then why had Casey apologized? Why did she withdraw? Had she felt Leslie's reaction? Was she embarrassed for her?

Leslie pounded her fist down in the water causing bubbles to fly. *You're engaged to be married. To a man, for God's sake.*

"Act like it."

And she tried. Later, when Michael came home and crawled into bed beside her, she didn't resist as his arms pulled her close, didn't resist as his hands moved over her body, moving her nightshirt aside as he fondled her breasts.

"You want to make love?"

She nodded, trying so hard to feel that passion that always eluded her when he touched her. She gave in to his kisses and his familiar touch, praying that it would be enough. But it never was. And when he parted her legs, when he hovered over her and entered her, he didn't seem to notice that she wasn't ready. She squeezed her eyes shut, fighting back the nausea that threatened. She let her mind go blank as she usually did when he made love to her. It hit her then. How did she ever think she could spend a lifetime like this? Drifting away as a man used her body for his release.

Thankfully, it was over quickly. She pushed him off her as he recovered, embarrassed by the tears she felt.

"I'm sorry. I couldn't hold it," he gasped. "I'll make it up to you."

She shook her head and sat up. "No. I'm fine." But he stopped her as she tried to get out of bed.

"What's wrong? Did I hurt you?"

"No, it's nothing," she said, unable to stop the tear that slid down her cheek.

"Leslie, what?"

"Just hormones," she lied. Like most men, he took that at face value.

"I'm sorry. I didn't know."

"No, no. It's not your fault. Not at all." She stood. "I just…I just want to take a shower."

"Okay." He got up too. "I'm wide awake now. I think I'll check the late news or something."

She nodded, disappearing into the bathroom once again and locking the door behind her. She stood under the hot water, scrubbing herself. And hating herself.

Why? Why now? After all these years, why now?

But as she dried off, she dared to meet her eyes in the mirror. The truth was there and she couldn't run from the truth.

"You're attracted to her."

Strangely, those words weren't nearly as frightening to her now as they were when she was nineteen. No, the problem was whether she was going to be adult enough to be able to talk to Casey about them. Because frankly, running and hiding from it seemed to be the logical choice at the moment.

Chapter Eighteen

After agonizing over it for most of the night, Casey was still upset by what she'd done the night before. She stood on her deck sipping a cup of coffee, much like she'd done last night when she held a wineglass.

Leslie had obviously been upset by it. Could you blame her? She'd practically manhandled her. It was totally inappropriate. She would never have done that if her partner were male. And a male partner would never have done that to her.

But she did it. She grabbed Leslie. She grabbed her and didn't let her go. Worse, she held her as if...well, as if it were an embrace.

"Jesus Christ," she whispered. *What the hell is wrong with you?*

Yeah, Leslie had been upset. They'd hardly spoken the rest of the night. And Casey had been too embarrassed to apologize properly. But she would do that today. First thing. She would apologize. And hopefully, Leslie wouldn't bring her up on sexual harassment charges.

"Idiot."

But her plans to get to work early in the hopes that Leslie would be there too failed when she got caught in traffic. By the time her police scanner gave the location of the accident, it was too late for her to take an alternate route. Now, twenty minutes late, she hurried into the squad room, nearly knocking Sikes down as she burst through the double doors.

"Where's the fire, O'Connor?"

"Sorry, man. Traffic was hell."

"There was an accident on Garland," Leslie said.

Casey met her eyes across the room, nodding. "Yeah." She made her way to her desk, her nerves nearly getting the best of her.

"I hear you guys thought you had our killer," Tori said.

"Huh?"

Leslie smiled at her. "I was telling Tori how I was ready to sprint from the bushes and arrest this guy before you stopped me."

Casey felt her cheeks flush and she tried to act normal, but knew she was failing. "Yeah. Our lone excitement of the night."

"I like the idea of cruising Deep Ellum though," Tori said. "Although I don't know if we can match you on off nights."

"Yeah, I know. Sam would kill me," Casey said.

"Sam would understand. It's Sikes I'm worried about."

They all turned to look at John.

"What?"

"You know what," Tori teased. She looked back at Casey. "John's in love."

"Oh, my God! Are you kidding?" She was pleased at the blush that covered John's face.

"I'm not in love," he said.

"Sure you are. You've had what? Four dates?"

"Four dates? With the same girl?" Casey glanced at Leslie. "John is one and out, normally."

"Well, how wonderful, John. Congratulations."

He glared at Tori. "I'm going to kill you."

"I think it's sweet."

"Shut up."

Casey laughed. "Don't be embarrassed, Sikes. Everybody should fall in love at least once."

"Yeah? What about you?"

Casey shrugged. "I'm still waiting. It'll happen someday." Her

101

smile vanished. "I hope." She looked up, surprised to find Leslie's eyes on her. She glanced at the others, but Tori had picked up the phone and Sikes had turned to his computer. She motioned to the hallway. "Can I talk to you?" she asked quietly.

Leslie nodded and got up, following Casey down the hall and into the ladies' room. Casey turned as soon as the door closed, facing Leslie.

"I need to apologize," she said.

Leslie frowned. "For?"

"Come on. We both know what for. It was inappropriate. I'm sorry."

Leslie raised her eyebrows. "What part, Casey?"

Casey dropped her head. She wasn't making it easy, was she? "If you were a guy, I never would have done that. And if your partner were a guy, he never would have touched you that way."

Leslie took a step closer. "Touched me that way?" she repeated.

Casey nodded. "I crossed the line. I don't know what happened. I just...I just did it. I grabbed you without thinking."

Their eyes met, holding. Casey tried to guess what was going through Leslie's mind. Was she remembering the way Casey had pulled her close, had pressed her body to her own? Casey swallowed, trying to clear her head, trying to forget how it felt.

"If it's all the same to you," Leslie said, "I'd just as soon not talk about it."

Casey shook her head. "No. It's not all the same," she said. "Please, we've got to talk about it. I feel like an ass. I just want to say I'm sorry and I want you to say you forgive me and we'll forget all about it."

Leslie turned her back to Casey. "And we'll just forget all about it, is that right?"

"Yes. It won't ever happen again. I'm sorry."

Leslie turned back around. "So the fact that I had a...a *reaction* to your touch doesn't matter?"

It was Casey's turn to stare. "*What?*"

"Maybe I should be the one apologizing."

102

Casey walked closer, her hand reaching out to grasp Leslie's arm. "What are you talking about? I did it, not you. You could file charges against me."

Leslie smiled. "Is that what you're worried about? Sexual harassment?"

"It's crossed my mind."

"Was it sexual harassment?"

"No, of course not. I swear. I don't know what came over me."

"And I don't know what came over me."

Their eyes met again and Casey was startled by what she saw there. She was unable to look away.

"I…I just had a…a *moment*," Leslie said quietly. "I thought you could tell. I thought you knew."

Casey couldn't drag her eyes away. All she remembered was the feeling of Leslie trembling in her arms. A trembling she assumed was from fear. "I guess…well, I guess maybe I had a moment too then."

They both broke into smiles and Casey relaxed, feeling somewhat relieved. At least Leslie wasn't pissed at her.

"Okay, so we had a moment," Leslie said. "And we won't talk about it anymore, right?"

"Right."

She nodded. "Okay. I can live with that."

But when the door opened and Tori walked in, they both took a step away from each other. Leslie's eyes darted from one to the other.

"I was just leaving," she said, then bolted from the room.

Tori stared at Casey, eyebrows raised. "Everything okay?"

Casey nodded. "Yeah, sure. We were…we were just having a moment."

Tori grinned and walked toward one of the stalls. "Yeah, Sam and I used to have moments in here all the time."

Their eyes met and Casey felt her face turn red. She followed Leslie from the room, hearing Tori's quiet laughter mocking her.

103

"Hey, Mac called," Sikes said when she returned to her desk. "Positive match on the knife wounds. And he said they got tox back on your homeless guy. He said to swing by if you wanted to chat about it, or he'd just e-mail you."

"Thanks. I think I'll swing by." She looked at Leslie. "You want to go?"

She noticed her hesitation and didn't blame her, but she nodded. "Yeah. Let's walk."

But their silence was unnerving and Casey finally stopped. "Look, are you mad at me?"

"No, of course not."

"Are you sure?"

Leslie took a step closer and Casey felt warm fingers grip her arm. "We're fine, Casey. But please, let's just forget about it, okay? 'Cause it's all fine." She squeezed her fingers tightly one more time, and Casey watched as her hand slipped away.

We'd be more fine if you'd quit touching me.

Leslie turned. "What?"

Casey's eyes widened. "Oh, my God. Did I say that out loud? I thought I thought that."

"Thought what?"

"Thought what you thought I said."

"Huh?"

She laughed. "I thought...well, never mind."

Leslie stared at her, then bumped her shoulder lightly as they started walking again. "You know, with a little perfection, we can take this comedy act on the road."

"Funny, Tucker."

Funny, yeah, but Leslie felt like she was going to explode if she didn't resolve this soon. Her admission last night, and her plan to act like an adult this morning and talk to Casey had gone out the window as soon as she laid eyes on her. It was easy to tell that Casey was eaten up with guilt and Leslie couldn't let her take all the blame. She also couldn't bring herself to say the

104

words *I'm attracted to you* either.

So they'd fumbled through the apologies, finally agreeing to forget about it and move on. Which would have been ideal, if not for one little problem.

She was attracted to her.

"What do you think?"

She blinked. "What?"

Casey tilted her head. "About the cocaine."

She frowned, meeting Casey's eyes.

"Okay. So you weren't listening," Casey said with raised eyebrows. "Tox came back positive for cocaine. Homeless people can't afford cocaine. Homeless people can't afford drugs period. So, where do you think he got cocaine?"

"Patrick?"

"If Patrick is homeless too, where'd he get cocaine?"

"Okay, so it's really a rhetorical question?"

Casey laughed. "No, I was hoping you'd have a guess."

"The way you've described this Patrick, he may be a carrier for a dealer. Could be why he's a little better off than the others," Mac suggested.

"But what dealer is going to trust a homeless guy with money?" Leslie asked.

"True."

Casey sighed. "Okay, Mac. Anything else?"

"Nothing else on tox."

"And the knife wounds are a positive match?"

"Yeah. I'll include photos from both in my report. I'll copy Hunter on the e-mail."

"Thanks. At least we know we have a link now."

Leslie sat quietly, watching as Casey brushed at her hair, unconsciously tucking the longer strands behind her ears. Her eyes lowered and she was horrified to find herself staring at Casey's chest. She pulled her eyes away, focusing on Mac instead.

"If you can find me a knife, we can match the cut."

"Yeah, and if I can find me a Patrick, maybe I can find you a knife." Casey stood. "Thanks for your time, Mac."

Casey held the door for her and Leslie walked through without a comment. Back on the street, she found herself keeping her distance from Casey as they headed back to their building.

"You know, tonight, there's really no need for both of us to be out," Casey said.

"Are you going to start that again?"

Casey glanced at her quickly, then away. "No offense, but there seems to be a little tension between us. And I hate it."

Leslie stopped, grabbing Casey's arm to make her do the same. "I hate it too. I'm sorry."

Casey ran her hand through her hair, staring skyward. "Look, I don't know what to do. I'm sorry for what happened. It's obviously made you uncomfortable to be around me."

"*What?*"

"That's why maybe tonight, we shouldn't be together."

"O'Connor, get over it already, will you? We're both adults here. And for some reason, you're not seeing the whole picture." She realized she was still gripping Casey's arm and she released her. *Christ, can't you keep your hands off her?*

Their stare was intense, neither pulling away. Finally, Casey took a step back. "Okay. I'll get over it."

"Thank you."

But not another word was spoken as they continued on to their building. At the door, she paused, shifting nervously as Casey waited.

"Look, I've got an appointment," she blurted out. She glanced at her watch. "Early lunch. I'll be back in an hour."

Casey frowned. "What?"

"Call my cell if you need me."

She left Casey standing at the door, but she had to get away. She sat for a moment in her car, trying to decide what to do. Then it hit her.

Sam.

But she almost lost her nerve as she walked into CIU. Sam and Tori were good friends with Casey. But who better to talk this out with than Sam? So she showed her badge and was pointed toward Sam's office without having to explain her business. At the door, she raised her hand to knock then stopped, closing her eyes for a moment before tapping lightly.

Sam glanced at the door, then called a quick come in. She was surprised when Leslie Tucker stuck her head inside.

"Sam, I'm sorry to barge in unannounced, but—"

"No, come in. Is everything okay?" Then her heart raced. "Tori?"

"No, no. Everything's fine. I just needed...well, I wanted to talk. It's personal."

Sam nodded. "Of course." She motioned to the visitor's chair across from her, wondering at the troubled look on Leslie's face.

"I know it's only ten thirty, but could you break away for lunch?"

Something about the haunted look in her eyes made Sam agree. "Sure. I can get away."

Leslie smiled her thanks. "And when I say lunch, I didn't mean to eat. I just...just..."

"Need to talk?" Sam grabbed her purse. "I understand. How about we walk down to The Palms? We can get some iced tea and find a table in the shade," she suggested.

"Perfect."

Sam stopped at the reception desk on her way out, letting Melissa know she'd be out. Once they were on the sidewalk, Sam leaned closer. "Want to tell me now or do you want to wait?"

"You already know, don't you?"

"Casey?" she guessed.

Leslie looked away. "I'm engaged to be married and I find myself attracted to another woman." She stopped up short on the sidewalk. "And I don't know what to do."

Sam took her arm. "Come on. We'll talk." At The Palms outdoor restaurant, she directed Leslie to an open table and then went in search of a waiter. Two teas and a spinach and mushroom quiche should serve as a light brunch. When she got back to the table, she squeezed Leslie's hand. "It's not the end of the world."

"I know." She twisted her napkin nervously. "What did you do when you found yourself attracted to Tori? I mean, you were with a guy then, right?"

Sam smiled at the memory. "Yes. And I was scared at first, I didn't really know what was happening. It obviously made me realize that what I felt for Robert wasn't it, you know? But we weren't living together, so that made it easier. And we weren't engaged. He wanted to get married, but I was never ready." She squeezed Leslie's hand again. "And of course, now I know why I wasn't ready."

"It's funny. When Michael asked me to marry him, I thought it would be good because he still had his friends and his games, and he wouldn't expect me to be with him constantly." Leslie tossed her napkin down and leaned her elbows on the table. "Isn't that an awful reason to agree to get married?"

Sam studied her, wondering what it was Leslie wasn't telling her. She didn't have to wonder long.

"I've had these feelings before." She glanced at her. "For a woman, I mean. Well, a girl really. We were nineteen. And without going into great detail, I ran from it. I just couldn't deal with it at the time. I didn't think I could *ever* deal with it." She paused as the waiter brought their tea. "I hid it away, I buried it, and I went on with my life. Truth is, I forgot about it. I mean, I'm thirty-two. Nineteen was a long time ago."

"But before Michael, I'm guessing there wasn't anyone?"

"No, not really. I dated but…how did you know?"

"Because before Robert, I was the same way. And when I met him, I thought, this isn't so bad. I mean, maybe this is all there is, you know?"

"Exactly. That's how I felt with Michael. It's been okay. But now, it's not okay." She looked at her. "Casey, I think about her all the time. I can't wait to get to work each day. I want to be near her, I want to *touch* her. And when I get home to Michael, I realize I don't feel those things with him. I never felt that *need* to be with him."

Sam nodded. "I know exactly how you're feeling. I just wanted to be with Tori all the time. I didn't care how or when."

Leslie laughed. "I know. I never thought I'd love all-night stakeouts."

They were quiet for a moment, Sam letting Leslie collect her thoughts. She finally leaned back in her chair. "So? Now what? Does Casey know?"

"Casey is either oblivious to it, or else she's pretending she's oblivious."

"Well, if it's anything like with Tori, I had to practically hit her over the head with it. But maybe that's not what you want? Maybe you want Casey to ignore it?"

"Like this is a phase and I'll get over it?"

Sam shrugged. "Perhaps. I mean, you consider yourself straight, right?"

"I did, yes."

"So did I. Until I met Tori. And I thought, how funny. What are the chances I could make it into my thirties and have never met a woman who stirred sexual attraction before? Must be an anomaly. But I couldn't shake it. All the things I was taught I'd feel when I fell in love, I never felt them until I met Tori. And once I accepted that and quit fighting it, it just all fell into place. Tori, on the other hand, was harder to convince. She had this huge wall around her. She wouldn't let anyone get close. She didn't want anyone to love her and she didn't want to love anyone. It was her way of not getting hurt." She sipped from her tea, wondering how much to tell Leslie. "I know you don't know them very well, especially Tori, but if you take them at face value, they seem so very different from each other. Tori is distant, she appears unapproachable to most. She doesn't make friends easily. Casey is just the opposite. She's very friendly, very open, and very approachable. And they both hide behind those traits. Tori lost her whole family when she was young." She paused. "They were murdered while she was made to watch."

Leslie's eyes widened. "I had no idea."

"She was twelve, but it took its toll. And Casey, well, she just had a crappy childhood. And her brother, well, let's just say he's a—"

"Bastard," Leslie finished for her. "She's told me some."

"Good. Then you can understand how they were both starving for family. So when the two of them get together, as different as they appear on the outside—when they drop their protective shields—they are so much alike, it's scary. They could be sisters. I tease them all the time, and despite their protests, I think they love it. They need each other." She stared across the table, wondering where she was going with this story. "I guess what I'm trying to say is that underneath that happy-go-lucky persona that Casey sports most of the time, lurks a fragile and kind heart, just like Tori's. And I don't want to see it get broken. She doesn't deserve that."

Leslie smiled. "No. But that would mean we'd have to actually talk about this."

Sam laughed. "Yeah. Good luck with that. Getting them to talk about their feelings is like pulling teeth."

Their waiter brought their quiche and Leslie looked up in surprise. "Lunch?"

"I missed breakfast." She felt her face blush, remembering just why she'd missed breakfast. "It happens quite often."

Leslie picked up her fork, then paused. "You won't say anything, will you? I mean, to Tori?"

"No. I promise. I won't say a word. This is between you and Casey." And she wouldn't. She sat there, watching Leslie, remembering her own plight, remembering how scared she was when she realized it wasn't Robert she was in love with but a woman. Scared, yes, but it had all been worth it. It hadn't been easy, but she wouldn't trade it for anything. Tori was her life. And she wanted nothing more than for Casey to find that same kind of love. Whether or not Leslie was the one, she knew they would have a rough road ahead of them.

But some things are worth it.

Chapter Nineteen

Casey pulled up beside Leslie's car, just like always. And like always, Leslie was waiting for her. She had two water bottles this time.

"I'm tired of you stealing mine," she said lightly as she handed one to Casey.

"And here I brought you an extra bag of potato chips," Casey said with a smile.

Their eyes met for a second, and Leslie nodded. Yes, they both knew what they were doing. And it was okay. Forget about yesterday. Start over. They could do that.

Casey pulled into traffic, driving slowly down Main, heading to Deep Ellum. Hunter and Sikes were already out, cruising the apartments. And with any luck, they'd find something. Because the idea of being out every night, cruising the streets, was depressing.

"Michael have plans tonight?" she asked.

"No. Actually, he was pissed."

"Told you."

"Doesn't matter. I told *you* that you weren't going out alone."

"Yeah, well, we can't keep this up indefinitely. You'll be divorced before you're even married and I'll *never* get a date."

Leslie laughed. "Those are our choices? Divorced and celibate?"

Casey pulled onto Elm, cruising slowly through the club district. "So, how pissed was he?"

"I'm apparently bordering on neglect."

"I see. Food or sex?"

"Both. He can't seem to order takeout on his own."

"But sex on his own is not a problem, right?"

Leslie laughed. "I wouldn't know. But we had quite the argument earlier."

"I'm sorry. Again—"

"Stop. Our argument had little to do with me being out again. It was just an excuse."

"I don't understand."

"When Michael has options, like a ball game, he doesn't care about my hours. But when he has nothing, like tonight, he cares. And as I told him, if I'd been left alone last night while he went to his ballgame, he wouldn't have considered it neglect that I was home alone. But apparently, since I'm out tonight while he's home alone, it's suddenly a big deal."

"So you left without having dinner and you're making him fend for himself?" Casey guessed.

"Pretty much. But he'll just end up going to Jeff's. They'll order pizza and play games, and he'll forget all about our fight by the time I get home."

And then you can make up with sex. Casey was surprised by the jolt of jealousy she felt at the thought. Good grief. They're engaged to be married. They're living together. They have sex. Get over it. They probably had sex last night. She glanced quickly at Leslie's profile. She was staring out the window, lost in thought. Yeah, they probably had sex last night. Casey was at home, agonizing over the little indiscretion she'd had, and Leslie was with Michael. Having sex.

She didn't realize the tight grip she had on the steering wheel until Leslie touched her arm.

"What's wrong?"

"Nothing. Why?"

"You have a death grip on the wheel."

112

Casey made herself relax. She took one hand off the wheel and reached for her water bottle, taking a long drink.

"Casey?"

"Hmm?"

"I like you a lot, you know."

Casey stopped at a red light, chancing a glance at her. But Leslie's gaze was straight ahead, staring out the window again. The light turned green and she went on, not knowing what to say.

And for the next hour, they cruised up and down Elm, and on the side streets, looking for anyone who caught their eye. They talked some, but their conversation took on a less personal tone. Which was fine. It was less stressful that way.

At ten thirty, just when she was planning her last drive down Elm, Leslie spotted him. She grabbed Casey's arm, jerking her around to her side.

"There. That guy."

He was young, tall and thin, and the only thing out of the ordinary was the long trench coat he wore. It was at least eighty degrees out. He ducked down a side street, walking quickly, hands shoved in the pockets of his coat, head down.

Casey turned down the street, following him at a distance. The traffic was light and she felt conspicuous. "I'm going to pass him. It's too obvious we're following if we stay back."

"Okay. But go slow."

And she did, moving past him at a steady speed, then turning on her blinker a block down and taking another street. She drove out of sight, then made a U-turn, and killed her lights. They waited.

"There he is."

He walked past the intersection of Baumer and headed north on Oak. Casey let him get a block ahead, then she pulled away from the curb. "You see him?"

"Yeah. He's up ahead."

"If he stays on Oak, he'll have to cross Gaston."

"Cascades? You think he's headed there?"

113

"Could be."

Casey waited until the light turned on the cross street before moving into traffic. She eased between two cars, going with the flow as they passed him again. At Gaston, she turned right. "Watch him."

Leslie turned in the seat, looking out through the back. "I've got him."

Casey drove as slow as she could without causing attention. One block up Gaston, at Hall, she crossed lanes, moving to the left. "Can you still see him?"

"No. He's out of sight."

"Goddamn," she muttered. She sped through the intersection, turning left again, trying to get back to Oak. "Where the hell are we?"

"We're on Swiss. Keep going. It intersects back with Oak."

And there they saw him again as he jogged across Swiss and turned onto Cobb, going north.

"Cascades is one block up," Leslie said. "Should we call Hunter?"

"Let's wait. Hell, for all we know, he lives there. He could have just had a night on the town and is going home." She drove past Cobb, taking the next street up. She saw the waterfall and turned into the entryway for the Cascades complex, parking in the first spot they found and then killed the engine and lights. "Duck down."

They both did, sliding low in the seat. And within minutes, he came into view, crossing practically in front of them as he ducked into the shadows, moving silently among the shrubs.

"He doesn't live here," she said.

"No. But he knows his way around."

"Let's follow."

They got out, closing their doors silently. Without thinking, Casey took Leslie's arm, pulling her, urging her to go first. She followed, keeping to the shadows, following him. Leslie stopped up short and Casey did the same.

"He went between the buildings," she whispered.

Casey nodded, keeping a hand on Leslie's arm. "Let's give him a minute."

And they waited. Casey could feel the tension between them. She squeezed Leslie's arm and she turned toward her, eyebrows raised.

"Ready?"

Leslie nodded, moving again, following him. They found him easily. He was beside a shrub, staring into an apartment, his hand inside his pants.

"Jesus Christ," she muttered. "He's jacking off."

"I think that's what Peeping Tom's do."

Casey pressed against the building, pulling Leslie with her. They stood face to face, their eyes meeting. "You stay here," she said. "I'll go around the side, keep him from running."

Leslie nodded, never taking her eyes away. But when Casey turned to go, Leslie pulled her back. "Be careful."

Simple words, but damn if they didn't tug at her heart. Casey's gaze dropped to Leslie's lips and she had such an overwhelming urge to kiss her, she panicked. She backed up, nearly tripping over the shrub, only to regain her balance when Leslie grabbed her.

"You okay?"

Casey grinned. "I'm an idiot. Other than that, I'm fine." She slipped away then, going back the way they'd come and down the sidewalk, and coming up from behind him. When she had him in view, she slowed her pace, walking purposefully toward him.

"Hey, man. What's up?"

He jerked his head around and they stared at each other for a second, then he bolted, taking off toward Leslie. She pulled her weapon, pointing it directly at him.

"Don't move."

He stopped, turning, but Casey was there and she grabbed his shoulders, pushing him against the wall of the building. "No, you don't," she said. "You're not going anywhere."

"Who are you?"

"Police. And you're being very naughty." Casey stepped back, looking at him. "Christ, man, put that shit back in your pants, okay?"

"I...I didn't do nothing wrong."

"Yeah? You think it's okay to watch girls and jack off while you do it?"

"But she leaves her blinds open."

"Whatever." Casey twisted his hands behind his back. "What's your name?"

"John."

"Well, John, you're under arrest." She slipped her handcuffs around his wrists. "Let's start with indecent exposure," she said, glancing again to his unzipped pants.

"I...I didn't mean no harm, ma'am."

"Uh-huh. And what's your last name, John?"

"Doe."

"Doe? Are you kidding me? You're going to give me *Doe*? John Doe?"

"What do you mean? That's my name."

Casey turned him around but she felt Leslie move beside her, felt her light touch on her arm.

"John? I'm Detective Tucker. This is Detective O'Connor."

"What's your name?" he asked.

She smiled. "It's Leslie. She's Casey."

"Pretty names. Mine is John."

She nodded. "Yes. We're going to want you to go with us to the police station, John. Is that okay?"

He shrugged. "She's got me tied up. I don't know if she'll let me go."

Leslie glanced at Casey. "She'll let you go. In fact, she's going to drive us."

"Okay then. I guess I can go, Miss Leslie."

"Good." Leslie turned back to her. "Okay?"

Casey nodded. "I'll call Hunter."

Chapter Twenty

"And his name is John Doe? Are you kidding me?"

"He's...well, he's a little slow," Casey said.

"And he's willing to give DNA," Leslie added.

Tori spun around. "Does he *know* he's giving DNA? If you said he's under arrest, has he requested an attorney?"

"No."

"So when you say he's slow, does he even know where he is?" Tori glared at Casey. "Christ, O'Connor, we can't screw this one up on a technicality."

"It's been by the book, Hunter." Leslie moved between them, feeling the need to defend Casey. "We told him he can request an attorney to be present. We told him he didn't have to talk to us. We told him he didn't have to volunteer DNA. It's by the book."

"Does he know *why* we want his DNA?"

"Yes."

Tori nodded. "Okay. I'm sorry. It's just—"

"It's been a long night for us all," Casey said. "Let's just do it and get it over with. Besides, he's not our killer."

"How can you be sure? Anybody can put on an act of being slow."

"I don't believe it's an act, Hunter. But we're getting the DNA, so that won't be an issue."

117

"And we can hold him overnight. I spoke with Mac. He called Emerson. They'll put a rush on it at the lab."

"Okay. Have we offered him a phone call?"

"Yes. He said he doesn't have anyone to call. We'll cut him loose in the morning."

Tori stared at them both, finally relaxing. "Okay. It's your case, your call." She turned to go, then stopped. "You let Malone know?"

"Yeah." She smiled. "He said to run it by you."

"Wonderful," she murmured with a sigh. "All right, I'm heading out. See you guys in the morning."

Casey slumped down in her chair as soon as Tori left, and Leslie couldn't stop herself from going to her. She slid her hands across her shoulders, squeezing gently, feeling the tense muscles under her fingers. She squeezed harder, eliciting a moan from Casey. A moan that caused a shiver to run up her spine. She closed her eyes for a moment, her hands still resting on Casey's shoulders. Then she moved, patting her arm in what she hoped was a friendly manner.

"Are you as tired as I am?" she asked lightly as she sat at her own desk.

"Mmm. And you could have put me to sleep with that backrub," Casey said, her eyes still closed.

Leslie watched her, unobserved, and she was free to stare. Casey's brow was furrowed, drawn. Her normally flawless complexion showed signs of stress tonight. Even her lips, usually curved upward in a smile, seemed lifeless. But then those blue eyes opened, catching her staring. They held her captive, refusing to let her go. Not that she tried to pull away. Because Casey's eyes were anything but lifeless.

"You should go home," Casey said quietly. "It's late."

"We've got—"

"I'll wait for Emerson. You go." She said, flexing her shoulders. "Michael's probably worried."

Leslie nearly flinched at the mention of her fiancé's name. Those moments when she stared into Casey's eyes, she'd

118

forgotten she had a fiancé. She wondered if Casey mentioned his name on purpose, just to remind her. Or perhaps to remind Casey that he existed.

God, it was suddenly getting too complicated.

So she nodded, getting to her feet. She picked her keys up off her desk and slipped them into the pocket of her jeans. She'd left her purse in her car earlier in the night. "I guess I'll head out then. See you in the morning."

Casey only nodded, her eyes slipping closed again. Leslie watched her for a moment, then left. But at the door, Casey called to her.

"Les?"

"Hmm?"

"We can do this. It'll be okay."

The words were spoken softly, surely. And they took her by surprise. She didn't have to ask her to explain. She knew exactly what Casey meant.

And she was scared to death.

Chapter Twenty-One

Casey was about two blocks from their building when her cell rang. It was Hunter.

"Mac has something for us. Why don't you just meet me at the lab?"

"Where's Tucker?"

"She's not in yet."

"Okay. Well, I'll meet you out front. I'm just parking now."

She sat for a moment, wondering if she should call Leslie. Of course, it wasn't late. Not even eight yet. She got out, looking around for Tori. She saw her just coming out of the building when her cell rang again. This time, it was Leslie. She took a deep breath before answering.

"Hey, it's me."

She smiled, feeling silly. "Good morning."

"I'm stopping for coffee. Want some?"

"Yes, please."

"So, I'm running a little late then."

Casey grinned. "Coffee's a good excuse."

"No excuse. I didn't sleep well." She paused. "You?"

Casey hesitated too. "No, I didn't really sleep well either." She heard the quiet sigh that Leslie uttered, so she forced a smile to her face. "But it's the weekend. We'll catch up."

"Yeah. I suppose." She cleared her throat. "Okay, well I'm

sorry I'm running late."

"No problem." She walked up to meet Tori, smiling a greeting. "Hunter and I are on our way to the lab."

"Results already?"

"Don't know yet."

"Okay. Well, I'll see you in a bit."

"Yep." She closed her phone, glancing at Tori. "That was Tucker."

"I see." She raised her eyebrows. "Just having a *moment*, are you?"

Casey ignored her. "She's getting us coffee."

"Great."

Casey noticed the smile Tori was trying to hide and she nudged her with her elbow. "Cut it out."

"I didn't say a word, O'Connor."

"You don't have to."

They walked on a few more steps in silence, then Tori turned to her. "So, are you completely insane or what?"

"Possibly. You should know."

"What's that supposed to mean?"

"Well, gee, Hunter, you've been here before. You tell me?"

"She's engaged."

"Yes, she is. So tell me what I'm supposed to do?"

"Sorry, kid. You're on your own on this one." She stopped before they got to the door. "But I know what you're going through, Casey. Just be careful."

And just like that, they'd talked about it without really talking about it. She and Hunter…damn, what a pair. Just like a couple of guys. She smiled as she followed behind Tori as they headed to Mac's office.

"Come on in," he called when Tori knocked.

"You're sure at it early, Mac," Casey said.

"Emerson called me at three this morning. He wanted me to check this." He shoved a graph across his desk. "It's a DNA sequence."

Tori stared at him, waiting.

"This is the DNA profile of the sample left at the murder scene. And this is the DNA profile of your John Doe."

Casey took the paper. "John Doe, that's his name. Not John Doe as in we don't *know* his name," she corrected.

"What? You're kidding me?"

Casey shrugged, looking at the paper. She then handed it to Tori. "We're just dumb cops, Mac," she said. "DNA sequence? We got a match or not?"

"We do not have an exact match, no." He took the paper from Tori and pointed to the chart. "But look at this. This is why Emerson called me. Not an exact match, but similar."

"Similar?"

"Without going into gene sequencing and losing you totally, in layman's terms, they're related. Father and son. Perhaps two brothers. Could even be an uncle to one. Related that way."

"You're serious? You can tell that from…just from this?" Tori asked, pointing to the graph he held.

"Yes. DNA profiling has come a long way. We've been able to break down the gene sequence for some years now. Why, if you give me—"

"Yeah, Mac, that's great," Tori said, interrupting him. "Let's get back to this."

"So John's not our killer, but someone he's related to is." Casey stood, pacing. "If he lives on the streets, it stands to reason that this relative does too." She stopped, staring at Tori. "Patrick?"

"Could we get that lucky?" She stood, too. "Let's go talk to John Doe." She nodded at Mac. "Thanks, man. Good job."

"Don't thank me. Emerson is one who stayed up here all night."

"So, you think if we push him, he'll give it up?" Tori asked.

"I don't know. Like I said last night, he's a little slow, but he's not stupid."

"So good cop-bad cop might not work with him?"

They stood in the doorway, watching Leslie and Sikes. A

cup of coffee sat on each desk. Leslie turned, as if sensing her watching.

"I think you should let Tucker talk to him."

"Why?"

"For one, he doesn't know you, and frankly, you're intimidating. And two, he took a liking to her. I think he'll talk to her."

"Okay. Your call. Sikes and I will observe though, if you don't mind."

"No, that's fine."

"Can't believe you're letting the new chick do this," Sikes said as he leaned against the wall.

Tori shrugged. "O'Connor thought it was best." She moved to the window, watching as John was led into the interrogation room. Sikes walked up beside her and adjusted the volume on the speakers, letting Leslie's voice drift into the room.

"Did you sleep well, John?" Leslie asked.

"Yes, Miss Leslie. It was soft." He looked at O'Connor. "Good morning, Miss Casey. Are you here to tie me up again?"

Casey smiled. "No, John. In fact, we're going to take you back down to the streets."

His face lit up. "Oh, goody."

"But first, we have a few questions. Then you can go. Is that all right with you? Can we ask you some questions?"

"I don't care."

Sikes nudged her arm. "He doesn't have a clue about his rights. A judge would throw this out in a heartbeat."

"We're not looking for him to testify. We just need some information."

"John, you live out on the street, right?" Leslie asked.

"Yes."

"Do you have a brother?"

He shook his head. "No. I don't have a brother."

"Does your father live with you, maybe?"

He made a face. "My father? I don't have a daddy."

123

"Okay. Well, is there anyone who lives with you?"

"You mean like my sister?"

"You have a sister?" Casey asked. "Not a brother, but a sister?"

He nodded.

"What's her name?" Leslie asked.

"Patty."

Casey and Leslie exchanged glances. "Patty? Does she have a last name?" Casey asked.

He made a face. "Duh. She's my sister."

Leslie hid a smile. "Patty Doe."

Sikes laughed. "Look at them. Do they have a clue yet?"

"What do you mean?"

"Oh, come on, Tori. I've already been through this with you and Sam, remember? Watch how they look at each other. They don't even know they're doing it."

"Yeah, I see what you mean."

"So? Do they have a clue?"

She shrugged. "Leslie's engaged."

There was a quick knock on the door and Malone stuck his head in. "Buzz them. He's posted bail."

"How?"

"I don't know. But his attorney is waiting. Kill the interview."

"He's homeless. *What* attorney?" Tori asked as Sikes buzzed into the interrogation room. Casey looked up at the window, then went to the phone.

"O'Connor, Malone says to cut him loose. His attorney is here."

They watched Casey's face, saw her *what the fuck* look as she hung up the phone. "God, I love her," Tori said without thinking. She looked at Malone and Sikes. "What?"

"I'll never understand you women," Malone muttered as he walked away.

"Hey, I didn't mean love like *love*, you know."

"Whatever."

She turned to Sikes. "Now he's going to think I'm having an affair with O'Connor."

"Yeah. Wait until he gets a clue about O'Connor and Tucker. That'll really spin his head." He grinned. "I know it's already spinning mine."

They walked out into the hallway just as Casey and Leslie came out with John Doe. Before Tori could say anything, two men in suits walked up behind them.

"Well, well. Detective Hunter. I should have known."

Tori turned, standing face to face with Robert, of all people. *Wonderful.*

"I understand you've been questioning my client without representation."

"He waived his right to an attorney."

Robert plastered a false smile on his face. "Let's see. Since when does *indecent exposure* require jail time? Or have you taken to harassing the homeless now?"

Tori tilted her head, aware of everyone watching them. "I wasn't the arresting officer." She took a step closer. "But I understand he was exposing himself while he watched a young lady in her apartment."

"I didn't expose nothing," John said. Then he smiled sheepishly. "Well, maybe just a little."

"You don't have to say another word. Let's get you out of here," Robert said. "I'll take you home."

"Who are you?" John took a step back. "Miss Leslie, who is he?"

"He's your attorney."

"I don't have no attorney. No. I don't want to go with him."

"Who posted his bail?" Tori asked.

"You're the detective," Robert said. "It'll give you something to do." He looked at John again. "John, I'm going to take you down to the shelter so you can get something to eat, okay? Then you can stay. You can go back to the street. You're not in trouble."

John looked at Leslie and she nodded. "It's all right, John. You go with him."

"Will I see you again?"

She smiled and touched his arm affectionately. "I think so.

Don't you?"

"I hope so." He turned. "Miss Casey, I'm glad you didn't have to tie me up again."

"Yeah, me too." She looked at the others. "But for the record, it was just handcuffs."

Sikes nudged Tori as Leslie reached out and squeezed Casey's arm. He leaned closer. "Told you."

They walked back to their desks in silence, then Leslie turned, facing them. "Who the hell *was* that?" she asked.

Tori stared as all eyes were on her. She shrugged. "Robert."

"Robert who?"

Sikes grinned. "Yeah. Robert who?"

"Shut up, Sikes."

Casey finally came to her rescue. "Robert is the defense attorney Sam was dating when…well, when…you know, when Tori and Sam…when they first…well, when they first…"

"You're a big help," Tori murmured. She looked directly at Leslie. "For the record, Sam broke up with Robert before we… well, before we, you know…before the first time we…well, we ever…"

Leslie laughed, looking at Casey then Tori with a shake of her head. "Good grief, you two are a pair, aren't you?"

Sikes stepped forward. "They were flirting with each other shamelessly, then Sam dumped Robert. I'd venture to say it was a very short time later that Tori and Sam slept together for the first time, making their affair official."

"Sikes!"

"What? I was here. I guess I know."

Chapter Twenty-Two

They sat at their desks—burger wrappers, chip bags and drinks littering each—as they tossed ideas about.

"Remember how some of the witnesses said the Peeping Tom was a woman," Casey reminded them. "Could have been this Patty."

"You're not seriously thinking that his brother *Patrick* is really his sister in drag and goes by *Patty*?" Sikes held up a chip. "I think that's too far-fetched."

"Oh, so you think it's just a coincidence that he calls his sister Patty? Come on, we told you what Mac said about the DNA. A relative. His *brother*."

"But he said he didn't have a brother," Sikes said.

"I think we're forgetting something here," Leslie said. "John is simpleminded." She grinned. "And I don't mean you, Sikes."

Tori laughed. "Good one, Tucker."

"Anyway, John sees things in black and white. So if this person in his life wears a dress and goes by *Patty*, to him, it's his sister. It may very well be his biological brother and most likely is, but he answered the question honestly. He doesn't have a brother, he has a sister."

Casey leaned back and folded her arms behind her head, staring at the ceiling. "But why would Patrick feel the need to dress up like Patty? And does he do it all the time? Obviously not. He must have been Patrick when he killed Rudy Bobby. They didn't say *Patty* killed him. They said Patrick."

"And who all knows that he dresses up?" Tori asked. "If it's something that he does once in a while, then John wouldn't say he had a sister. John said he had a sister as if he dresses like Patty all the time."

Casey closed her eyes, still thinking. They had more questions than answers. But at least they *had* questions. At least they had somewhere to go now.

"Oh, I had Sam make some calls. The Homeless Alliance bailed him out. Seems Robert volunteers there," Tori said.

"How would the Homeless Alliance even know he was arrested?"

"Sharon down in booking. She's a volunteer too."

"What? It's like a little network of volunteers? All waiting around for us to arrest one of them so they can send in the troops?" Casey shook her head. "Amazing."

"Everybody's got a cause, O'Connor," Tori said as she wadded up her foil wrapper and tossed it at her. "What do you guys think of canning the surveillance of the apartments? I think it may be a waste of time."

"I don't agree," Leslie said. "If Patrick is our killer, then he has to do some kind of reconnaissance on his victims. They're not random."

"Actually, it makes sense," Casey said. "He's a lot less likely to cause suspicions if *he's* a she, you know. You see a woman walking around, you don't think anything of it. You see a guy snooping in apartments, you call the cops."

"But there's too much ground to cover. And you guys just lucked into John Doe. If you hadn't, then he'd have been at Cascades doing the dirty and no one would have been the wiser. We were cruising six blocks away."

"And maybe we'll luck into Patrick doing surveillance," Leslie said. "At least we'll be out there. If not, then we're just waiting on his next murder."

"Let's all do it every night," Casey said. "With both of us

out, we can cover more ground." Her suggestion was met with a groan from both Hunter and Sikes. "Oh, I forgot. I'm the only one without a life."

"No, no. It's a good idea," Tori said. "Sam will understand." She glanced at Leslie. "Can you swing it? I mean, your fiancé might—"

"I can swing it," she said without hesitation.

"Okay then. John? Will it mess up your new love life?"

"Hell, yeah, it will. But I guess if Sam can handle it, Kristi can."

"Kristi? How sweet," Casey teased.

"But Friday nights, no, waste of time," Tori said. "There's too much activity on the weekends. I can't imagine he'd take a chance at scouting out apartments then. Too many people around." She looked at Leslie. "When you pulled your Peeping Tom reports, what days had the most hits?"

"Wednesdays and Thursdays."

"But I think we should still go out on Monday and Tuesday too," Casey said. "Don't you guys agree?"

"Yeah, yeah. Every damn day, O'Connor. By the way, we're going out on the boat tomorrow, spend the night. Sam wanted me to invite you."

"Are you sure?"

"Yeah. She made up a big pan of lasagna last night. Come on. We've got to take advantage of the lingering summer weather while we can."

"Cool. I'm in." Casey glanced at Leslie. "You guys have big plans?"

"We're going to Austin. A college friend of Michael's is getting married. I don't really know them."

Casey looked away. "Well, you can maybe get some pointers for your wedding then."

"Not necessary. Michael's mother already has it all planned, remember?"

There was an uncomfortable silence in the room, then Sikes cleared his throat. "So, have you set a date yet?"

Chapter Twenty-Three

The sun was high and hot, and Sam shaded her eyes as she watched Casey climb on board. She smiled, shaking her head. Tori and Casey greeted each other with an arm bump. She walked over, wrapping her arms around Casey in a hug instead.

"Glad you could come." She kissed her cheek affectionately, pleased to see the slight blush that covered Casey's face.

"Thanks for including me." Casey pulled out a bottle of red wine from her bag. "For dinner."

"Excellent. Thanks. Now go put your cooler in the shade. Tori's anxious to get out on the water."

"I'm going to start her up. You guys ready?" Tori called from the control deck.

"See what I mean?" Sam looked at Tori and gave her the thumbs-up.

They sat in the anchored deck chairs while Tori sped across the lake. She accepted the beer Casey offered her, then slipped her sunglasses on her head. She wanted to talk to Casey and she wanted to do it now, in private. She was dying to know about Leslie.

"Everything okay?"

"Yeah. Why do you ask?"

"You seem a little...well, quiet. Distracted."

"Do I?"

Sam smiled. "Want to talk about it?"

"Oh, I'm okay. It's nothing really."

Sam reached over and squeezed her knee. "You know, I don't tell Tori *everything*. And I'm a good listener."

Casey took a deep breath. "It's just...I'm an idiot," she finally said.

Sam laughed. "Okay. So I'm going to guess it involves a woman."

"Yeah." Casey nervously twisted her beer bottle in her hand. "Actually, it's Leslie," she said quietly.

"Your partner?"

"Yeah."

Sam nodded, wondering how many questions she could ask without Casey clamming up. "Want to elaborate?"

"I've committed the ultimate sin." Casey looked at her, meeting her eyes. "I've got a crush on my partner."

"Not to burst your bubble, but I can relate."

"No, you can't. Tori wasn't straight."

"No, but I was. Or I *thought* I was."

Casey sighed. "I don't know what it is. We just clicked. We can talk, you know? Stuck in a car every night, we can talk. We're comfortable together."

"Friends can talk too. Friends can be comfortable together."

Casey grinned. "Yeah. But I want to jump her bones."

Sam laughed. "Yes, that does cross that friendship line."

"And of course, she's engaged to be married. That kinda puts a damper on things."

"Does it?"

"It would, if she didn't touch me all the time. And God, Sam, sometimes she looks at me and...well, I *feel* something."

"Like what?"

"Like...well, like my heart does the pitter-patter thing. It's disgusting."

Sam bit back a smile, knowing how vulnerable Casey must feel at the moment. So she tried another approach. "You know, you've only known her a few weeks. Maybe—"

131

"I know," Casey said quickly. "That's why I'm telling you I'm an idiot."

This time Sam couldn't hold back her smile and she leaned over and hugged Casey. "You're not an idiot." *You're just falling in love*. But she couldn't say that without Casey jumping overboard. "Maybe it's just…I don't know—"

"A phase?" She rolled her eyes. "I'm attracted to my partner, who's engaged to be married. To a man. And instead of coming to my senses, I'm *jealous*."

"Okay, let's change gears. What about Leslie?"

"I think she knows. I'm pretty sure she knows. I mean, like I said, I'm an idiot."

"I see. So do you think she *feels* anything too?"

"Christ, Sam, when I was holding her, I swear she felt something. And she said she—"

"Wait, wait, wait. What do you mean, when you were *holding* her?"

But Casey didn't answer. Her eyes were fixed on Tori as she made her way down the ladder to the deck. She turned to Sam. "I'll be fine. Thanks for letting me talk."

"But—"

"Isn't this great?" Tori asked, spreading her arms. "I love late summer weekends like this. Not many boats on the water, don't have to fight anyone for our favorite cove. It's perfect."

"More perfect if you had a beer, though, right?" Casey asked, going to their cooler.

"A beer and fishing pole." She walked to Sam. "And a kiss."

Sam's lips lingered, then moved to Tori's ear. "I love you," she whispered. She pulled away. "Now, go enjoy yourself. I'm going to sit here in the sun and read."

She pulled a lounge chair out and laid a towel on it, then relaxed, slipping her sunglasses back on. But the crime novel couldn't hold her attention as much as the two women within her sight. She loved times like this. It made her feel as if her world were perfect. Tori and Casey had stripped off their shirts. They both stood at the railing—clad in skimpy sports bras and shorts, their feet bare—holding a rod and reel in one hand and a beer in the other.

She was so happy Casey came into their life. Casey and Tori, while so different, were so much alike. They were good for each other. More importantly, they *knew* they were good for each other. Tori finally had that best buddy she needed, and Casey, well, Casey had the big sister—and the family—that had been missing in her life.

Now if we could only get her love life settled. Sam smiled and opened the book again. She liked Leslie. She didn't envy her having to go through what Sam suspected she was going through. Sam remembered how difficult if had been. The uncertainties, the fear. And the excitement of falling in love.

But falling in love with a woman for the first time could be shocking. Not only to yourself, but to those who knew you.

She should know.

Chapter Twenty-Four

Leslie twirled the wineglass methodically between her fingers, trying so hard to listen to the conversation—to be *interested* in the conversation—but truthfully, she was bored to tears. She'd obviously been to weddings before, but for the life of her, she couldn't remember there being this *endless* discussion of weddings and proceedings. And honeymoons. *My God.* They'd dissected it to death. Surely there were more interesting topics to discuss?

Like famine in Africa, for instance. She smiled to herself, glad she hadn't lost her sense of humor this evening, even if her feet hurt from the high heels she'd chosen to wear.

She watched those around her, all cute couples paired up nicely, talking animatedly in groups. The bride and groom were the *perfect* match. Or so she'd been told a hundred times. *And you and Michael look so happy. When's your big day?* She swore if one more of Michael's friends asked her that question, she was going to throw up.

And there he was, chatting away with his buddies from college. They all hung on his every word as he was no doubt describing a new computer game he was working on. Suddenly, she couldn't take it any longer. She bypassed the wine table, which was free to the wedding party, and headed to the bar instead.

Who has a wedding at a bar anyway?

"I'm complaining?" She shook her head. *No.*

She chose a barstool on the corner, away from people, away from the TV where a group sat watching a college football game. Instead, she stared into the mirror behind the bar, meeting her eyes, not surprised at what she saw.

Confusion, and just a hint of depression. These were Michael's friends, Michael's people. Not hers. She didn't know them. And judging from the conversations she'd been subjected to, she didn't *want* to know them.

"What can I get for you?"

She leaned her elbows on the bar and rested her chin in her hands, smiling at the bartender. Yes, indeed. What could he get for her? She lifted a corner of her mouth in a smile, trying at least. "Something strong," she said.

"Straight up on the rocks?"

She shook her head. "Better kill it with something."

"Double Crown with a shot of Coke?"

"Perfect. And run me a tab."

"Sure thing."

She turned, watching the wedding guests through the double doors. *Good Lord.* Again, who has a wedding at a bar?

"Are you with the wedding?" he asked as he placed the glass in front of her.

"Sort of." She picked up the glass and took a sip, nodding at him. "Perfect. What's your name?"

"Thank you. It's Paul." He pulled a rag out and wiped the wet spot in front of her, then tossed the rag behind him. "So, are you *in* the wedding?"

"God, no." She leaned closer. "Who gets married in a bar anyway?"

"They met here."

"So?"

"They come here a lot."

"His family owns the hotel, right?"

He laughed. "No. But I think it's kinda romantic. You know, they meet here as strangers one night, fall in love, then come back often for dinner, a few drinks, a room upstairs in the hotel.

135

Why not tie the knot here too?"

"Good thing they didn't meet at the dry cleaners," she quipped.

He laughed and moved closer. The look in his eyes was one she'd seen many times before. And mostly at bars.

"So? You here alone?" he asked.

She picked up her drink again, staring at him. "No." She took a sip. "Because if I was alone, I wouldn't be here."

"Weddings aren't your thing, huh?"

"Leslie, there you are. I've been looking for you."

She met Paul's eyes. "That would be Michael. My fiancé," she added.

"You don't look like you go together," he whispered.

"I'm beginning to see that." She turned as Michael grasped her shoulder.

"What are you doing in here?"

"I got tired of wine," she said as she held up her glass. "Paul is just the best bartender."

"I'll take your word for it. But they're ready for dinner."

"We're having dinner here, right?"

"In a private room, yes. I'm sure Paul won't mind if you bring your drink."

"Do you mind, Paul?" she asked as she fished out some money from her purse and laid it on the bar.

"Not at all. I hope you'll come back later."

"Absolutely," she said as Michael led her away.

"What's wrong?" he whispered.

"Nothing. Well, other than I'm trying to get drunk. Why?"

He pulled her up close. "What the hell's the matter with you?"

"For God's sake! I've been stuck in a group discussing weddings and honeymoons for hours. It would drive the freakin' Pope to drink. If I'd had my weapon with me, I may have shot someone."

He laughed. "Aren't you exaggerating just a bit? Besides, I thought the wedding was perfect. I hope ours goes as smoothly."

He led her by the arm back to the wedding party. "I think it was a great idea to have it at the hotel. Everything's right here. Your guests just grab an elevator to their room. You don't have to worry about partying too much and then driving." He looked at her. "I like it."

She stared at him. "You're not serious?"

"Why not?"

"Well, for one, your mother will kill you."

"It's our wedding, not hers."

"Since when?" She finished the last of her drink, feeling a slight buzz from the double shot. Paul was a good man. She just might be able to make it through the night.

He pulled her close again. "Please don't embarrass me."

"You mean tonight? Or at our wedding?"

He smiled. "Both."

She took a deep breath. "I'm not drunk, Michael. This is my first drink. I was just escaping…all this," she said, waving her hands at his friends.

"They're really fun people, Leslie. Give them a chance. I think you'll like them."

She took a deep breath. "Sure, Michael. I'm sorry. I'll try."

But as she pushed the food around on her plate, she was convinced she would *never* be friends with these people. Not that they didn't try. It was her. She simply wasn't interested. And after another hour of trying to fake conversations with strangers, she escaped again. But not to the hotel bar this time.

She found herself on the third floor where the outdoor patio bar overlooked the pool. It was still crowded on this Saturday night, despite the late hour. She walked to the edge, leaning over the railing, looking down at the pool then up into the night sky, blocking out the chatter around her. She closed her eyes for a moment, finally letting in thoughts of the one person she'd been trying to keep at bay all weekend.

Casey.

Trying to keep her away, yes, but she'd been there all along. She pulled out her cell, looking at the time. After eleven. Was she still awake? She was out with Tori and Sam, out on their boat. Could she dare call? If they were all three awake, how would she ever explain it?

She closed her phone. *Don't do anything stupid.*

But as she stared overhead, seeing the faint twinkling of stars above the city, she opened her phone again, her thumb punching through the numbers, stopping when Casey's number came up.

She squeezed her eyes shut for a moment, then pushed the call button. She only wanted to hear her voice.

The air, while warm, still had a freshness about it. Maybe it was simply being on the water, but it lacked the stifling effect it had in the city.

Casey tilted her head up, watching the stars. She loved it out here. The gentle rocking of the boat, the light breeze over the water, the sounds of the frogs and insects, the sounds of night.

It had become a ritual. Ever since she'd been joining Tori and Sam, she'd made it a point to stay up on deck after they went to bed. Privacy. She didn't want to get into theirs. So, as was her habit, after they went to bed, she pulled out the wine and brought it on deck with her. Some nights, she'd sit only for an hour. Other times, she'd still be out in the early morning light. Just sitting. Thinking.

Like now. Thinking.

She smiled. Or trying *not* to think.

But her heart skipped a beat when her cell phone vibrated against her leg. She pulled it out of her pocket, squinting in the moonlight to read the name.

Leslie. Damn.

"Casey," she answered quietly.

"It's me."

Casey held the phone tightly. "Is everything okay?"

"Yeah." A pause. "Are you alone?"

"Uh-huh. Are you?"

"If I don't count the thirty or so people on the patio, yeah."

Casey grinned, looking out over the water. "Okay, so let's don't count them."

There was only a beat of silence, then she heard the quiet sigh. "I miss you."

She gripped the phone tighter. "I...I miss you too."

Again, a sigh. "I shouldn't have called. I just needed to hear your voice."

"It's okay," Casey whispered. *Christ*, she didn't know if it was okay or not. She didn't know *anything* anymore.

"Is it, Casey? Is it okay really?"

"I don't know," she admitted. She heard a quiet laugh.

"Yeah, I was afraid that would be your answer." She cleared her throat. "I should go."

Casey stared up at the stars again. Yes, go. *Back to Michael.* "Enjoy the rest of your weekend," she managed.

"See you Monday."

And so she sat, phone still held lightly in her hand, listening as the sounds of the night faded away and all she heard was the steady beating of her heart. And the quiet words that echoed in her brain. *I miss you.*

Chapter Twenty-Five

When Casey walked into the squad room, she was determined to make everything as normal as possible. She would forget the phone call Saturday night. She would forget the conversation she'd had with Sam. And she would forget how her heart skipped a beat at just the sight of Leslie Tucker. Because—as she'd finally convinced herself last night—Leslie was off limits. An engagement ring tended to do that. So she forced a smile to her face as she walked in, holding up the two bags in her hands. One with coffee, one with pastries.

"Thanks, O'Connor. I was hoping you'd bring coffee," John said, flashing her a smile. "You're the best."

"Uh-huh." She put the cappuccino on Tori's desk, noting the empty chair. "Where's Hunter?"

"She's not in yet," Leslie said, reaching for the cup Casey handed her. "Thanks. I needed this."

And just like that, just one glance, and her resolve crumbled. Because the look in Leslie's eyes was haunted, as haunted as her own had been that morning. She took the lid off her coffee, sipping it, trying to convince herself that Leslie Tucker was her partner, nothing more, nothing less. A late night phone call during a weak moment meant nothing. At least, that's what she told herself. But when Leslie turned those soft brown eyes on her, she was no longer sure.

I miss you.

Christ! She put her coffee cup down and leaned closer. "What's wrong, Les?" she asked quietly, unable to stop herself. She saw Leslie glance at John, then back at her.

"Nothing, O'Connor. Everything is fine."

"Okay." The fake smile Leslie gave her failed to convince her, but obviously Leslie didn't want to talk. *Fine.* It was probably safer that way anyway.

She'd just taken a bite from her pastry when her phone rang. "O'Connor," she said with a mouth full.

"It's me. Grab the team. We've got a homicide. I don't know if she's ours or not."

Casey stood, snapping her fingers at Sikes and Tucker. "Where?"

"Cascades."

"Cascades? That's where we picked up John."

"I know. I'll meet you there. And, O'Connor, bring my cappuccino." She slipped her phone back into the clip on her belt and grabbed her coffee. "Another woman. Cascades." She pointed at Tori's coffee. "Sikes, bring that for her, will you?" She looked around. "Where the hell's Malone?"

"He's out this morning. Doctor," Sikes reminded her.

"Which is why Tori got the call," she murmured, hurrying out the door with the others.

She and Leslie automatically went to her truck, then stopped, looking at John. While it was a large truck with extra cab space behind the seats, no way he could fit back there. They all looked at each other, waiting.

"Look. I'll take my own. It'll just be easier," he said. "Meet you there."

As she got inside, she wondered why they just didn't all ride in John's car, but he was already pulling away. Fine. They could do this. They were adults.

"I'm sorry," Leslie said unexpectedly.

Casey started the truck and backed out. "For what?"

"For earlier. For calling you the other night. For—"

"You don't have to apologize. Forget it."

"Forget it? Forget what, Casey? What should I forget?"

Casey turned, meeting her eyes. "Everything. Let's just forget everything."

She heard rather than saw the smile. A smile, but a sad smile. "How is it we manage to talk about *it* without really talking about it, Casey?"

"Because *it* is very scary, that's why."

"Are we afraid to say it out loud?"

"Apparently." She sped up, just missing the light on Gaston. She took a deep breath. "So, how was your weekend?"

"Is that your not so subtle way of changing the subject?"

"Yes." She felt Leslie turn away from her and she wanted to apologize for being so abrupt. But she didn't.

"Okay. We won't say it out loud then. We'll change the subject, O'Connor." She shrugged. "Wonderful weekend."

"Good."

"Yeah. Good."

Casey turned sharply, practically tossing Leslie against the door as she pulled into the Cascades parking lot. Three units, a fire truck, an ambulance and the ME's van. Plenty to attract the attention of the neighbors. She got out without waiting for Leslie, needing to escape her presence, if only for a few moments.

But it was short-lived. As they rounded the corner, she felt Leslie's hand on her arm, stopping her.

"Look. It's the same apartment."

Casey stopped. "You're right. Goddamn," she whispered.

"Hey, guys, over here," Tori called. "Apartment one thirty-four. First floor, just like the others."

"What was her name?" Leslie asked.

"Rhonda Lampton," she said.

"Hampton," Sikes corrected her.

"Right. Hampton. Rhonda Hampton. Age twenty-four."

"We were here," Casey said.

"What? When?"

"The other night. We were here." She turned, pointing to the shrubs lining the small patio. "This is where we found John."

"The same goddamn apartment?" Tori stared at them. "What the fuck?"

"What the fuck what?" Casey said loudly. "He was jacking off, staring in this apartment. Are we supposed to know his brother is going to hit the same goddamn apartment?"

"Hey, guys. Calm down," Sikes said, grabbing Tori by the arm and pulling her away.

"I'm sorry, O'Connor. It's just—"

Casey plunged her hands into her hair. "I know. Hell, I know."

Leslie stepped forward. "If we can discuss this *rationally*," she said, looking at both Tori and Casey, "perhaps we can figure out how Patrick knew this was the apartment. Does John do recon for him? Does John brag about him being able to watch women without getting caught? Is this how Patrick might know who lives alone and who doesn't?"

"Without having him evaluated, we don't *really* know whether John is slow or not, or is just faking," Tori said. "Because this," she said, pointing at the apartment, "is just too goddamn much."

"He's not faking it," Leslie said.

"You can't be sure. He could be playing you."

"No. I don't think so. He never changed his demeanor, his speech. It all came too naturally for him."

Tori glared at them. "Find him. Bring him in."

"On what charges?"

"Make something up. I don't care," she said as she stormed away. "Just find him."

"Why the hell is she pissed at us?" Leslie asked.

Casey smiled. "That's just Hunter. That's just what she does."

"She's scary."

"Yeah, she is. But I love her anyway." She looked quickly at Leslie. "Come on."

Leslie drove down Elm for what felt like the hundredth time

143

that day. She felt like she was as familiar with the surrounding streets now as she was the back of her hand. They'd been at it all day. And they'd not seen even a trace of John Doe. They'd taken a break at five, meeting back up at seven. Leslie knew Casey was tired from driving all day, so she volunteered her car for the night shift.

And the night was proving to be as quiet as the day. Quiet as in Casey wasn't saying much. Quiet as in she was about to snap.

"Are you asleep?" she finally asked. It had been at least a half hour since they'd spoken and Casey was in the same position, staring out the side window.

"No. Not asleep." Casey flexed her shoulders and shifted in the seat. "Just watching, that's all."

Leslie endured another long silence, long enough to travel down Elm twice more and make a circle over to Gaston. And she'd had enough.

"Casey, I want to talk about it," she blurted out. "I can't stand this."

"There's nothing to talk about. You're engaged to be married." She turned to look at her for the first time in hours. "So there's nothing to really talk about."

Leslie stared at the road, not knowing where to start. "Speaking of engaged, they want a December wedding."

Casey's head jerked up. "December? *This* December?"

"Yes. Three months." She could feel Casey withdraw from her even more, could feel the tension in the car. But she didn't care. She wanted to talk about it.

"Wow. Three months," Casey said quietly. "I guess you'll be busy between now and then."

Leslie pounded her hand on the steering wheel. "Goddammit, Casey! This is ridiculous. You know as well as I do that I'm not getting married in December."

"Look—"

"No, *you* look. I'm tired of ignoring this." She snatched up her phone, scrolling until she found Tori. It rang only twice. "Hunter? It's Tucker. Listen, we haven't had any luck. We're going to call it a night." She nodded. "Good. See you tomorrow." She glanced at Casey. "They're done too."

"What are you doing?"

"I'm taking you to get your truck, then I'm going to follow you home. We're going to talk."

"Les, please. There's nothing to say. This is what it is. End of story."

"Why do I feel like we're talking in code? Why do we talk around it?" She looked at Casey, then back to the road. "I'm attracted to you. There. I've said it out loud."

"Leslie, please...don't."

"Don't what? Don't be attracted to you?" She turned into their parking lot, stopping beside Casey's truck. She turned in her seat, facing her. "But I *am* attracted to you. And you *know* I'm attracted to you." She reached over and took Casey's hand, holding it tight when she tried to pull away. "And I know the feeling is mutual," she whispered. "I'm tired of pretending this isn't happening." She felt Casey stiffen, but she refused to release her hand.

"Okay. So we've said it out loud. And yes, the feeling is mutual. But we've got two problems here. One, we're partners. And that can't happen. And two, you're *engaged*, for Christ's sake."

She finally released Casey's hand and pushed the button to unlock the doors. "Please, Casey. Let's don't have this discussion in my car. Can we go to your place and talk? Please."

She could see the indecision cross Casey's face, could feel her hesitation. Finally, she nodded.

"You're right." Their eyes met. "We should talk."

"Thank you."

145

Chapter Twenty-Six

"Here," Casey said, handing Leslie a glass of wine. She was pleased that her hand didn't shake. She turned her back to her, leaning on the railing instead, looking out over the water. She liked it better when they were ignoring it. At least that way she didn't feel quite so *school girlish*.

She heard Leslie get out of the chair, felt her move up beside her. She mimicked her pose, resting her arms on the railing, staring out into the darkness.

"What's wrong? Are you nervous? Or embarrassed?" Leslie guessed.

Casey smiled. "Both, I guess. I've just committed the cardinal sin for lesbians."

"What's that?"

"Not only are you straight, you're also engaged. Double whammy."

Leslie tilted her head slightly as she watched her. "Oh, I get it. You assume you're the first woman I've been attracted to and I'm going through some freakish curiosity phase before I get married. Is that it?"

"Is that *not* it?"

"Don't you think I'm a bit old for a game like that?"

Casey turned to face her. "Are we going to talk in circles again? Or are we going to just talk?"

Leslie smiled. "Oh, *now* she's brave."

Casey nodded. "Let me start by telling you a story."

"How much wine do you have? Because I have a story too."

"You want to stay out here or go inside?"

"No, it's nice out. Tell me your story."

"Well, it's about the cardinal sin," she said. "I met this woman when I was in the Academy. We hit it off right away. Turns out she'd just broken up with her boyfriend. I should have run right then." Casey sipped from her wine, surprised that the memory of that time still smarted. She'd been so naïve. She glanced at Leslie, still feeling very naïve at thirty-three. "But I didn't run. I was infatuated with her. And she with me. And our affair lasted nearly a month. Until she went back with her boyfriend. She said her curiosity about having sex with a woman had been satisfied. And the fact was, her sleeping with another woman *really* turned her boyfriend on."

"Wow."

"Yeah. So you see, I've committed this sin before. I got involved with somebody I worked with, somebody with a boyfriend." She turned slowly, meeting her eyes. "And I don't want to do it again."

"I understand."

Leslie moved away, going to the other end of the deck, into the shadows. Casey waited as she rested a hip against the railing, watched as she took a sip of her wine. Now who was nervous?

"I was nineteen," Leslie said finally. "And I had this grand plan for my life. I thought it was grand because it was nothing like my mother's life had ended up. And I knew without a doubt I didn't want to be like my mother, one loser husband after another." She moved, coming closer again. "I would graduate college, get a good job, marry a nice man who would be good to me and live happily ever after. It seemed simple enough." She drank the last of her wine and set the glass on the railing beside her. "I didn't count on Carol Ann coming into my life."

Casey kept quiet, only moving to refill Leslie's wineglass.

"We were roommates in the dorm. And she was a lesbian.

And I was totally and completely enamored by her." She took the wine, staring into the glass. "And the first time we kissed, I knew. It was so different than kisses I'd shared with boys. My body came alive." She smiled. "My body came alive, and I freaked out. It wasn't in my *plans* to fall for a woman." She moved again, back into the shadows. "It didn't matter. I couldn't resist her touch. But I couldn't allow myself to fall in love with her either. So each night when she came to me, when our touches grew bolder, when I simply *ached* with wanting her, I would turn her away. I couldn't let her do it. I saw my mother. And I remembered my plan. And Carol Ann wasn't in it. So I pushed her away."

Casey stared at her, trying to find her eyes in the shadows, wanting to see her face, but Leslie stayed hidden.

"I pushed her away. I pushed all those feelings away. And I went about my life. I never let myself get close to another woman. I had very few women friends. I couldn't take a chance. Then I met Michael and it seemed okay. It was good enough." She paused, staring out at the lake. "But it's not good enough," she said quietly. "I'm not in love with him. I've never been in love with him. I thought maybe it would come. He's good to me, and he thinks it's all good with us. So I thought...well, I thought I could be happy." She turned to Casey then. "I knew the first day I saw you, I knew that you would be the one to throw my plan into shambles," she said with a quiet laugh. "I knew I was attracted to you. But I ignored it. Until that night when you held me. I couldn't ignore it any longer."

"I'm sorry. I'm so sorry."

Leslie came out of the shadows, smiling. "Oh, God, Casey. So now you're going to feel guilty because you've come in and screwed up my plan?" Her hand moved between them, gently touching her arm. "Obviously, my plan was flawed," she said lightly. She dropped her hand, putting some space between them.

Casey didn't know what to say. Shocked by the story, yes. Should she be though? Wasn't there something about the way Leslie carried herself? Confident and sure. Never playing down a level like some women did whenever a man was around. She closed her eyes. There was still one problem with her story.

"You have a fiancé."

"Yes, I do." She walked past Casey to get the wine bottle. "For all of my complaining about him, he's really a nice, decent man. And he's going to be extremely hurt." She paused. "But what I said was the truth. I'm not in love with him. And this is going to hurt him badly." Instead of refilling her glass, she put the bottle down. "You're right. We have two problems. I have a fiancé, and you and I are partners." She took a deep breath. "And I'm very tired."

Casey nodded.

"I should go." She turned around, facing Casey. "Thank you. Thank you for talking," she said.

"Did we resolve anything?"

"No. I don't guess we did." She walked closer. "I just didn't want this distance between us. No matter what, we should be able to be friends, right?"

"Right."

"Good." She paused. "So, I'm going to go. It's late."

Casey stood there stupidly, wondering…what? But Leslie smiled sweetly and took the couple of steps necessary. Their hug should have been brief. At least, that's what she told herself. But when she felt Leslie slip into her arms, when her own arms closed around her, brief was the last thing on her mind. Long dormant feelings roared to life as they held each other, as they listened to their heartbeats, as their bodies melted together.

Leslie was the one who pulled away, her eyes dark, excited. She took a step back, but Casey felt her trembling. Or was it herself she felt?

"Friends?" Leslie murmured.

Casey nodded. "Friends."

Chapter Twenty-Seven

"How can someone just disappear?"

Leslie smiled. "Again, a rhetorical question?"

They'd been at it all week, looking for John Doe. They'd cruised the streets, day and night. They'd shown his picture around and were met with blank stares. They'd staked out the shelter at meal times to no avail. It was almost as if he didn't exist. Even Maria—who said John ate there most days—hadn't seen him.

So here they were again, Friday afternoon, driving down Elm. They had driven Deep Ellum and the surrounding area so much, she thought she could find her way with her eyes closed. She turned slowly, watching Casey's profile as she drove. It had been a week since they'd had their talk. A week. And they hadn't mentioned it since. Oh, it was there. When they looked at each other, when they'd touch—however innocent—it was there. But at least the tension, the distance, was gone. But in its place was an artificial cheeriness, both of them going out of their way to make things seem *normal* between them. And it wasn't quite normal.

Because there was Michael.

She turned away from Casey, looking again out the window, her eyes darting over the pedestrians who strolled down Elm Street. Yes, there was still Michael. But in her defense, when is a good time to tell the man you're engaged to that you're not in love with him? Do you just blurt it out over dinner one night? Not that they'd had a chance to have dinner, of course. Not when she was working, day and night. And Michael, for his part, had ceased his complaining that she was never home. He was out having fun with his friends. In fact, more often than not, she beat him home each night. And more often than not, he would wake her up, wanting to make love.

And she was running out of excuses. Tired, headache, just got her period, not in the mood. She'd used them all. But the weekend was here. There would be no more excuses. She would have to tell him. And then what? Was she ready to admit that her life had just been one big charade? At thirty-two, could she finally accept what she'd already known at nineteen?

She looked again at Casey, letting her eyes linger.

Yes.

She was a lesbian.

"You okay?"

She nodded. "Yes."

"You're kinda quiet."

"Mmm."

Without thinking, she reached across the console, resting her hand on Casey's arm, letting her fingers tighten. Such an innocent touch, yet she could feel the electricity between them. For just a second, blue eyes captured hers. A second, that's all. But that's all it took. In that short instance, everything made perfect sense to her. This woman sitting beside her—this beautiful woman— could set her soul on fire.

Yes, she was a lesbian. And yes, this is the woman she wanted. Her partner.

She closed her eyes. Yes, the second of their two problems. They were partners.

"It's going to be okay."

She opened her eyes, listening to Casey's words. Had she read her thoughts? She turned to her. "Do you think so?"

"That's going to be my mantra anyway," she said with a laugh, easing some of her fears.

Leslie smiled too. Her world was slowly turning upside down, but yeah, it would be okay. Living a lie, as she had been, was slowly zapping the life out of her. She could see that now. Whatever the future held, it had to be better than a lie.

"Hey. Check out that woman."

Leslie turned, looking where Casey was pointing. A tall, thin woman walked along the sidewalk at a brisk pace. "Yeah? And?"

"Does that walk look familiar to you?"

"Oh, my God. Pass her."

She did, driving slowly past the woman. "It's John," they said at the same time.

Casey whipped to the curb in front of him, stopping. Leslie wasn't sure if Casey expected John to run or not. But he didn't. He stared at them through the window, his face breaking out in a grin.

"Miss Leslie! Miss Casey!" He waved, then hurried over to the truck. But his smiled vanished. "Miss Casey, you're not going to—"

"I'm not going to tie you up, no." She pointed at his outfit. "But John, what's with the dress?"

He glanced around nervously, as if making sure no one was around to hear, then stuck his head back in the window. "I'm the sister today."

Leslie hoped the surprise she felt didn't show on her face. "You're the *sister*?"

Casey leaned across the console, looking up at John "So your sister then, she's now—"

"My brother."

"Oh, dear God," Leslie heard Casey murmur. She wanted to echo those words. Instead she said, "John, you want to maybe ride around with us and talk?"

He tilted his head. "I'm not supposed to."

"Why not?"

"Because he said not to."

"He?"

"Robert Attorney."

Leslie hid her smile as she glanced at Casey.

"Do you know Robert Attorney?"

"No. I don't think I like him. He was mean."

"Okay." Leslie smiled, trying another approach. "Where are you going?"

"To the park."

"Exall?"

"Yeah." He leaned closer. "To watch the pretty girls." Then his eyes widened. "But not to…you know. I don't want to get tied up again."

"No, no. You're fine," she said. "Can we go to the park with you?"

"Oh, sure."

"John, isn't it going to look funny if you look at girls and you know, you're in a dress?" Casey asked.

He laughed, a delightful childlike sound. "Just as funny as when you look at Miss Leslie that way."

Leslie couldn't contain her own laughter. The look on Casey's face was too priceless.

"Clever boy," Casey murmured. "So, you want to ride with us to the park?"

"I like to walk. There are more things to see that way."

"Okay. Well, let me park on the street over there and we'll walk with you. Cool?"

As they pulled away to park, Leslie whispered, "What the hell do you think is going on?"

"I'm almost afraid to find out."

"Should we call Hunter?"

"No. She'll make us arrest him for something, remember?"

"When she finds out we finally found him, she's going to be pissed." Leslie lowered her voice. "You don't think she'll shoot one of us, do you?" Casey's laughter rang out, causing Leslie to join in. "I wasn't really joking," she added.

"We both know we can't arrest him. He's done nothing

153

wrong."

They parked and got out, waiting for him to join them. "I like him," Leslie admitted.

"I know."

"He's—"

"Sweet."

"Yeah, he's sweet. Innocent."

"Or so it seems," Casey said, smiling as John hurried along the sidewalk to catch up with them.

"This is going to be fun," he said. "I wish I'd bought some chocolate."

"Chocolate?"

"Yeah." He stopped, looking around. Then he opened his blouse and pulled out a small leather wallet. "Look here," he said, opening it for them to see. "Thirteen dollars," he said excitedly.

"Where'd you get it?"

"My brother gives it to me. But I save it. I don't really need money. I can eat at the shelter." He walked on. "And Miss Maria sometimes will let me have three showers a week instead of two. But I like to buy chocolate. And sodas."

"Speaking of your brother, the other night when we picked you up, remember we asked you if you had a brother. But you said you didn't."

He shook his head. "No, that time I didn't. Today I do."

"So, what's your name today?" Casey asked.

"It's John, silly."

Leslie could tell Casey was losing her patience, so she bumped her lightly with her shoulder, tossing a *be nice* look her way.

"Okay. But you said your sister's name was Patty. So today, if your sister is your brother, is her name still Patty?"

"No. I just never found a girl name I liked."

"But she did?"

"Yes. Patrick."

"So when he's your brother, he's Patrick. And when he's your sister, he's Patty?"

"Uh-huh." He stopped, pointing. "Oh, look! The ducks are

154

here," he said, breaking into a run.

The pond that made up the center of Exall Park was surrounded by flowering trees and shrubs, manicured lawns and a small boardwalk. Four ducks swam lazily by until John ran up to them and they squawked loudly, fluttering away to the other side of the pond.

"I see people feed them bread sometimes," he said. "I always wish I had some. I'd like to feed them too."

"Well, you know, maybe the next time you buy chocolate, you could buy some bread," Leslie suggested.

"I could, couldn't I?" He spun around quickly. "Come on, Miss Leslie, let's find a bench." Then he stopped. "And you too, Miss Casey. I didn't mean you couldn't come."

She smiled. "Right behind you."

But Casey hung back and Leslie looked at her over her shoulder, seeing the thoughtful expression on her face. Casey, like herself, must have a hundred questions for him.

"John, I'm curious. How did you know you'd be the sister today?"

"Because the dress was there."

"Where?"

"Where I sleep."

"How often are you the sister?" Casey prodded.

He looked up at the sky, his eyes darting about, thinking. "Not too much," he finally said.

"Once a week?"

He looked at her strangely. "A week?" Then he looked away, embarrassed. "I lose track of the days." Then his eyes lit up. "But I know when Sunday is. That's when I hear the bells."

Leslie smiled. "Yes. The church bells."

"That's Sunday," he said proudly.

"Okay, John, but back to the dress," Casey said. "Patrick leaves the dress for you?"

"Uh-huh."

"So, do you live…like, in an apartment?"

He gave Casey a look that made Leslie laugh out loud. She

couldn't help it, but Casey fishing for information from this boy—and that was what he was, a boy in a man's body—was just too comical. So, like you would do with any child, you asked directly.

"John, where do you sleep?"

"Depends on the weather. If it's not too cold, I like to be with Sammy."

"Who's Sammy?"

"He's my friend. He let's me sleep by him sometimes."

"Out on the street? In an alley?"

He nodded. "It's not so bad."

"Does Patrick sleep with you?" Casey asked.

He shook his head. "He likes it dark."

"What do you mean?"

"He's always inside. But it's cold there. Cold and dark. So I like it outside."

"Inside where?"

He stared at her for moment, frowning. "I'm not sure." His eyes lit up. "Look! Here they come." His voice lowered. "I think they're dancers. They're so pretty."

Leslie followed his gaze, seeing the group of young girls running across the grass. Dancers, indeed. But it wasn't a musical. It appeared to be some sort of exercise class.

"They don't come all the time," he said. "But sometimes when I'm here they come."

"John, listen," Casey said. "Do you think you could introduce us to Patrick?"

He made a face. "I don't think he'd like that."

"Why not?"

"He gets mad sometimes." He paused. "But I don't see him that much."

"Why not," Leslie asked.

"He's opposite."

"Opposite? You mean, like sometimes he wears the dress and sometimes you do?"

John laughed. "No, silly. I mean he's opposite of me."

156

Leslie looked at Casey, wondering if she had any idea what he was talking about.

"Okay. Opposite…like you're a boy and he's a girl?" Casey tried.

"He's mostly a girl. I'm mostly a boy. Sometimes we're both boys. But we're only a girl one at a time."

"Okay." Casey stood, moving in front of John. She squatted down, looking at him. "Opposite like…you like chocolate and he doesn't?"

John laughed. "No. Like I like day and he likes night."

Casey frowned. "Huh?"

"He sleeps when I'm up," he said, holding his hands out to the sunshine. "I sleep when *he's* up. Opposite."

Casey looked at her, a pained expression on her face. *Help.* Leslie smiled at her, having to stop herself from simply bending closer and squeezing her tight in a hug. Instead, she bumped John's shoulder with her own, sitting close to him on the bench.

"Opposite. I get it. So right now, he's sleeping."

"Yeah, I guess." He tilted his head. "We should be alike, but we're not."

"Because you're brothers?"

"'Cause we're twins. But we don't like anything the same. He doesn't like chocolate."

Casey's eyebrows shot up. "You're twins?" She grabbed the bridge of her nose. "Twins. Imagine that."

"Where is he now?" Leslie asked.

"He's in the hole, I guess."

Casey touched his knee. "What hole, John?"

"The hole in the wall." He broke out in a smile. "Look! The ducks came back." He jumped up, running again to the pond.

"Christ," Casey murmured. She looked at her. "What do you want to do?"

"We can't keep pushing him. He's like a child. He's going to clam up when he's tired of talking."

Casey nodded. "Twins. Didn't see that coming."

"Twins. But not identical twins," she said.

157

"How do you know?" Casey asked.

"Because identical twins have the same DNA." She shrugged. "I took a couple of forensic classes."

"So even though they're twins, they might not even look alike."

"Right. But because they switch out on being the sister, I'd guess that they do favor each other."

"Well, at least we've got some sort of relationship with him." Casey grinned. "I think he has a crush on you."

Leslie stood. "And I think he's scared you're going to tie him up," she teased.

"Okay. Let's try to find out where he goes during the day and why the hell we couldn't find him all week."

"Yeah. But why do you think Patrick does the dress thing? And why would he make John wear it occasionally? It makes no sense."

"If there's another murder, CIU will get involved. And then we'll have profilers and shrinks reviewing the case. We'll know soon enough why he does the dress."

"That's the problem. The why of it isn't going to really help us catch him."

Chapter Twenty-Eight

"Give me a break, Hunter," Casey said. "On what goddamn charges?" She flicked her glance at Leslie, rolling her eyes. "He hasn't done anything wrong. We found him, we talked to him, end of story." She frowned. "Because we goddamn believe him, that's why."

Leslie watched her, having learned how Casey and Tori spoke to one another when they appeared to be upset. Which, in reality, they weren't really upset with each other. It was just Tori's way of venting, and Casey let her. To a degree.

"Yeah, yeah. Love to Sam." She closed her phone. "She drives me insane. I swear, I think she does it on purpose. Anyway, Malone's trying to get approval for a twenty-four hour tag detail, hoping John can lead us to Patrick. I'll get with Hunter sometime this weekend and go over what all John told us."

"Well, at least we know more than we did. I'm glad we can call it an early night for once." As soon as the words left her mouth, she wanted to take them back.

"Yeah. Short night." Casey forced a smile. "And a Friday. I guess you and Michael have big plans?"

Leslie bit her lip. Casey hadn't mentioned Michael's name all week. "No, Casey, that's not what I meant. I just…it's been a long week. That's all."

"Yeah, it has." Casey glanced at her quickly. "I'm sorry. So,

I have laundry planned for the weekend. And I promised Mr. Gunter I'd mow his yard for him." She took a deep breath. "What do you guys have going on? Anything fun?"

"Stop it."

Casey put her blinker on, waiting for a car to pass before turning into the parking lot. "I'm sorry," she said again. "You're right. It's been a long week. It's none of my business anyway."

"Casey?"

She looked at her and Leslie was shocked by the sadness she saw in her eyes. She reached a hand out, but Casey pulled away.

"Don't," she whispered.

"Casey? What are we doing here?"

"I don't guess we're doing anything. I'm sorry. I'm very tired. I know you are too." Casey stared out the windshield. "Have a good weekend. I'll see you on Monday."

As far as dismissals went, Leslie was sure she'd had colder ones. She just couldn't think of any at the moment. So she nodded, torn between trying to explain things to Casey and her need to get home to Michael. Because it was time. It was time she told him. She *needed* to get this over with. And she wanted to do it without Casey knowing. She didn't want her to feel guilty. She didn't want her to feel pressured. She didn't want the fact that she'd ended things with Michael to be a consideration when it came to their own relationship.

"Casey—"

"Goodnight, Leslie." She lowered her head. "Please," she whispered. "Just goodnight."

Leslie sighed. "Okay."

She got out, closing the door quietly behind her. Casey turned and their eyes met for a second, then Casey drove off, leaving her standing there, the memory of those haunted blue eyes etched in her brain.

She clenched her hands into fists, watching the red taillights of Casey's truck fade from view. "Oh, Casey," she whispered. She took a deep breath, letting it out slowly. *Michael will have to wait.*

She simply couldn't leave things like they were with Casey.

So she hurried to her car, speeding away down the street after Casey.

Chapter Twenty-Nine

"Idiot."

Casey sank down in her chair, trying desperately not to think about Leslie with *Michael*. The rational part of her brain said they couldn't possibly still be sleeping together. *Right?* But the other part, the part that was fueling her jealously, said why else was Leslie rushing off to be with him on a Friday night.

Idiot.

Jesus! You *never* fall for a straight woman. *Never.* She thought she'd learned that lesson ten years ago. Apparently not. *Straight women are just curious.*

Okay. She could get past this. They were partners. They were friends. That's where it ended. This silly crush—this attraction—would simply go away over time.

Surely.

"Idiot."

"Who are you talking to?"

She nearly fell out of her chair and was embarrassed by the gasp—and scream—that left her lips.

"Jesus Christ! You could get shot doing that!"

Leslie laughed. "Yeah. I see how quickly you pulled your weapon."

Casey spun around. "What the hell are you doing here, anyway?"

"I came to talk to you."

Casey shook her head. "No. Come on, Les. Please, let's don't do this. This is silly. You're engaged. You live with a guy. And I'm an *idiot*," she said.

Leslie walked closer. "An idiot because you're attracted to me?"

"I'm trying to get over that."

"Are you now?"

"Yeah. In fact, I'm going to work on it this weekend."

"Why?"

Casey raised her eyebrows. "Did you forget about that cardinal sin?"

"So you're going to go back to the argument that I'm just curious? A straight woman playing a little game with you?" She moved closer. "Is that what you really think?"

It's what she *wanted* to think. Her insecurities told her that's what it was. Her insecurities told her that this beautiful woman who was engaged to be married couldn't possibly find her attractive, couldn't possibly *desire* her. But when their eyes met, she thought no such thing.

"Curious is not the right word, Casey. I don't want to touch another woman's breasts. But I want to touch yours. I'm not curious to know how another woman's skin tastes, but I want to know how yours tastes," she whispered. "And I don't want to kiss another woman, Casey. But God, I want to kiss you, and I want to make love with you."

With their eyes locked together, Casey was unable to speak, unable to think.

"So you won't get over it this weekend. But you have got to give me some time to get my life sorted out, Casey. Please don't run from this." She closed her eyes. "Please don't doubt me. I'm doing the best I can here."

Casey finally moved, lifting her hand and touching Leslie's face. She let her fingers move gently across her skin, aware it was the most intimate touch they'd shared. "I'm sorry," she whispered.

"It's not a game for me, Casey. But I'm not ready for this yet, and I don't think you're ready." She covered Casey's hand with her own, holding it close. "I don't want to screw this up. I don't want to hurt you *or* me, and I don't want to ruin our new friendship over this. But we're not ready yet."

"I know." She reached for her. "Come here."

She was right. Everything she said was so right. No, they probably weren't ready for a physical relationship. Because it wasn't going to be just physical. And they had a working relationship to deal with as well. It occurred to her that any sane person would have ended things right then before they even got started. But a sane person hadn't looked into her eyes, hadn't seen the glimmer of desire, hadn't been innocently touched by her, causing her own desire to flare. A sane person couldn't possibly see past the fear in her eyes to see the promise.

So she pulled her close, wrapping her arms around Leslie's body and just held her, letting their bodies get acquainted with each other. No, they weren't ready. But it felt so *good* to hold her, to hear her heartbeat, to feel her breath, and to feel her tremble, just from being close.

Imagine what making love would be like.

She pulled back, needing to end this before her body took over, but Leslie's fingers threaded through her hair, touching her, pulling her back, pulling her close again.

"Kiss me."

Casey stared at her lips. Was it a command? Or had she only imagined it? But no, Leslie's lips parted, Leslie's hand at her neck guided her, beckoning her. She didn't resist. She took what was offered. She just wasn't prepared for the softness, for the aching sweetness that greeted her. She moaned. Or was it Leslie? She lifted her head, staring into those dark eyes that were swimming in desire, wondering if Leslie's thoughts were as jumbled as her own at the moment.

But then Leslie pulled her back down, and a fire was ignited. Her mouth opened, her tongue demanding entry, and Leslie complied, her hands roaming freely, pulling Casey tight against her. Any restraint she was clinging to vanished as her own hands slipped down to Leslie's hips, grasping her, pulling her hard against her body.

She felt Leslie's hands digging into her back, heard the nearly primal sounds coming from her throat as their hips melded together. She pulled her mouth away, needing to breathe, needing to think, but Leslie's thighs parted, and she lost her will to think. She clutched Leslie's hips, pulling her hard against her leg, imagining the wetness she would find there as Leslie ground herself against her.

Mentally they weren't ready, no, but God, physically, they were about to explode. When was the last time she'd felt this kind of fire from kissing a woman? They were so close, clinging to each other, she wasn't even sure where her body ended and Leslie's began. But when Leslie lifted her shirt and she felt the cool night air against her skin, when she felt the burning warmth of Leslie's fingers as they crept higher, she knew they should stop. She could tell by Leslie's actions that her body had taken over her mind, overriding her sensibilities as their passion raged.

But this wasn't how she wanted their first time to be, a hurried encounter out on her deck, as if they were sneaking around, as if it was some sort of an affair. No. She wanted Leslie to be able to give herself freely, not have to feel guilty for making love so hurriedly just because their need to touch had become too much. So she tore her mouth from Leslie's, taking her hands and holding them between their bodies, trying to still her racing heart.

"Oh, *God*," Leslie whispered. "I'm sorry. I—"

"Shhh, no. And stopping has nothing to do with being gallant on my part." She bent her head, lightly brushing Leslie's lips with her own again. "I just didn't want our first time to be like this."

Leslie stepped away, her eyes wild. "I completely lost my mind there." She tried to smile. "I knew it would be like that with you. I knew my body would react like that." She walked to the railing, leaning over, catching her breath. "I've never wanted someone so much before like that." She turned back around. "I thought I would be afraid."

"Afraid of me?"

"Afraid of this," she said. "Of *us*."

"We can take it as slow as you need, Les."

She smiled. "Slow? I don't think my body understands that word." She straightened. "I should go. Before we…"

Casey nodded. "I know."

Leslie stopped when she got to the steps of the deck and turned back around. "You're an awesome kisser, by the way."

She fled then, leaving Casey smiling after her.

Awesome, huh?

Chapter Thirty

The nonchalance she tried to exhibit to Casey as she left faded as soon as she got in her car. She sat for a moment, holding the steering wheel, her mind spinning.

"My, God," she whispered.

Was it supposed to be that intense?

Without thinking, she shoved her hands between her legs, squeezing hard, her body still reeling from Casey's touch. She could feel the unfamiliar wetness between her legs, could still feel the heat., and her body cried out for release.

"Oh *God*," she groaned as she pressed the seam of her jeans tight against her. *Stop!*

She jerked her hands away, trying to calm herself. She glanced at her reflection in the mirror, hardly recognizing the look in her eyes.

"I want her," she whispered. Then she smiled. *You don't say?*

But her humor faded as she drove away. She had to tell Michael. *How* she was going to tell him, she had no idea. Because she had no desire to hurt him. But what man would understand this?

When she got home and found it quiet, she assumed he'd gone up to Jeff's. She hadn't called him. He would have had no idea it was an early night for her. Her hope that he was gone, giving her a chance to rehearse what she needed to tell him, was short-lived, however. She screamed as he grabbed her from behind and pulled her against him.

"Michael! You're wet."

"I just got out of the shower." He spun her around, kissing her hard. "And I'm feeling frisky. Come on, we haven't had sex in ages."

"Michael, what are you doing? *Now*?"

"Yes, now. Why not now?" He kissed her again. "Let's do it before you get a headache, or claim you're too tired, or any other excuse you can think of."

Leslie forcibly pushed him away. "I didn't know that I needed an excuse not to have sex. It's still a choice, right?" She wiped her mouth with the back of her hand, his bruising kiss replacing the soft touch of Casey's.

"Come on. You know what I mean. You always have some reason lately. The last time we did, you started crying." He leaned against the wall. "You want to tell me what's going on?"

This wasn't how she envisioned having this talk. Not with him wanting sex and her having to defend herself. She looked away for a second, remembering Casey's touch, her kiss. No, she couldn't put it off any longer.

"Michael, I don't want to have sex with you," she said quietly. "It just doesn't feel *right* to me."

"Right? What doesn't? *Sex*?"

She tucked her hands under her arms, not able to look at him. "Not just sex, Michael. Everything. Us. I'm having second thoughts about this," she said weakly, hating herself for not being able to just tell him.

"About the *wedding*?" He took a step closer. "Are you kidding me?"

"Michael, it's just not right with us. Can't you feel that?" She finally looked at him, meeting his eyes. "I mean, what are we doing here? I feel like we're just going through the motions."

"What are you talking about?"

"I'm talking about *us*, Michael. Can you name me one thing we have in common? Just one," she said. She watched as his brow furrowed and he wet his lips nervously.

Finally he smiled. "We both like movies."

"*You* like movies."

"All right. Well, we both like to go out to eat."

"Good Lord, Michael, that's because neither of us cooks." She grabbed his arm, squeezing hard as if that would make him understand. "The closest thing we have in common is when football season comes around and I like to watch the game with you. With you and Jeff and Miles and Russell, that is." She dropped her hand. "Don't you see, Michael? You love your games, your big TV, your season tickets, your *friends*. We're here in this apartment because Jeff and the guys live here. We could afford a house, but you didn't want to. Because you love it here."

"It's a nice apartment. I didn't see the need in rushing into a house."

"Oh, Michael, that's not the point. It's us. Do we even really know each other?" She raised her hands. "Do I want to have kids?"

He shrugged. "I don't know. I guess."

She stared at him. "Do you?"

"Well, someday, yeah. I guess so."

She gave a sad smile. "Isn't it strange that we never talked about that? Who plans to get married and they don't even know if the other wants kids or not?"

"Leslie, I think you're blowing this a little out of proportion here, don't you?" His eyes narrowed. "Did you start your period again?"

"No, Michael, this isn't about my hormones." She took a deep breath. "I'm trying to tell you that I can't marry you." She knew he would be upset. She expected that. But the look of devastation that crossed his face was nearly too much for her. "I'm sorry," she whispered.

"You want to call off the wedding?" he asked quietly. "You want to...*break up*?"

She met his eyes. "Yes." And of course, his next question was not unexpected.

169

"You've met someone, haven't you?"

But she'd inflicted enough wounds for one night. There was no need to tell him about Casey or about the lie she'd been living. So she shook her head. "This has nothing to do with meeting someone else, Michael. It's just about us. And we just don't fit together."

He slammed his fist down on the counter. "And you've just now come to that conclusion? Just woke up one morning and it hit you?"

She deserved his anger, yes. But it was still shocking. He'd never once raised his voice with her. She kept her voice even, her gaze steady. "I think we should stop right here, Michael. Before either of us says something we'll regret."

He lowered his head. "I'm sorry. I just can't believe this," he whispered. "It's just out of the blue."

"Think about it, Michael. Is it really out of the blue? Think about it."

He rubbed his head, brushing the hair off of his forehead over and over again, his eyes darting nervously around the room. "Well, I…I can go stay with Jeff. You can stay here. We can—"

"No. This is your apartment, not mine. I'm just going to pack a few clothes and I'll get a room for the weekend. Next week, we'll talk. We'll see about our stuff," she said. God, how can breaking up be so civilized?

But no, it wasn't. Suddenly, the look in his eyes changed. He grabbed her arm tightly.

"I think we're just giving up too fast. We're not fighting for this. Let's go to counseling," he said, holding her in front of him. "We've got too much invested to just throw it away like this."

She stared at him. "No, Michael. Counseling will not help."

"Why not? Why won't you even try?" He dropped his hands from her, still staring at her. "I don't understand how you can just *quit* on this without trying? Don't you care even a little?"

"Michael—"

"I'll set us up an appointment. We can go to a couple of sessions, just see what we can do to change things. Come on," he

170

pleaded.

"No. We can't *change* things."

"Yes, we can," he insisted. "We can. If we—"

"Michael, stop it!" she said, grabbing his arm. "Michael, we can't change, because…because I'm a lesbian."

Michael's mouth opened, but no sound came out. He stared at her, questions flooding his eyes. But the silence was too much.

"I'm sorry," she said.

"No. You're just saying that. You're just using that as an excuse. You're no *lesbian*. My God, we've been living together, we're fucking *engaged*. Lesbians don't get engaged," he said loudly.

"No. I guess normally they wouldn't get engaged." She swallowed hard. "I take full responsibility, Michael. And all the blame. You have done nothing wrong."

"No! Lesbians don't have sex with men," he yelled. "I just can't believe you think you're gay." He laughed bitterly. "Is that the excuse you came up with to break up with me? That you're *gay*?" He ran his hands through his hair again. "Jesus, Leslie. How about you want to become a nun or something? I might believe that. But no, you're not fucking *gay*." He pointed his finger at her. "And don't you dare tell any of our friends that. I won't let you make a joke out of me." He spun away, and she heard him in their bedroom, pulling on jeans and shoes. Soon, the sound of his keys jingling and the front door opening.

And then the slam.

She knew it was coming and she still jumped from the force of it. She took a deep breath, rubbing her face with her hands, trying to get rid of some of the tension. It didn't work.

"That didn't go well," she murmured. But she couldn't blame him. She would be just as shocked if he had announced *he* was gay.

But surely he could tell. Over the years, couldn't he tell that she wasn't as responsive to him as she should be? He'd slept with plenty of women before her. Surely he knew what it was supposed to be like? Surely he could tell she was faking it.

"Oh, *God*." She felt like such a fraud. Which she was, of course.

And he had every right to hate her. In reality, she'd just wasted nearly four years of his life.

And four years of yours.

No, truth be told, she'd wasted nearly fourteen years of her life, ever since she rejected Carol Ann and all that she stood for. Ever since she tried to hide under the heterosexual cloak and pretend she was perfectly happy. Ever since she ran from what she was and tried to be something she surely was not.

A straight woman.

So, without ceremony, she slipped his ring from her finger, clutching it in her palm for several long seconds before opening her hand, watching the light bounce off the diamond, mocking her. Strangely, just the simple act of removing the ring seemed to free her.

Chapter Thirty-One

"Oh, my," she whispered, lowering her sunglasses to take in the full effect of Casey mowing the lawn in nothing but a sports bra and skimpy shorts. Her body was as tanned and toned as she suspected it would be. And the sight of it caused her libido to stir to life. *Oh, my.*

She got out of her car, smiling a greeting at an older man sitting on his porch watching Casey. This must be the Mr. Gunter whose lawn needed mowing. She walked up the sidewalk, past the perfectly manicured flowerbeds that were still overflowing with lush flowers even this late in September. The man stood when she reached his porch, holding out his hand in a friendly greeting.

"I'm here for Casey," she explained.

He nodded. "Sit," he said loudly as the buzz of Casey's mower came closer.

She saw her then and Leslie noticed the startled look cross her face. Startled because she was sitting in a chair beside Mr. Gunter, or startled to even see her at all, she wasn't sure which. Leslie smiled, then in an exaggerated show, let her eyes follow the length of Casey's body, past the ridiculously charming bright purple bra, the smooth, tanned stomach, the tiny baggy shorts that hugged her hips, and down the seemingly endless length of legs to a pair of old, ratty, grass-stained shoes. *Oh, my.* And the blush that covered Casey's face at her appraisal simply added to the allure. Casey held up two fingers and pointed to the yard. Leslie nodded.

"She's just about done," he said.

Leslie leaned closer to him. "You must be Mr. Gunter. I'm Leslie Tucker," she said loudly. "A friend of Casey's."

He smiled and nodded, then leaned back in his chair, his eyes following Casey around the yard. At first, she assumed he was enjoying the sight of Casey in near undress—much like she was. But then she realized there was a bit of pride in his eyes, much like a father might watch a daughter. She wondered what their relationship was. Obviously friendly enough for Casey to mow his lawn. Was he a widower?

After two more spins around the yard, Casey killed the mower. She leaned casually on it, watching her.

"To what do I owe the pleasure, Detective Tucker?"

"I thought maybe I could take you to lunch, Detective O'Connor."

"Lunch?" She came closer, her smile widening. She glanced at Mr. Gunter. "What do you think, Ronnie?"

"She's pretty," he said. "I'd take her up on it if I were you."

Casey nodded in agreement. "She is pretty, isn't she? Okay. Lunch."

Leslie wrinkled up her nose. "But you are going to...you know," she said, pointing at her.

"Shower? Yes, I'm going to shower. I'll let Ronnie entertain you." She pushed the mower back across the lawn, then stopped. "And, Ronnie, no secrets," she called over her shoulder. "She doesn't need to know everything."

Leslie laughed. "Oh, I think she opened a can of worms there. Just what secrets do you know?"

He smiled, the skin around his eyes crinkling. "You want some lemonade?"

She looked at the empty glass in his hands and nodded. "Sure, if it's not too much trouble." But before he could get up, the door opened and an older lady came out with two full glasses. Ah, so he wasn't a widower.

"Ruth, this is Leslie. A friend of our Casey's."

Leslie took the offered glass of lemonade, then gently shook the woman's frail hand. "Nice to meet you, Ruth. Thank you for this. I can't believe how hot it still is." She took a sip, her eyes widening. Not just lemonade, but homemade lemonade. "Delicious."

"Oh, I've been making lemonade for years." She smiled sweetly. "Casey enjoys it too." Pulling the housedress away from her chest to fan herself, she pointed back at the door. "I think I'll go back in where it's cooler. Nice to meet you, Leslie."

He leaned closer when the door had closed. "She doesn't come out much anymore," he said quietly with a quick glance at the house. "Last few years, she just wants to stay inside."

Leslie didn't know what to say. "Well, some people can't stand the heat. And I know it's September, but it still feels like August," she said lightly.

"That's not it." He pointed to her flowers. "She used to love her flowers. Love to plant them, love to sit here and watch them." He shook his head. "Not anymore. It's like she's lost interest." He motioned to Casey's house and smiled. "The highlight of her week is when we drag Casey over and Ruth can cook for her."

"Casey hasn't lived here long, has she?"

"No, no. Just this year. I think it was late spring when she moved in." His eyes crinkled again as he smiled. "I was trying to get some bags of mulch out of my car. It was time for the flowers, you know. Anyway, Casey pulls up with her truck all loaded down, sees me struggling with the bag and comes right over, fussing that I was going to rupture something if I wasn't careful." He laughed. "I called her a young know-it-all and told her to mind her own business."

Leslie laughed with him, seeing the genuine affection for Casey in his eyes.

"Oh, she put me in my place. Said it was her business if she was going to have to come over and do CPR all the time just because I was being a stubborn old cuss." He laughed again and slapped his knee. "Oh, she was feisty that day. Then Ruth told me to quit arguing with the neighborhood kids. Casey got a kick out of that, all right." He leaned closer again. "She invites me over for a beer every once in a while. We sit on her deck back there and talk."

"Ruth doesn't mind?"

"No." His eyes looked far away. "She doesn't mind much of anything now."

"I'm sorry."

He shrugged. "Just a part of getting older, I guess." His face brightened as he looked at her. "So, you and Casey are friends?"

"Yes."

"That's good. I was beginning to think she didn't have any."

Leslie frowned. "Really?"

"You're the first one she's had over. Well, except for that cop friend of hers."

"Tori?"

"Tall woman. Hunter, she calls her."

Leslie nodded.

"Yeah. She comes by some. They sit out back and drink beer or wine. Not that I'm spying or anything."

"No."

"And you know, it wasn't until recently that we found out she was…well, you know…that way. A homosexual."

Leslie tried to hide her smile. "I see."

His eyes fixed on her. "Are you a homosexual too?"

"Me?" Leslie felt the blush that quickly covered her face. "Well, yes. Yes, I am."

His eyes drifted away again. "You know, as old as I am—pushing eighty—I don't think I ever knew a homosexual before. It was kinda shocking. Casey, I mean. I wasn't quite sure how to take it." He glanced back at her. "She's been more family to us these last six months than our own grandkids have been. She's nothing like all the stories we used to hear in church, you know." He laughed and rubbed his hair. "I expected to see horns growing on top of her head or something. But like I said, she's like family.

She's a good person."

"Yes, she is."

"Well, you better go on over there." His eyes twinkled as he stared at her. "I'd surprise her as she got out of the shower, if I were you."

Again, Leslie felt a blush cover her face.

"That's what I used to do to Ruth," he said, laughing again. "Of course, I was sixty years younger."

"Well, actually, we're just friends. We're just getting to know each other," she clarified.

"No. I saw Casey's eyes light up when she saw you. That wasn't no look at a friend."

Leslie couldn't help but smile at him, and she squeezed his shoulder lightly as she stood. "I guess I should go see about that, then." She placed her glass beside his. "Please thank Ruth for the lemonade."

"I will. Come back and visit."

"Thank you."

She walked around to the back of Casey's house and to the deck, pausing to look out at the lake.

He called me a homosexual.

She lowered her head, but couldn't hold her laughter. A week ago she'd have fainted dead away if someone had said that. This week? No, this week she was being encouraged to spy on Casey as she got out of the shower. Encouraged by an eighty-year-old man!

She went inside, not intending to take his advice. Not really. In fact, she wasn't even sure where Casey's bedroom was. She'd only been inside the house once, and that was a quick walk-through as they went to the deck for their *talk*. Last night, she'd gone straight to the deck, knowing that's where she'd find her. So now, she took the time to glance around, not really surprised at the mix-and-match furniture Casey had put together. The sofa was a solid neutral brown. The chair was a striped brown and maroon. The coffee table was light oak. The end table appeared to be mahogany. And the leather recliner jet black. Not that anything was old or worn. In fact, the recliner looked new. But it appeared to all have been purchased at different times, different seasons, for different homes. And by the prominent position of the recliner facing the TV, she'd assume it was the newest purchase, probably when she bought the house.

She walked through the living room, her hand gliding across the leather as she looked around. She tilted her head, hearing the shower turn off, then whistling. She smiled, picturing a very naked Casey whistling as she dried off.

How cute.

Yes, cute. And no doubt Casey was wondering what she was doing here, barely noon on a Saturday. Lunch had been an excuse. She really just wanted to see her, to talk to her, to be with her. After her talk with Michael, she'd packed enough clothes for a week and gotten a room at the new Dallas Suites on the expressway, but still close to downtown. She'd use the week to find an apartment. As she'd told Michael, that was his place, not hers. She'd rather get something new, something that was only hers. Someplace where she wasn't likely to run into Michael or his friends in the parking lot.

And so today, after she'd looked through the paper for apartments, after three cups of coffee…and after reliving Casey's kisses from last night for probably the hundredth time, she had to see her. So lunch was just an excuse.

"Hey."

Leslie turned slowly, finding Casey standing at the edge of the hallway holding up leather sandals in one hand and Nikes in the other. But Leslie only gave the shoes a cursory glance. Her eyes traveled past her still damp hair, past the white T-shirt that was tucked into khaki shorts, and lingered instead on the long, tanned legs that had held her attention earlier.

"I wasn't sure where you planned to go," Casey said, holding up the shoes.

Leslie looked up and frowned. "What?"

"Lunch?"

She lowered her eyes, embarrassed. "Right. Lunch." She gave

a short laugh, then looked up again. "I forgot I was…starving," she said, her voice dropping to a whisper as Casey's eyes bored into hers. She swallowed nervously, then felt her breath catch as Casey let both pairs of shoes drop to the floor.

"I'm starving too," Casey said as she moved closer.

Leslie's throat felt dry, and again she swallowed, her eyes locked on Casey's as she moved in front of her. The tension in the room was electric as they stood a foot apart, watching each other. Leslie saw Casey's pulse beating rapidly in her throat, saw her chest rise and fall, startled that she was the cause of it—just her mere presence, for they had not touched. Her brave words from last night seemed to mock her. *I'm not ready for this*. But, oh, yes, *she was*. It had been too many years of pretending, too many years of forced passion, and too many years of longing for the fiery touch upon her skin that would set her free. Casey's touch would do that, she was certain. Casey's touch would no doubt send her places she'd only dreamed of.

"I lied," she whispered.

Casey seemed to understand exactly what those words meant, and her eyes gentled in response. There was no longer a question in those blue depths, no hesitation, and no veil in place to hide her emotions. Casey's eyes were open, revealing plenty. When Casey's hand lifted, when trembling fingers brushed against her cheek, Leslie knew then and there that this was the woman she'd been waiting for. She just *knew*. Deep in her heart, deep in her soul. And all it took was this light touch upon her face to know that she was about to be freed from her self-imposed chains.

Casey drew her closer and Leslie's eyes slipped closed, her mouth waiting for Casey to claim her. But she felt Casey hesitate and her eyes flew open again.

"Are you sure you—?"

"Yes. I want to know. I want to know how soft your skin is," she whispered. "I want to know how your breasts feel when I touch them." She licked her lips. "I want to know *everything* about making love with you."

There was no more discussion, no more hesitation. She

slipped into Casey's embrace as if it were the most natural thing in the world, meeting her mouth without the guarded urgency of last night. Her arms moved over Casey's shoulders, pulling them closer just as Casey's arms wound around her back, slipping to her hips. She moaned against her mouth, letting Casey's tongue capture hers, her hips jerking in response, pressing tightly against Casey.

Oh, God. She wanted to rip her clothes off, she wanted to touch flesh. She moaned again as she felt Casey's hand slide up her hips to her waist, slipping under the short blouse she'd worn. She leaned back, her breath coming in quick gasps, her eyes locked on Casey's as her hands moved across her skin.

"I want to touch you," Casey whispered, as if asking permission.

"Yes," she breathed. *Please.*

But her eyes slammed shut when she felt Casey's fingers brush against her breasts, moving over them as if reading Braille, her fingertips lightly touching. Leslie leaned her head back, offering herself to Casey. *God.* Casey finally took what she offered, cupping her breasts fully, her thumbs rubbing against her taut nipples, making them ache, making them yearn for more.

"*Casey*, please, I'm going to fall down," she finally said when Casey's mouth found the pulse in her neck and nibbled there. She felt Casey smile against her skin and Leslie pulled her closer, loving the quiet, unhurried passion that simmered between them. "I'm dying to see you naked," she whispered into her ear.

Casey pulled away, her hands releasing her breasts, her eyes still dark with desire. "Bedroom? Is that okay?" Then she hesitated. "I mean—"

"Yes," Leslie said. "I want to make love with you. I want everything, Casey." She was surprised at the quick intake of breath, the quiet moan. Casey appeared to be as nervous as she was. But then Casey smiled, that lazy half-smile that lightened her features.

"Our next meal may be breakfast then."

But her smile faded when Leslie moved closer, her lips

lingering. "Teach me how to love you. Show me."

And without another word, Casey took her hand and led her into her bedroom, her bare feet silent on the floor. She stopped, looking at the bed, then back at Leslie.

"I'm nervous," Casey finally confessed.

"Because I've never been with a woman before?"

"What if it's…I mean, what if I don't—"

Leslie silenced her by placing a finger across her lips. "Are you kidding me? I'm about to explode here. I don't think you have to worry about that." She tugged at Casey's T-shirt. "Now please, take this off."

And Casey did, pulling it over her head, leaving her in a tight black sports bra. But before Leslie could touch her, Casey was unbuttoning her blouse, urging it off her shoulders. Casey's head lowered, her lips moving against her skin, her tongue touching the edge of her lace bra. She groaned, her hands slipping behind Casey's neck, pulling her closer, *aching* to have her mouth on her breasts.

"Oh, *Casey*," she breathed when Casey's mouth finally covered her, only the thin material of her bra separating them. But then Casey released her bra, pulling her mouth away long enough to shed the garment, then going back, this time without an obstacle to block her. Again, Leslie was afraid she was going to fall. The wet swirling of Casey's tongue as she teased her nipple, bringing it to life, nearly was her undoing. The mouth at her breast was gentle, teasing, then demanding as she suckled her, her teeth raking against her nipple. Leslie held her tight, silently begging her to take more. Her head fell back and she stood there, mouth open and gasping for breath as Casey feasted on her breast.

So lost was she in the feel of Casey's warm mouth devouring her that she didn't realize her shorts had been unbuttoned, didn't realize Casey's hands were on her flesh until she felt them slide inside her panties, cupping her buttocks hard, kneading them. She groaned when Casey's mouth left her breast and moved to her ear, her tongue snaking inside hotly.

"Are you wet for me?" she whispered.

Involuntarily, Leslie's hips pressed forward, touching Casey, desperately seeking relief. Her hands moved across her back and into her hair while her lower body tried to mold itself to Casey. *Was she wet?* She was beyond wet. She was absolutely *throbbing*. And *damn*, it felt so good. So she pulled her head back, finding Casey's lips this time, and she smiled against them. "Why don't you touch me and find out?"

They pulled apart, their eyes meeting. Leslie nearly collapsed right there from the pure look of desire that reflected back at her. No one had ever looked at her this way. No one had ever *wanted* her this way. And certainly no one had ever brought her to her knees with passion. Passion for her.

While she watched, Casey stepped back and stripped off her bra. Leslie stood there, her chest nearly heaving, her eyes fixed on Casey's breasts. Unconsciously, she wet her lips as she watched her nipples harden, beckoning her. Then her gaze shifted downward as Casey's hands unzipped her shorts and slid them past her hips, down her thighs and to the floor. When her hands reached for the last remaining item of clothing, Leslie stopped her.

"No."

Casey raised her eyebrows and Leslie shook her head. "Let me," she whispered.

Her own shorts, which already hung low on her hips, slipped easily down her legs, and she tossed them aside. They stood facing each other, naked except for the clothing covering the one place they both wanted to be. Then Leslie stepped forward, nearly embarrassed by the shaking of her hand as she reached out to touch Casey for the first time. She watched in fascination as Casey's nipples hardened even more from her light touch.

"Your skin is so soft," she murmured, wondering if she'd spoken the words or only thought them. But her touch grew bolder as she cupped both of Casey's breasts, feeling her eyelids grow heavy from her desire. "I want...I want to kiss them," she said shyly.

Casey simply nodded, waiting.

Her heart was beating so loudly, it blocked out all thought.

She lowered her head, a soft moan slipping out as her mouth closed gently, taking Casey inside, letting her tongue swirl across the taut nub in her mouth.

"*Yes*, harder," Casey whispered, holding her firmly against her breast.

And Leslie did, her mouth opened again, letting her hunger guide her as she sucked hard on Casey's breast, both her hands cupping her, holding her to her mouth.

"Now I may fall down," Casey said, gently easing Leslie away. "*My God*," she whispered. "Bed."

Leslie wasn't sure she could make it to the bed. Her legs felt wobbly, her mind fuzzy. She stared at Casey, lost in a passion she'd only dreamed of, barely conscious of Casey slipping her panties down her legs.

Then Casey led her to the bed, laying down and pulling her on top. The long-buried memories of lying with another girl, of shyly exploring another girl's body under the cover of darkness in a tiny dorm room, could never have prepared her for this. She let her weight settle on Casey, was conscious of Casey's thighs parting, making a space for her. But then conscious thought left her when Casey's hands gripped her hips and pulled her close, both of them arching, touching.

"You feel so good," Casey whispered as her mouth once again found hers.

The bed spun and Leslie found herself on her back with Casey's smoldering eyes boring into hers. Then Casey's knee urged her legs apart and she pressed her hard thigh tight against her. Any coherent thought she still clung to fled as she lost herself in Casey's hands and mouth. Again, a hot tongue circled her nipple, teasing it until Leslie was trembling. But the hands that moved across her skin so softly—so slowly—were driving her to the very edge of sanity.

She arched her hips, her legs opening wider, trying desperately to bring some relief to her heated body. She groaned as Casey pressed down hard against her clit, then gasped as Casey's teeth raked across her nipple.

"*Please,*" she begged. "I can't take any more." She felt Casey's mouth gentle as she moved her lips to her other breast. "It's agony. *Torture,*" she breathed as Casey's mouth closed over her. She grabbed Casey's hips, jerking them forcefully against her. "Please *touch me.*"

She felt Casey's weight shift off her, then whimpered as Casey's hand moved past her waist to her hips. *Hurry, hurry, hurry.* Never had she *needed* like this, never had she been on the verge of begging someone to make love to her before, never had she thought she would *die* from the want of it. In agonizing slowness, Casey's fingers danced across her skin, driving her mad with desire, with need, with a *hunger* that demanded to be satisfied. Just when she thought she couldn't take any more, Casey's fingers dipped lower, brushing through her wetness, touching the inside of her thighs lightly, pushing her legs apart.

She felt Casey pause and she opened her eyes, finding Casey's.

"Yes." *Yes to everything.*

And then, finally, Casey touched her, her fingers gliding into her, filling her. *God, yes.* She arched, taking Casey inside, holding her there. Then she lowered her hips again, feeling Casey withdraw—almost—then those fingers took her again, filling her, moving with a rhythm that Leslie set, her hips rocking gently with each stroke. She tried to open her eyes, she wanted to watch Casey as she took her, but her eyes refused to cooperate, remaining shut as her hips moved faster and faster, feeling Casey taking her harder and harder.

The only sounds the slick wetness as Casey plunged inside her and frantic breathing of both of them. *Yes, yes, yes, yes,* she silently chanted as she felt her body drift away from her, pulling at her soul, threatening to rip her apart. When she was certain she would literally explode, when her brain simply ceased to function any longer, she felt Casey's fingers withdraw, replaced immediately by her mouth. Hot lips closed over her aching clit, and she grasped the sheets in her fists, trying to hold on, but Casey took her over the edge. Her scream—a deep guttural sound—came from her soul, and in her haze she wondered if she'd ever really had an orgasm before.

But she had no time to recover. Casey gathered her hips to her, her mouth still feasting, suckling her, her tongue delving deep inside her. No, she couldn't possibly respond again, her body was too spent, her mind too drained. But she did. Like a slow crescendo, it built, tugging at her, pushing her forward. She opened her eyes, watching as Casey nestled between her legs. The sight of this woman pleasuring her—making love to her—was her undoing. Her hips jerked once, hard against Casey's face, then she squeezed her thighs together, holding Casey, letting her take the last of her orgasm in her mouth...and then she collapsed.

Casey leaned on her elbow, watching Leslie as she caught her breath, unable to stop her hand as it found its way across her body, lightly caressing Leslie's skin, moving to her breast. The nipple hardened against her palm, and she squeezed, feeling Leslie stir. Brown eyes opened, then closed again as a contented smile touched her lips.

"Is *wow* an adequate enough description?" Leslie asked as she rolled toward her. "I thought I was going to pass out."

"Mmm."

Casey lay back, pulling Leslie's warm body to her, her own eyes closing as Leslie's hand shyly cupped her breast, teasing her.

"Your skin is so soft." Leslie leaned closer, her lips moving across her breast, finally closing over her nipple.

Casey moaned, forcing her eyes open as she watched Leslie at her breast. Was it too soon? Had they rushed things? She let her eyes slip closed as Leslie moved to her other breast. No, it was inevitable. Today, next week, it didn't matter when.

"You like that?"

Casey smiled. "Mmm."

"Can I...can I touch you?"

Casey finally opened her eyes, forgetting this was Leslie's first time. She pulled Leslie to her, kissing her slowly, hearing her moan. "I want you to touch me," she whispered.

Leslie didn't need any more encouragement as her hand glided down her body, past her hips. There was no hesitation, she simply parted her thighs, her fingers moving through her wetness, touching her.

"Oh, *God*," Leslie breathed, her eyes finding Casey's. "Can I touch you with my mouth?"

Casey merely nodded, unable to speak. There was a hunger in Leslie's eyes she'd not seen before. A look of sheer desire, of longing. She was suddenly terrified she wouldn't be able to stand it.

Again, there was no hesitation as Leslie slid down her body, her hands and mouth moving across her skin, nearly burning her where they touched. She spread her legs, her back arching, silently begging Leslie to hurry. Leslie's mouth moved across her stomach, leaving light kisses behind, finding the sensitive spot at the curve of her hip, causing her to moan.

"Yes." *Oh, yes.*

She felt Leslie cup her hips, felt her settle between her thighs, felt her breath against her wet skin. She forced her eyes open, watching. Then Leslie looked up, meeting her gaze.

"I've been dreaming of you my whole life," she whispered.

Any reply Casey had was lost as Leslie lowered her head, her tongue slipping inside her, her mouth covering her—kissing and tugging—driving out all thought except for the reality that this woman was nestled between her thighs, devouring her.

Chapter Thirty-Two

Leslie stared at herself in the mirror, wondering why she didn't look different this morning. She certainly *felt* different.

Would anyone know? Would anyone know she'd spent the last two days in another woman's bed? She gripped the countertop hard, still not used to the flood of desire that stole over her every time she thought of Casey making love to her, and her loving Casey. *Just once more*, she'd begged Casey.

Just once more.

One more kiss, one more touch. But it was never enough. And Saturday turned into Sunday while they explored every inch of each other, finding the secret places, driving each other over the edge again and again.

And it was still not enough.

She turned on the faucet, splashing her face with water, remembering every kiss, every touch, every time she screamed out Casey's name.

"*Good Lord,*" she murmured. Even now, she could still feel her desire, could still smell Casey, *taste* her. Could still imagine her fingers as they slid into her wetness, stroking her, making her come again and again.

She turned the water off, again staring at herself. How was she ever going to get through the day? When she saw Casey, how was she going to stop from touching her? How was she going to be able to look at her and not *want* her?

Why hadn't they discussed it? Had they even talked at all? No, not really. Certainly not about Michael. They didn't have to. Casey had touched her finger where the ring had been. There was no need to bring Michael into their weekend.

But the rest? No, they'd not talked about *it*. Like Casey had said once, *it* was very scary. But what do they do now? They acknowledged their attraction, yes. They acted on that attraction. Now what?

Panic and fear crowded in at once, nearly choking her. Was that it? One weekend? Was Casey satisfied? Or would they date now? Or would Casey think that they needed to see other people?

Does she think I want to see other women?

She took deep breaths, wondering why everything suddenly seemed so complicated. So they had sex. It was just a natural progression. They were attracted to each other, so they had sex. Nothing more, nothing less.

Right. Then why did her insides feel all jumbled up? Why was her heart lodged in her throat? And why was she hiding out in the ladies' room at seven thirty in the morning?

Before an answer came to her, the door opened. She looked up, catching the reflection in the mirror. In that one glance, her fears subsided as quickly as they'd come. Because the look in Casey's eyes was the same look she'd seen all weekend. Desire. Understanding. And the barely veiled look of longing. She turned slowly, absorbing the warmth and affection she found there, surprised she was able to stop from flinging herself into Casey's arms.

"You okay?"

Leslie nodded, afraid to speak.

Casey let the door close behind her, then came closer. Too close. This time Leslie couldn't stop and she moved her hand, capturing Casey's fingers with her own.

"We probably should have talked," Casey said, her lips hinting at a smile.

"Yes. I'm not sure how I'm supposed to act this morning."

They stared at each other, their fingers still touching. Then Casey finally did smile, squeezing her fingers before moving away. "We'll be fine," she said. "We're partners." She went to the door, then stopped, turning back around. "I had a fantastic weekend. How was yours?"

Leslie laughed, feeling the tension leave the room. "Yeah. It was a wonderful weekend."

"Good." Casey stepped out, then stuck her head back inside. "Maybe we could do it again? Soon?"

"Yes. I'd like that."

"Good." Then she winked at her. "See? We've talked about it."

The door closed behind her and Leslie turned back to the mirror, meeting her own eyes again. There was a different kind of fear in them this time.

I think I'm falling in love with her.

Of course, considering how she just spent the weekend, she hoped it was more than just lust that had kept her in Casey's bed for two days.

Chapter Thirty-Three

They crowded around Malone's desk, shuffling the visitor's chairs to fit them all. Tori tipped her chair back, leaning against the wall as she watched O'Connor and Tucker. There was *something* going on with them. First of all, they sat as far away from each other as possible, which Tori found strange. Normally, they were practically joined at the hip. And secondly, they weren't looking at each other. She arched an eyebrow as she casually glanced at Leslie's hand. No ring.

No ring?

"Okay, let's go over it," Malone said. "I finally got the approval for the twenty-four hour tag on your John Doe. I had to pull in favors on this one, seeing as how he's not even a suspect."

"His brother—"

"Yes, the mystery brother—or *sister*, depending on his mood." Malone looked at Casey. "O'Connor, I understand you two talked to him on Friday. Why don't you fill us in?"

O'Connor crossed her legs and glanced over at Leslie quickly. "Well, as everyone knows, we'd been looking for John all week. We finally spotted him Friday afternoon. In a dress."

"What the hell?"

"He said it was his turn to be the sister. Basically, whenever Patrick wants him to be the sister, he leaves the dress. So when John wakes up and the dress is there, he knows he's to be the sister."

"And what's the purpose of that?" Sikes asked.

"We have no idea," Leslie said. "John doesn't know why, and he doesn't ask. He merely does as his brother tells him."

"You think it could be for an alibi?" Tori asked. "I mean, if John is seen on the street in the dress, they'll just assume it's Patrick, like always."

"I think the dress is a quirk of Patrick's," Leslie said, "but I don't think it's the norm for him."

"John kept saying they were opposite," Casey said. "When he's awake, during the day, Patrick sleeps. At night, he sleeps, and Patrick is out and about. And they don't normally sleep together."

"John said Patrick stays inside, where it's cold and dark. The hole in the wall," Leslie said.

"A warehouse?"

"There are plenty of abandoned buildings. They would be cold and dark."

"John is like a child," Leslie said. "He sees things in black and white. When we asked him where Patrick slept he said the hole in the wall. That's because that's what he sees. He doesn't see a building or a warehouse, or whatever. To him, he sees Patrick going into a hole in the wall."

"And I got the impression he was afraid of that hole," Casey added.

"Tell Malone about the twin part," Tori said.

"Oh, yeah. Not just brothers. He said they were twins."

"Identical twins?" Malone asked. "Are you kidding me?"

"Not identical," Leslie said. "Their DNA is different."

"I don't understand."

"Yeah, I checked with Mac," Tori said. "Identical twins have identical DNA. John's DNA sequence suggests it's a relative, thus his brother. Mac said identical twins come from one egg that splits, so it's essentially two of the same egg. Fraternal twins start out as two separate eggs. They could end up looking alike, but they won't be identical."

"Mac told you all this and you actually understood?" Casey teased.

"Hey, I'm not as dumb as I look," Tori said as she tossed a pen at her.

"No. It's just that I've been with you before when Mac's explaining DNA. I've seen the blank look on your face."

"Kids, can we focus on this, please?"

"Sorry, Lieutenant," they said in unison.

"Okay, we have three murders associated with this. The other case…four months ago now?" He shuffled through his files. "The one Donaldson and Walker had. Yes, Christine Farmer. Twenty-six. Cascade apartments. Then we go nearly three months before we got Dana Burrows, the college student, at Stone Ridge apartments. Now, Rhonda Hampton, again at Cascades. All women in their twenties, all lived alone."

"All on ground floor units," Sikes added.

"None of the women were raped, yet semen was found on each victim," Tori said.

"Don't forget about Rudy Bobby," Casey said. "Our homeless guy was killed with the same murder weapon as our girls."

"And the matching fiber," Leslie reminded them.

"Right. There was a fiber found on Dana Burrows," Malone said. "It matched the blanket covering the homeless guy."

"Tox on Rudy Bobby showed cocaine. Something that John said," Casey said, glancing at Sikes. "Not you. The other John. He said Patrick gives him money. And he said Patrick is out and about at night, not during the day. Piece that together with the fact that the others on the street are afraid of Patrick—"

"Drug dealer?"

"I wouldn't say dealer. I'm guessing more of a carrier. And I'd bet Rudy Bobby stole some from Patrick and that got him killed. Maybe Rudy Bobby was following him around, saw stuff he shouldn't. Maybe he followed him to the apartment, saw the murder, went inside—"

"Unknowingly left a fiber," Leslie said.

"Or maybe he saw the murder and blackmailed Patrick,

trading his silence for cocaine," Sikes suggested.

Casey nodded. "Might be more plausible than stealing it, you're right."

"I still don't get the dress thing," Malone said. He looked at Tucker. "You said a quirk of his, but not the norm. What are your thoughts?"

"I think, like Tori said, it's some sort of alibi. I wouldn't be surprised if he's in the dress when he kills his victims. We've all been wondering how he gets inside their apartments. Dressed as a woman, a young woman at that, would probably be fairly easy to get them to open their doors." She looked at Casey. "If anyone spots him coming or going, they've spotted a woman."

"And maybe getting John to wear the dress occasionally allows Patrick to be on the streets during the day posing as John. I got the impression from John that Patrick is rarely out and about during the day. So on the occasions when he does want—or need—to be out, he gets John to wear the dress, and Patrick morphs into John, leaving the real Patrick still under cover."

Tori stared at her, shaking her head. "Jesus Christ, O'Connor, I think you've taken a few too many psychology classes. He *morphs* into John? You don't think he's just a punk who gets off dressing like women?"

"I think Casey's right," Leslie said. "It goes beyond playing dress-up. And I know we've never met Patrick, don't even know what he looks like, but I would think, as John says, they are quite opposite. I think he's very intelligent, whereas John is not. I would assume he is calculating, meticulous. John is childlike, simple, and therefore easily manipulated. I think the dress is just part of the game. I don't believe he does it for any *emotional* reasons."

Malone leaned back in his chair, slowly rubbing his bald head, watching them. He met Tori's eyes and raised his eyebrows. She shrugged.

"Captain wants us to bring CIU in, along with a profiler," he said. "Personally, I hate when CIU gets involved." He glanced quickly at Tori again. "Sorry. No offense to Sam."

Tori smiled. "I feel exactly the same way, Lieutenant."

"Good. Then let's try to wrap this up. Twenty-four hour detail. You decide how you break it up. No one goes out alone," he said, casting a look at Casey. "If we need help, I can try to pull someone from another squad. I'd suggest Donaldson and Walker, but—"

"We can manage, Lieutenant," Tori said quickly. "Like you said, let's try to wrap this up."

"Very well. But I want you to keep me posted. I've got a meeting with Hagen over at Narcotics, want to see if maybe this Patrick guy is on their radar."

"Yes, sir."

"I mean it. Let me know what you get. The captain wants an update by the end of the day. I'm guessing we have a couple more days before CIU and a profiler come calling."

"Well, Leslie and I are going to head over to the shelter," Casey said. "We want to talk to Maria again. She knows John. She may not know Patrick, but maybe she knows *Patty*."

"Looks like Sikes and I get the first shift then," Tori said as she stood. She pointed at Casey and Leslie. "You two need to get some rest this afternoon if you're taking the night shift."

"An afternoon nap?"

"Yeah, O'Connor, you're going to wish you had a nap when two a.m. rolls around and you're cruising the streets."

"Okay. So we'll switch out at what? Seven? Eight?"

"Let's say eight. And take a radio in case we need dispatch."

"Ten-four," Casey said with a grin.

Tori walked out with Casey, nudging her shoulder. "So? You have a good weekend?" she asked quietly. She was surprised at the slight blush that colored Casey's face.

"Yeah. Good," she said. "You?"

"Uh-huh. Sam hauled me around looking at houses."

"Sorry I missed that."

"Yeah. I was hoping you'd call me and persuade me to go to the lake yesterday."

"Yeah, well, I had…you know, laundry and stuff to catch up on."

Tori laughed. "You're so damn cute, O'Connor."

"What the hell does that mean?"

"That means I'm a detective, hotshot."

Casey arched an eyebrow.

"She's not wearing her ring."

Casey blushed again. "Look, *please* don't say anything," she whispered, then took a step back as Leslie walked over.

"I'm ready if you are."

"Yeah, sure. All ready." She walked away, then turned back. "See you at eight, Hunter."

Tori watched them go, smiling.

"What's up with you?" Sikes asked.

"Nothing."

"Did you notice Tucker didn't have her ring on?"

Tori laughed. "Oh, yeah. I noticed."

"What's up with that?"

"What would be your guess, Sikes?"

Chapter Thirty-Four

As they made their way up the sidewalk to the shelter entrance, Leslie grabbed her arm and stopped her.

"Casey, can we talk for a second?"

Casey turned around, nodding. "Sure. What? You want to do the questioning? That's fine. Maria—"

"No. No, that's not it." Leslie pulled her to the side. "Why are we doing this?"

"Doing what?"

"Casey, are you...I don't know...nervous because of what happened over the weekend?"

Casey laughed and realized it did sound nervous. "I may be a little, yeah. I didn't think it showed."

Leslie smiled slightly. "We had such a pleasant ride over here, talking about such diverse topics as the weather and our lingering summer temperatures. But I'm wondering why we're avoiding—and totally ignoring—the fact that we, well, that we spent the weekend together. *Naked.*"

Casey ran her hand through her hair, another nervous gesture, so she plunged it into the pocket of her jeans instead. Yeah, she was nervous. "I'm just not sure how we go about this," she said. "Like I said, the weekend was fantastic. But then—"

"But then now what?" Leslie turned and pulled her again to the side of the building, away from traffic. "I was thinking I should be the one nervous as this is all new to me, but it's really new to you as well." Leslie moved closer. "We should have talked about this before I left your bed yesterday."

Casey nearly stumbled from the impact of those words. *Before I left your bed.* She closed her eyes for a brief moment as images of their lovemaking flashed through her mind. "Let's do this interview, do our job, then please come home with me," she said quietly. "We'll talk. We'll get some rest. We'll get ready for tonight."

"If I come home with you, we're not going to get any rest."

Casey swallowed. "Of course we will. We'll talk. We'll decide where we go from here." She took a deep breath. "And we'll... we'll sleep."

"Okay. But I'll warn you now. If I get into bed with you, sleep is not going to be the number one thing on my mind."

She turned, going back to the sidewalk, leaving Casey staring after her.

No, sleep wouldn't be on her mind, either.

"Maria?" Leslie smiled. "Detectives Tucker and O'Connor."

"Of course. I remember. You have some news about Rudy?"

Casey stepped forward. "We'd like to talk to you again, if you don't mind. Do you have a few minutes?"

Leslie looked around the large room, most of the tables empty now as breakfast had already been served. A handful of volunteers busied about, clearing off tables. She turned back to Casey and Maria, waiting.

"The kitchen is very busy now. They are preparing lunch. Let's go into the storeroom. We should have privacy there."

They followed her, weaving their way between the tables to the other side of the room and down a hallway. The smell of soap and steam hit them as they rounded a corner. The showers, no doubt.

"How many do you feed at a normal meal?" Casey asked.

"There are no normal meals, Detective. Not surprisingly,

197

lunch is the busiest meal. Some are still sleeping off the bottle of booze they scored and miss breakfast. And others start their evening prowls early and miss dinner. But lunch usually brings them all around." She stopped at a door. "In here."

The storeroom was large and nearly bursting at the seams. Leslie walked into the room, turning a circle. "Wow. Lot of stuff."

"Yes. We're stocking for winter. That whole wall there," she said, pointing, "is mostly blankets and coats. And of course, when we have a food drive, this is where the canned goods end up." She closed the door behind them. "But I'm sure you didn't come to inspect our inventory."

"We have some questions," Casey said. "About John Doe."

She smiled. "Oh, yes. John is very sweet. One of my favorites. He hasn't been coming regularly though."

"When he does come in, does he ever have anyone with him?" Leslie asked. She glanced at Casey. "Someone who looks like him? A girl that might hang with him?"

"No. I've never seen him with anyone. But he's friendly with most of the others." She frowned. "What is it you're asking?"

"John has a brother. Or a sister," Casey said. "Actually, it's a brother who dresses as a girl occasionally."

Maria's eyesbrows lifted in surprise. "No. There's been no one with him."

"Okay. But does John always seem like John?" Leslie asked. "I mean his personality," she explained.

"Everyone has bad days, Detective. I don't expect John to always have that childlike happiness about him. Life is hard on the street. Some days, I wonder how old John is, he looks so young and carefree. Then other times, his eyes have a hardness about them, making him seem much older. He's not always friendly, not always sociable. Sometimes, he doesn't even speak to me." She shrugged. "But like I said, life on the street, you have good days and you have bad days."

"But when he's sweet, happy, friendly," she coaxed.

"Yes. Then he always speaks to me. He calls me Miss Maria."

198

She smiled. "Yes, that's the John we know."

"And you've never seen John in a dress?" Casey asked.

"No. Why would John wear a dress? And what does this have to do with Rudy?" Her eyes widened. "You surely don't think John had something to do with his murder?"

"No, no," Leslie assured her. "We're just trying to piece together all of our information."

Casey turned, apparently inspecting the shelves filled with canned goods, her back to them. "Tell me, Maria, when John doesn't seem like John, does he *look* like John?"

"Well, yes. He—" she paused, glancing between them. "Oh, my goodness," she said quietly. "No. The hair."

Casey turned around. "The hair what?"

"John has light hair. But sometimes it's darker. I don't know why it didn't register before. The other day when he was here, when he didn't speak to me, I went over to ask him if he was okay. There was something different about him, his expression, the look in his eyes. And his hair. It was dark. Like he had dyed it." She frowned. "What's going on?"

Leslie glanced at Casey who nodded. She moved in front of Maria. "John has a brother. A twin. His name is Patrick."

Her eyes widened. "You don't mean the Patrick that—?"

"We believe so, yes. He also dresses as a girl sometimes. John calls him Patty on those days," she said matter-of-factly. "We just can't seem to find anyone who knows Patrick. Our belief is that when he's out, he wears a dress so he won't be recognized. And when he does dress as a man, he pretends to be John."

"Which is why sometimes John speaks to me and sometimes he doesn't," Maria said, her voice trailing away. "Sammy. John hangs with Sammy at night. If anyone would know, he would."

"Where can we find him?"

"Sammy comes for dinner. Never misses."

"Do you have a description of him?" Casey asked.

Maria smiled sadly. "Yeah. An unkempt old man with a shaggy beard and torn clothes. You can't miss him."

"I'm sorry," Casey said. "I didn't mean—"

199

"It's okay, Detective. I know you're just doing your job. And honestly, despite my description, they do all have their own look, their own personality. Even the street can't take that away."

"What time is dinner?" Leslie asked.

"Starts at five thirty. By seven, we're out of food."

"Would it be too much trouble for you to call us when Sammy shows up?" Casey asked. "I don't want to stake out the place for hours. No sense in making everyone nervous," she said.

"I can do that," Maria said. "Sammy is usually here by six."

Casey handed over her card. "We'll wait for your call. Thank you."

Chapter Thirty-Five

After a call to Hunter to let her know they'd be on duty by six, Casey tucked her phone away, glancing once at Leslie who sat quietly beside her, her eyes fixed on the passenger window. They hadn't spoken, and no doubt they were both nervous. Would they sit on the sofa and talk? Perhaps out on the deck? Or would they simply rip their clothes off and forget all about talking?

"Casey?"

"Hmm?"

"It's not always going to be this awkward between us, is it?"

"I don't think so, no."

Leslie finally turned away from the window, shifting in her seat. She reached across the console and touched her arm. "We need to talk, I know. However, I can't seem to get past the fact that I want to make love to you again."

Casey smiled. "Yeah, I was trying to decide if we could possibly sit on the sofa and talk like mature adults, or if I would just rip your clothes off and drag you to bed."

"I vote for the latter."

Casey didn't say anything as she turned on her street. She didn't know why she was so nervous. Whether they talked first or last, it didn't matter. But at some point, they were going to be naked. Naked, touching…and making love. She pulled into her driveway and stopped. They both sat still, waiting. Finally, she turned. Her breath left her as she saw the unguarded look in Leslie's eyes.

"Are you scared?" Leslie whispered.

Casey nodded. "A few days ago you were wearing an engagement ring. Yes, I'm scared to death."

Leslie smiled. "I was scared too. This morning, I was scared. *What have I done? What happens next? Will people know? Did Casey enjoy it?* All random thoughts running through my mind." She took a deep breath. "But then you came into the ladies' room, and just your presence calmed me. You were trying to be confident, in control." She smiled. "You had that *attitude* going. But then I looked into your eyes and saw that you were as nervous as I was. And when you left, I think I was more scared than before. Because I realized I was falling in love with you and I was *terrified*." She took Casey's hand and squeezed. "I'm not so terrified anymore," she said. "Because you're falling in love with me too. Aren't you?"

Casey couldn't pull her eyes away, and she certainly couldn't deny the statement. Was it too soon to feel that way? Could one weekend of passion propel them into love? Years ago she would have scoffed at the idea. Sex was sex. And the part of her that was terrified wanted to claim that it *was* only sex. Of course her mind was still cogent enough to realize the reason she was terrified in the first place. She was scared because it *wasn't* just sex. So she gave in to what her heart already knew. It would serve no purpose to deny it.

"Yes, I'm falling in love with you."

Relief shone in Leslie's eyes, and she wondered if perhaps Leslie thought she might refute it.

"Can we go inside now?" Leslie asked quietly. "I'll tell you why I'm not wearing a ring anymore, and I'll tell you what I told Michael." She squeezed her hand again. "I'll tell you anything you want to know. We can talk as much as you like." She smiled. "Or as little."

Yes, Casey wanted to know about the ring. She wanted to know what Leslie had told Michael. But that could wait, she thought, as she pulled Leslie through the house and into her bedroom. Talking could wait. They'd be stuck together in a car for twelve hours. They could talk then. Now, she just wanted her naked.

When she stopped and turned, Leslie was there, slipping into her arms. Their kiss was not gentle. It was hungry and demanding, needy and insistent. And as intoxicating as she remembered. They pulled apart, their breath uneven, both gasping for air. Without a word, they tugged at clothing, tossing it where they may, hurrying to get naked, to feel skin on skin, wetness on wetness.

Casey guided Leslie to the bed, a blinding need coursing through her as her fingers found Leslie, filling her, watching her face as pleasure transformed it. Leslie's hips rose, taking her inside, and Casey glided into her, her hand pumping faster, meeting each stroke as Leslie's hips rocked against her.

"*Yes*," Leslie breathed. "*Take me…*"

Casey did.

Chapter Thirty-Six

The quiet beeping of her phone roused her from sleep and she rolled, gently untangling Leslie's arms as she reached for it.

"O'Connor," she said sleepily.

"It's me."

She opened her eyes, squinting at the clock. Had they overslept? "Uh-huh."

"I thought I'd wake your ass up," Tori said. "You were asleep, right?"

"Right," she said around a yawn.

"But not alone, I'm guessing. Hope it was fun."

"Shut up, Hunter." She rolled her eyes as Tori's laughter rang out.

"Sorry, kid. Couldn't resist."

"Any luck?" she asked, changing the subject.

"Nope. We've driven a twelve-block radius all day and not one sign of the little bastard. Twenty-four hour tag only works if we're actually *tagging* him."

Casey's comment died when she felt a warm hand slide across her stomach and cup her breast. She rolled her head, finding Leslie's eyes half-closed, a sated look on her face as her fingers gently traced her hardening nipple. It was after five, they'd only slept a few hours, and still her hunger for this woman was as fresh and raw as if they'd never touched. She felt the phone slipping

204

away as she leaned closer, finding soft lips, touching them lightly with her tongue.

"O'Connor? Did you fall back to sleep or what?"

She felt Leslie smile against her mouth and she picked up the phone which had slid down between them.

"Yeah, Hunter. Sorry. What did you say?"

"Forget it. But you don't have time for sex, O'Connor. Pull away from her, take a shower—*alone*—and try to keep your hands off each other tonight." She laughed. "Sikes wants a full report in the morning."

Casey smiled. "You're evil. Both of you."

"Yeah, yeah. But…well, be careful, O'Connor."

Casey nodded. The words had a double meaning, she knew. "I will. Thank you."

She closed the phone and pulled Leslie closer, sighing as she felt her lips move across her breast.

"I take it they know," Leslie murmured as her tongue raked across her nipple.

"*Mmm.* Yes, they know."

Leslie lifted her head. "Are we in trouble?"

"No. Not yet. Not until Malone finds out." She rolled them over, pressing her weight into Leslie. "Tori informed me we don't have time for this. But we must take time for a shower." She raised her eyebrows. "Share?"

"My God, there's so many," Leslie said, her eyes scanning the dining room of the shelter. Row after row after row sat people— mostly men, mostly disheveled—quietly eating their dinner.

"Yeah. You don't see all this when you're just cruising the streets." Casey pointed to the serving line. "There's Maria."

"We stick out like a sore thumb, you know." She could feel eyes on them.

"I know."

Leslie caught Maria's attention, who nodded at them, motioning them to the side. They waited patiently while she found someone to relieve her in the serving line.

"I told Sammy you wanted to speak with him. It's only fair he know," she said.

"I understand. Is he still willing?"

"Yes. Rudy was a friend of his. I told him you had questions about that. I didn't mention John."

"Good. Thank you." Casey looked over the crowd. "Where is he?"

"Oh, no. He won't meet you in here."

"How will we know him?"

"He'll find you outside." She shoved a paper bag into her hands. "He left without eating. Please give him this."

Leslie nodded. "Of course, Maria."

"So he doesn't want to be seen talking to cops?" Casey asked. "Should we have been more discreet coming in here?"

"No, it's fine. Cops come in all the time. Mostly uniforms, but still, after what happened to Rudy, it's not unusual for there to be questions." She turned to go, then stopped. "Sammy's a good man. But like the others, he's more afraid of the evil on the street than he is the cops. He'll only tell you what he wants."

"We won't harass him, if that's what you're alluding to," Leslie assured her. "We want to get the evil off the street as much as anyone."

"Yes. I believe you do." She motioned to the door. "Just walk back to your car. I'm certain he watched you arrive. He'll find you."

"Thank you, again, Maria." Casey nodded curtly at her. "Again, if you hear anything that might be useful to us—"

"I'll be certain to let you know." She wiped her hands on her apron. "Now, if you'll excuse me, I must get back to work."

Leslie followed Casey outside, pausing to look back into the shelter. "I admire people like her," she said. "I doubt her salary is much above the minimum, yet she probably cares about her job more than most people making four times as much."

"Yeah. I wonder if it's personal for her."

"What do you mean? Like her father or something?"

Casey shrugged. "Perhaps. I knew a woman once whose older sister lived on the street. She didn't have to. The family had money. But the sister, I think she was diagnosed as bipolar. She would pop in and out of their lives. They'd get her on medication for awhile, then she'd disappear back to the street." She stopped at the truck and pushed the remote to unlock it. "They'd be driving along and they'd see her panhandling."

"What happened to her?"

"She died. She was buried as a Jane Doe. When they found out, they had her body moved, but it was all very sad. But anyway this woman, Sharon, she volunteered every spare minute she had after that. It consumed her."

"All their faces. They just looked so hopeless."

"And maybe they are," Casey said as she opened the door. "Living day to day. No happiness, no love. Just existing."

Leslie got into the passenger seat and closed the door. "Of course, you don't have to be homeless to have those symptoms."

"No, I guess you don't."

They sat quietly for a moment, then Casey started the truck. "What do you think? Drive around the block or something?"

"It's still daylight. If he doesn't want anyone to see him, I doubt he'll be waiting on the curb for us."

"Then let's make the block."

But they didn't have to go far. At the next intersection, he was leaning against the stop sign. Full beard, the skin around his eyes weathered, his long hair hidden by an old cap. Casey stopped and lowered her window.

"Sammy?"

He stared straight ahead, not looking at them. "Meet me on the corner of Walton and Worth."

Casey nodded. "That's just a few blocks north of here. What time?"

He shrugged. "Don't own no watch." He turned without another word, walking slowly back toward the shelter.

"I forgot his bag," Leslie said, holding it up.

"We'll give it to him later." She looked at her watch. "Six thirty.

I guess we go to Walton and Worth and just wait for him."

"You want me to check in with Hunter?"

"Yeah. And see if they ever found John."

"Here he comes."

Casey glanced in the mirror, nodding. They'd been waiting forty-five minutes. Long enough for them to doubt he'd show. Hunter and Sikes had spotted John finally. They caught him buying a burrito from a street vendor on Elm and followed him to the old historical cemetery that hadn't seen a burial since way back in the Sixties. There on a wooden bench, he sat and ate his dinner. From there, back on the street, he disappeared into one of the alleys in Deep Ellum.

"We might be better served to follow Sammy tonight instead of looking around for John," she suggested.

"Of course there's always the possibility that John is out cruising apartments. Let's don't forget, he likes to watch girls."

Casey lowered her window, waiting until Sammy passed by. Again, he didn't stop to look at them.

"Let's walk," he said, his feet still shuffling along the sidewalk.

"Well, he's careful, I'll say that."

"I was about to say he's watched too many spy movies," Casey said. "But then, maybe not."

They got out of the truck, moving behind him, then up beside him on either side. They kept to his slow, steady pace, not speaking. They were in a residential area, older homes with large yards and mature trees. Before they reached Baumer, he ducked into a line of hedges nearly eight feet tall.

"Come, come. Out of sight," he said.

They crawled in among the limbs and leaves, Casey meeting Leslie's eyes in the shadows. "How cozy," she murmured.

"Sammy? I'm Detective Tucker. This is Detective O'Connor," Leslie said.

"I know. John told me. Miss Leslie and Miss Casey." He turned to Casey. "You're the one who ties him up."

"I don't tie him up," she said, ignoring the quiet laugh from Leslie. "We need your help, Sammy. We need to find John's brother. Do you know where he stays?"

His eyes darted around nervously as he shook his head. "No. Don't see him much. Don't *want* to see him."

"He killed Rudy," Leslie said. "He's also killed others. Young women who live alone. We've got to find him."

"Do you ever see him with John?" Casey asked.

"I don't know where he goes, where he stays. He just shows up. I think John is scared of him."

"Are you scared of him?"

He laughed nervously. "Hell, yeah. I ain't stupid."

"What did Rudy do?" Leslie asked. "What did he do to make Patrick kill him?"

He shook his head. "I ain't talking about that. I don't have nothing to do with that mess."

"Drugs?" Casey asked.

"Yeah, drugs. And I told Rudy to leave it alone. But no. He followed Patrick one night. Saw him make a deal with some kid. So he follows the kid and shakes him down. As if the kid wouldn't go back to Patrick." He shook his head again. "Patrick came for him the next night. I heard the screaming. We all did. Then he wasn't screaming no more."

"Did anyone actually see Patrick kill him?"

"We didn't have to *see*."

Casey looked past the shrubs to the street, dusk finally settling on the city. She turned back to Sammy. "Are you afraid to be talking to us?"

"Yeah. Like I said, I ain't stupid."

"But you like John?" she guessed.

"John is just a boy. Don't care how old he is, he's just a boy. He doesn't know any better. I tell him not to go out at night. I know what he does."

"At the apartments?" Leslie asked.

"He watches them."

209

"Do you think Patrick watches him watch them?"

Sammy stared at her. "I don't know about that."

"John wears a dress sometimes. What's up with that?" Casey asked. "I don't know. I don't know nothing." He looked at the street. "I gotta go. I been here too long."

"Sammy, wait," Leslie said. "Miss Maria gave me a bag to give you. It's in the truck."

"I don't need it. I just need to get back." He walked out of the hedge, then stopped. "And don't come looking for me again. I don't know anything else." He left then, hurrying back down the street, his old coat pulled tight around him, even on this warm evening.

"Is now a good time to talk about the absurdity of the situation?" Leslie asked.

"What do you mean?"

"We're hiding in shrubs, O'Connor," she said with a laugh.

"Oh, yeah, I guess we are." She laughed too. "Interrogating a homeless man who knows more than he wants to know."

"More than he's telling us, for sure."

Casey stepped out onto the street and held her hand out for Leslie. "Do you get the feeling that the only way we're going to find Patrick is if we just stumble upon him?"

"Yeah. And maybe tailing John wasn't the answer. I mean, they apparently don't hang together, don't sleep together."

"No. But something you said to Sammy, about Patrick watching John watch the girls. I think that's an excellent theory."

"Perhaps. But no way to prove it."

"Well, other than watching John."

Leslie stopped at the truck, looking across the back at her. "You mean look for Patrick while he's watching John watch the girls?"

"Yeah."

They got inside the truck, but Leslie touched her arm. "But that would mean that John is the one who triggers the killings."

Casey frowned. "How so?"

"Because the Peeping Tom reports come in spurts. So if he's watching John, he has to wait until the…well, until the *urge* hits him. And the past patterns indicate that the incidences increase in frequency, like daily, before the killing."

"The murders are increasing in frequency as well. A three-month span between the first and second, then two weeks."

"Why don't we pull data on that three-month span? I mean, maybe John was going out, but Patrick wasn't interested."

"And we're assuming all the Peeping Tom reports from this area are John. We both know that's not likely," Casey said as she started the truck.

"Not likely all, no. But these apartments, within our radius, are most probably John."

Casey drove back down toward Elm, not feeling confident they'd hook up with John tonight. Tori said they'd lost him as he ducked down the alley behind the Captain's Chair Seafood Bar. And if they didn't find John tonight, didn't find Patrick, then CIU and their profiler would be all over the case.

"If we get a profiler involved, get CIU involved, then John can no longer be protected," she said.

"I don't know what good a profiler is going to do."

"Well, technically, Patrick is only a name. We've never seen him. He's like a ghost that haunts the streets." Casey glanced at her. "We have DNA, that's it. And Rudy Bobby? Sammy said it best. No, they didn't *see* Patrick kill him, but they all know it was him. What the hell good would that do us in court?"

"We've got the fiber," Leslie reminded her.

"A fiber that potentially puts Rudy at the murder scene of a young woman. It hardly implicates Patrick."

Leslie leaned back against the seat, turning her head slightly. "So we drive around all night hoping we stumble upon him?"

"That's how this whole case is going, isn't it? We stumble upon John. Get his DNA, thinking he's the one, only to stumble upon the fact that no, it's not him, but a relative, possibly his brother."

She turned right on Elm, back to Deep Ellum. Traffic was heavy, like it usually was, but the pedestrian traffic was still light at this early hour. The after-work crowd that gathered for happy hour was gone, and the late night regulars had not yet arrived. Because even on a Monday night, there would be partiers.

"Gonna be a long night."

Casey turned, nodding. "Yeah. And we didn't exactly sleep today."

Leslie smiled. "Not exactly, no."

"Well, we can take turns driving. I know that's not the most comfortable place to take a nap, but feel free."

"Maybe in a little while. I'm okay for now."

Casey nodded and turned her attention back to the streets. No, they hadn't slept much. Some, but not much. Certainly not enough to sustain them for a twelve-hour shift. But it was nice, wasn't it? Holding her while they slept, waking up with her. Is this how falling in love felt? Because if so, everything else before paled in comparison. Sex was just sex. But not any longer. A handful of dates didn't make a relationship, and living with someone didn't mean they were your life partner. But now? She glanced again at Leslie and found her eyes on her. She smiled and looked away, feeling so *giddy* about the possibilities, she was nearly embarrassed.

Then a soft hand touched her arm, the fingers rubbing lightly across her skin. She turned, catching Leslie's warm gaze. Neither said anything.

They didn't have to.

Chapter Thirty-Seven

Leslie heard talking and she tried to force her eyes open. She rolled her head, the cold glass of the truck window bumping her forehead.

"We got nothing, Hunter. We talked to Sammy. The only thing he told us was Rudy apparently hit up a kid that Patrick had sold cocaine to. He partied with it and Patrick killed him."

She turned, finally opening her eyes. The sun was nearly up and she stretched, managing to stifle a yawn.

"I'm telling you, Patrick is like a ghost. I hope you guys have better luck today."

Leslie studied Casey, seeing her nod.

"Okay, yeah. We're going to crash. Been a hell of a long night." Casey looked at her and smiled. "Later."

Leslie smiled sheepishly. "Sorry. I fell asleep."

"No problem. I napped when you were driving."

"You napped for maybe a half-hour. Judging by the crick in my neck, I'd say I've been out for awhile."

"Not quite two hours. But it was quiet."

"So we're off the clock?"

"Yeah. They're already down on Elm hoping to spot him early." Casey headed north, crossing over Gaston. "You hungry?"

"I can't decide if I'm more hungry or tired. You?"

"I'm too tired to be hungry. I just want to sleep." She glanced at her. "Come home with me?"

Leslie raised her eyebrows.

"Sleep," Casey clarified. "I don't have the energy for anything else."

"Okay. Sleep. We'll worry about eating later." And she supposed she'd worry about her living arrangements later too. The hotel room was paid for the week, and she'd have to make a run by there to get clothes. She really needed to go by Michael's apartment to get more of her things. She didn't know when she'd have time, not with them working these crazy hours.

The vibration of her phone against her waist startled her. Only one person would call her this early. She leaned to the side and unclipped her phone, glancing at the number. No, not Michael. Worse.

She took a deep breath, then answered.

"Good morning, Leslie. It's Rebecca. I wanted to catch you before you started your day."

"Actually, I'm just ending my day. I worked the nightshift." She met Casey's gaze and mouthed *Michael's mother*.

"I'm sorry. Is this a bad time?"

"No. What's on your mind, Rebecca?"

"Well, what a silly question, dear. I guess you know what's on my mind."

"No offense, but really, this is between me and Michael."

"He's just devastated. I've never seen him more upset. Surely you can't just walk away from this engagement without trying to reconcile your differences."

She rolled her eyes, wondering just what it was Michael had told her. "There is no reconciling. You want me to be blunt, I will. I'm not in love with him." She glanced at Casey who was being polite and at least pretending not to listen. "I'm not going to marry him."

"And you think telling him you're *gay* is going to appease him? How could you tell him such a thing?"

"So he doesn't believe I'm a lesbian? If I told him I was having an affair with another man, he'd believe that?"

"Oh, Leslie, what are you doing? Was it that bad that you need to ruin his life? What about all the plans? Why, I practically had your wedding arranged."

Leslie sighed. "Yes, you did. And I'm sorry. But things happen. I wasn't happy with Michael, and if he's honest with you, he'll tell you that he wasn't really happy with me. This is best, Rebecca."

"No, I don't believe so. I want you to reconsider. The least you can do is go to counseling like he suggested. You owe him that much."

"Oh, no. You're not going to guilt me into this. I don't *owe* him anything." She looked again at Casey. "We all deserve to be happy in life. I'm not going to settle. Neither should he."

"I just don't understand why you—"

"Rebecca, I am extremely tired. Trust me when I say there is nothing either you or Michael can say that would change my mind."

"But—"

"Good-bye." She closed her phone and leaned back in the seat, eyes closed. It was a conversation she didn't need to have in front of Casey. She'd not actually told Casey about her talk with Michael yet. And after listening to her end of the conversation, she was most likely filled with curiosity.

But still, she said nothing, her eyes fixed on the street. Finally Leslie could stand it no longer. "I know you want to know. Why haven't you asked me?"

Casey laughed. "I was trying to be polite and mind my own business."

"After everything we've…well, *shared* the last few days, don't you think it's your business?"

"Everything we talked about before this, I knew you wouldn't come to me until you'd ended things with Michael. How you ended it, what you told him, I don't think that's my business. I don't know him. That part of things was just between the two of you." She smiled. "And apparently his mother."

Leslie stared at her. "You're very trusting."

"I like to think I'm a good judge of character." Casey looked

215

at her quickly, then away. "Am I wrong?"

"No. You're not wrong. I told Michael I wasn't in love with him and couldn't marry him. When he insisted we go to counseling to try and fix things, I told him they couldn't be fixed. I told him I was a lesbian." She smiled. "Of course he didn't believe me."

"Was that hard?"

"Saying the word *lesbian* out loud? Yeah, it was. A little. But saying it out loud, especially to Michael, made it all real to me. It wasn't just something in my mind any longer. It wasn't just something I thought about when I was with you. Saying it out loud made it true."

"I don't imagine it's going to be easy. You have people in your life who have known you as a straight woman. A change like this, it's a shock to most people."

"Yes. And I'm hoping Sam will be willing to talk with me. She seems so strong about everything."

"She's strong about it because she's sure of their relationship. Tori was the one balking when they met. But then you'd have to know Tori. She had this idea that no one could love her."

"So she didn't trust Sam?"

"I don't think she believed someone like Sam would love her. Of course, the Tori we know now was not the same person back then. As Sam says, she had *issues* to work through." Casey pulled into her driveway and stopped. She smiled tiredly. "My issue right now is can I make it into the bedroom before I fall asleep."

They didn't say anything else as they went into the house and down the hall. In the bedroom, they stripped, but there was nothing sexual about it. Casey pulled the covers back and got in, holding them up for her. She climbed in beside her, letting Casey wrap her naked body around hers.

"I love sleeping with you," Casey murmured before her even breathing signaled she was fast asleep.

Leslie sighed contentedly, pulling Casey's arm more firmly around her and letting her eyes slip closed.

Chapter Thirty-Eight

"There he is," Tori said, motioning down an alley where John emerged, hand held above his face as if squinting from the sunlight. "About damn time."

"Wait a minute. Dark hair." Sikes reached in the back and pulled out the folder with Tucker's spreadsheet. Inside was a shot of John from their interrogation. He held it up. "Blond. What did O'Connor say about the hair color?"

"Maria, the lady at the shelter, said John had dark hair the last time she saw him, but he didn't act like John." Tori drove slowly, keeping him within sight. "O'Connor's thinking Patrick has dark hair." She glanced at Sikes. "You want to pull him in?"

"Christ, Hunter. On what charge? We don't even know what Patrick looks like. This guy," he said, pointing, "looks like John with dark hair. So you pull John in again and you get his attorney, *Robert*, breathing down your neck, then we're in the paper for harassing the homeless. No. I don't want to pull him in."

"We should call O'Connor. They've spent the most time with the guy. They'd know if this was him or not."

"They haven't slept in how many days now? No. Let's just follow him. That was the plan."

"I got a bad feeling, Sikes."

"Turn up here," he said.

"Can you still see him?"

"Yeah. I'm guessing he's heading to the shelter for breakfast."

"Okay, good. At least we'll have a fix on his location."

Tori turned, intending to meet up with him on the next block, past the clubs, when Sikes squeezed her shoulder hard.

"What?"

"There's a John in a dress too. My God, they look just alike."

"Are you *fucking* kidding me?" She sped to the curb, jerking the binoculars out of his hand. "Jesus Christ," she muttered. "They look identical." She lowered the glasses. "Mac said they can't be identical. He said if their DNA is not identical, they're not identical twins."

"Maybe just from this distance they look alike. Up close, maybe not."

"Call for patrol units to back us up, then let Malone know. I'm going to wake up O'Connor. Who the hell knows which is which?"

"You think they'll know?"

"If not, we haul them both in and let the DA deal with a judge in getting DNA." She pulled her phone out and continued driving, hoping the two Johns would materialize at the opposite end of the alley.

"Oh, God *no*," Casey mumbled, fumbling for her phone, eyes still closed. *I'll kill her.* "This better be good, Hunter."

"We got them spotted."

Casey opened her eyes. "*Both* of them?"

"Yeah. They just cut through an alley behind the Rat Club. We think they're heading to the shelter. One of them is in a dress."

Casey sat up, ignoring the sheet that slipped to her waist. "Maria said she'd never seen them together. And she'd never seen either of them in a dress. Maybe assuming they're going to the shelter is too hopeful." She nudged Leslie with her leg, smiling at the groan she received in response. "You want us to come?"

"Yeah, I need you here. We can't tell them apart. Maybe you two can. Regardless of what Mac said, they look identical to me.

And they both have dark hair."

Casey tilted her head. "John's got blue eyes. Blond hair, blue eyes."

"Okay, so you're assuming Patrick is naturally dark with brown eyes? Is that how we'll tell them apart?"

"I'm not assuming anything. I just know John is blond and blue." She stood, bending to pick up the jeans she'd discarded such a short time ago. "They could both be naturally blond and blue and Patrick just colored his dark for some reason. Or colored both of them."

"Okay. Head to the shelter. I'll call you back if it looks like they're not heading that way."

"We still have the radio, don't forget. Quicker."

"Yeah. With more ears. But keep it with you."

Casey struggled into her jeans with the phone tucked against her shoulder. "We're on our way." She sat on the edge of the bed, gently shaking Leslie. "Come on. We have to go."

"You're kidding, right?" Leslie asked, her face still burrowed into the pillow.

"Sorry, sweetheart. But they have Patrick spotted."

Leslie rolled her head, her eyes blinking. "For real?"

"They saw John and Patrick together. Both with dark hair."

Leslie sat up, shaking her head. "John has—"

"Blond hair, I know. They don't know who is who. I'm sure we can pick John out though." She got up, collecting her clothes from the floor. "I wish we had time for a shower, but we don't."

"We look like hell."

Casey laughed. "I'll be nice and say you're as beautiful as ever."

Leslie tossed the covers off and stood. "And you'd be lying."

Casey stared as Leslie walked naked to the bathroom. "Not lying, no."

Chapter Thirty-Nine

"Where the hell are you?" Casey asked as she scanned the street, looking for Tori's Explorer.

"Christ, O'Connor, are you blind?"

Casey pulled the phone away from her ear and stared at it, then flicked her gaze to Leslie. "She's a smartass," she said quietly. She put the phone back to her ear. "I've had about six hours sleep in the last four days, Hunter. I shouldn't even be driving."

"Perhaps you should *pace* yourself then, O'Connor. You can have sex anytime. Take a night to sleep instead."

"You are *so* funny," she said as she whipped her head around, finally spotting them. "You could have said you weren't on the street."

"Oh, yeah. We're in the Rat's Club parking lot."

Casey handed her phone to Leslie. "I can't deal with her in this mood. You can have her."

"Okay. But I'm not in much better humor." Leslie took the phone. "Hey, Tori. It's Tucker. You want us on the street or what?"

Tori was just having some fun, Casey knew. And under normal circumstances, she'd have played along. But today, no. She was tired, she was cranky, she was stressed about the case, and she wished she was back in bed tangled up with Leslie.

"How long have they been in there?"

"In where?" Casey asked.

Leslie covered the phone with her hand. "In the coffee shop," she said quietly before removing her hand. "Yeah, well I don't think—"

"Wait...there," Casey said, pointing. "It's John."

"Hunter, we have a visual," Leslie said. She shook her head. "No, in a dress." She looked at Casey. "What do you think?"

"I don't know what the hell to think." She grabbed the phone from Leslie. "They're both out, Hunter. One in a dress, one not. Hell, they look alike."

"I told you."

"I thought Mac said—"

"Yeah, yeah. But we don't have time to argue about Mac now. If you can't make a positive ID on which one is John, then we take them both."

Casey nodded. "They're heading down Elm, away from you."

"Shit," she murmured. "Okay, we're on the move. Fucking follow them, O'Connor."

Casey pulled away from the curb, driving slowly, keeping a safe distance away from John and Patrick. "What do you think, Les? Which one's John?"

Leslie stared at the pair and shook her head. "They look so much alike. But the dress. We just saw John in a dress. Remember how he walked? Like he wasn't used to it. But this one, the one in the dress, he doesn't look uncomfortable at all."

Casey watched them. "I agree. Hunter, you hear that? We think Patrick's in the dress."

"We're right behind you."

Casey nearly slammed on her brakes as both men stopped and turned, looking right at them. "Fuck, they made us," she said as she felt adrenaline flood her body.

"Goddamn," Tori muttered.

"They're running!"

"Follow them, O'Connor! We've got patrol cars right behind us."

"They're in the alley."

"Follow them."

Casey pulled to a stop and jumped out, running fast into the alley. She heard the others behind her. John and Patrick weren't far ahead. Patrick was slowed by the heels.

"Police! Stop!" she yelled. John turned around and looked at her, then nearly stumbled as he hit a trash can. "John! Stop!" At the corner between buildings, they split up. Patrick took off down the side alley and John headed for the street.

"O'Connor, get John," Tori yelled. "We've got the other one."

Casey stopped, nodding at Leslie to follow Tori. She sprinted after John, running into the street, dodging traffic as horns blasted around her. "John, hold up!"

He slowed finally, looking over his shoulder as he ran.

"What the hell's wrong with you?" she yelled. "We're trying to help you."

He finally stopped, bending over at the waist to catch his breath. She stopped too, breathing hard.

"Why did you run from me?" she gasped.

He shook his head and took a step away from her. "Don't hurt me. Don't hurt me, okay?"

"I'm not going to hurt you. Jesus, have I ever hurt you?" She took several deep breaths. "Come on."

"Where?"

"We've got to go back, John."

He shook his head again. "No. You're going to hurt me."

"I'm not going to hurt you. But you have to come with me."

He hesitated. "What are they going to do to my brother?"

"They just want to talk to him, that's all. They just have some questions. Like when we had questions for you that time. Remember?"

He eyes were wide with fright. "Yeah. Okay."

"Good. Now come on." She started walking back, looking over her shoulder as he followed a few steps behind her. He looked scared, but she couldn't blame him. He probably didn't know what the hell was going on with everyone yelling and chasing after him. When they got back to the street, traffic had been blocked off and six patrol cars were facing the alley.

She jogged over and held up her badge. "Any word?"

"No. They're in one of the warehouses."

She pointed at John who stood several feet away. "Keep an eye on him, will you?" she asked, squinting at his nametag. "Officer Staton?"

"Yes."

"Put him in the back of your car. He's not under arrest, but I don't want him running off."

"Yes, ma'am."

She hurried off, then turned. "John, you stay here." She didn't wait for a reply as she dashed into the alley. She knew what she was looking for. A hole in the wall. But she stopped up short, something nagging at her.

Don't hurt me.

"I can't see a goddamn thing," Sikes said as he hugged the wall.

"Tucker?" Tori whispered.

"Behind you."

"Sikes, go right. Tucker, go left. I'm going up front."

She waited as they moved away, then slowly walked into the warehouse, her eyes adjusting to the darkness as only tiny beams of light penetrated through pinhole imperfections in the metal walls. It looked like it had been abandoned years ago. The boxes that littered the floor smelled old and stale and were coated in dust. She heard scuffling up ahead and stopped, tilting her head. She turned slowly to her right, hearing faint footsteps running along the concrete floor. She gripped her weapon tighter, her palms damp with perspiration.

"Sikes?"

"I heard."

She moved in that direction, hearing Sikes's careful footsteps ahead of her. They were inside the warehouse now and the boarded up windows let in enough light to chase some of the shadows away. She saw Sikes, maybe ten steps ahead of her. She stopped, looking to her left. Tucker was moving slowly, her weapon drawn, eyes straight ahead.

They all three moved steadily deeper into the warehouse, looking for movement. But when he jumped up from behind two boxes, they didn't have time to react. He was on Sikes in an instant.

Don't hurt me.

Casey frowned. Not *don't tie me up*. But *don't hurt me*. John never said that. John said *don't tie me up, Miss Casey*. That's what John always said. And John had friendly, smiling blue eyes. Not hard like these. Not lifeless like these appeared.

"Son of a *bitch*!"

She turned, running as fast as she could back to the patrol cars. "Where the fuck is he?" she demanded, her eyes darting between the cars. She grabbed Staton by the arm and spun him around. "Where the *fuck* is he?"

Christ, she should have known it wasn't John. She should have known.

"Sikes!"

But he was too quick. The knife flashed, slashing across John's neck an instant before blood poured from his wound.

Tori fired without thinking, sending three rounds into Patrick, barely registering his flailing body before she ran to John, pressing both hands hard against his neck, trying to stop the blood.

"Officer down! Officer down!" she yelled as loud as she could. "Officer down!" She saw Tucker come up beside her, saw her fumble with her radio, repeating *officer down, officer down*. She motioned behind her to Patrick. "Check on him." Then she bent low to John, knowing her hands were trembling as she felt his blood seeping between her fingers. "You goddamn hold on, Sikes. You hear me? You goddamn hold on." She lifted her head again. "Where's the fucking ambulance?" she yelled.

Casey turned at the sound of the shots. They all did.
Officer down. Officer down.
"Oh, God, no."
She took off running again, her heart beating so wildly in her chest, she thought it would explode. She found the hole in the wall, a piece of metal lifted up from the bottom, hidden by a Dumpster. The Dumpster had been shoved to the side. She drew her weapon and stepped inside.

Leslie kicked the knife out of Patrick's hands, startled at how similar he looked to John. If not for the nearly black hair, she'd—
His hand twitched and she watched in amazement as his eyes fluttered opened. Blue eyes. *Oh, dear God.*
"Miss Leslie," he whispered. "I'm sorry."
"John?"
"He...he made me."
She fell down beside him, cradling his head, unable to stop the tears that formed in her eyes. "Oh, John," she whispered. "No..."
"He said...he said he'd go after you if I didn't." He coughed and blood spewed from his lips. "I...couldn't let...him do..."
She felt his body go limp as the life faded from his eyes. She held him tightly in her lap, looking over at Tori who still held fast to Sikes, a pool of blood surrounding them.

Casey stood in the shadows, the scene unfolding in front of her like a bad movie. Her feet felt glued to the floor as she watched Leslie holding him. John. She knew it was John. And only a few feet away, Tori knelt beside Sikes, her hands covered in his blood.

Oh, God. No.

Then voices penetrated and she was shoved out of the way as the room filled with paramedics and police. She watched Tori stand helplessly aside as they took Sikes from her. Tori glanced at Leslie, her brows drawn together.

"It's not Patrick," Leslie said. "John."

"What the hell?" She whipped around, eyebrows raised as she glared at Casey.

Casey shook her head. "No. He got away."

Chapter Forty

Casey stood by the door in the waiting room, watching Tori stare broodingly out the window, her back to the room. Sam was seated in one of the visitor's chairs, her hands folded in her lap, her eyes staring at nothing. Casey made herself move. Sam looked up and offered a weak smile as she sat down beside her.

"How's she holding up?"

"I'm not sure. She won't talk to me." Sam leaned closer, resting her hand on her thigh and squeezing. "I'm scared. For the first time, she doesn't *see* me, she doesn't *hear* me. I can't seem to reach her." Sam leaned into her shoulder. "For the first time, I can't reach her."

Casey put her arm around Sam and pulled her close. "She's in shock. Sikes is like her brother, you know. And she's got her hands on his throat, trying to stop the bleeding, trying to keep him alive. She's still in cop mode, Sam. It's nothing to do with you."

"I know. I just can't stand to see her like this. It's like she's gone to another place." Sam pulled away slightly and looked at her. "I imagine it's the same place she went to when her family was killed. A place where there's no comfort. And I don't want her to go there alone."

"She'll be okay, Sam. She'll come back."

Sam didn't say anything as she leaned her head on Casey's

shoulder again.

"I don't suppose there's any news?" Casey asked.

"No. We haven't heard a word." Sam turned. "Where's Leslie?"

"She went to her old apartment to get some clothes. I think she needed some time alone. John—John Doe—was special. She took it very hard."

Sam sat up again. "What do you mean, *old* apartment?"

Casey smiled sheepishly.

Sam laughed quietly. "So Tori was right." She nudged Casey playfully. "Good for you."

"I like her a lot."

"And it's mutual?"

"Yes."

"Wonderful. Now I'll have someone to play with while you and Tori fish."

"Thanks, Sam. She's...well, I think she feels a little lost. And I imagine she's going to need someone to talk to."

"And maybe you underestimate her. Love is a very powerful thing, once you accept it. Leslie seems very strong and level-headed to me. I don't think you need to worry about her *adjusting*, if that's what it is."

Casey smiled. "No, she's adjusted quite well. I just mean how to deal with coworkers, friends, family."

"I've found that people, as a rule, just want you to be happy. Now family—"

"Oh, that's right, you still haven't told yours."

Sam blushed slightly. "It's not something you casually mention in a phone call. And it's not like I've been to Denver to see them."

They both turned when the door opened. Leslie stood there, her eyes red and puffy. Casey got up and went to her, pulling her into a hug. She didn't say anything. There was nothing to say.

Leslie squeezed her tight. "Thank you," she whispered.

Casey nodded and pulled away. "Come sit with Sam." She motioned to the window where Tori stood. "I need to go talk to her."

Leslie squeezed her arm affectionately. "Yes, go. I'm fine."

Casey walked quietly over, standing next to Tori, staring out the same window, wondering if Tori saw anything or was simply lost in her own mind. She stood silently by her, letting Tori feel her presence. Finally, she nudged her shoulder gently. "I love you, you know."

There was a moment of silence, then she heard Tori take a shaky breath. "It's my fault. I really fucked things up."

"No. I'm not going to let you bear the burden of this."

Tori turned away from the window, her eyes swimming in tears. "I'm sorry," she whispered.

Casey moved without thinking, pulling Tori into her arms and holding her tight. She'd never seen Tori cry before, never seen her break down. She doubted anyone had. Not like this, with deep sobs choking her throat. Casey didn't know what to say, so she said what she thought she'd want to hear if it were reversed.

"You did what you had to do. He had a knife. We all thought it was Patrick. Even if you knew it wasn't, you still had to take the shot. I'd have taken the shot too, Tori."

She felt Tori's grip loosen, felt her sobs subside. She finally pulled away.

"Thanks, O'Connor," she said as she wiped her eyes with both hands. "If you tell anyone about this, I'll kill you."

"It's between us."

Tori took a deep breath, then wiped her nose with her hand. "Sikes, man. I just can't believe it. He lost so much blood. I should have never sent him—"

"Stop it right now, Tori. Don't you start second-guessing. You can't control everything. You know that."

"They haven't told us a thing. I mean, what if he's brain-dead or something? Then that's my fault too. I kept him alive."

"Yeah. You kept him alive. That's all I'd ask for you to do for me." She met Tori's eyes. "The rest is up to him. He fell in love. He's got someone waiting for him. He'll fight."

Sam watched them, her eyes filling with tears. Tori was in pain and she wasn't reaching out for her. She was reaching out for Casey. She turned to Leslie.

"Casey's being the sister." She wiped at her eyes and smiled. "I love her, you know. She's special."

"I think so."

"Yeah. Look at her. She's trying to bring Tori back to me. Tori wasn't Tori there for a minute."

"It was…it was terrible, actually," Leslie said. "It all happened so fast. I saw what was happening and I couldn't respond fast enough. But Tori, it was like she processed everything in a millisecond and fired. Before I even realized what had happened, she was on John, trying to stop the bleeding."

Sam nodded. "She has a gift. She…she saved me once from a…a situation." Was *situation* a good word for rape, she wondered? But Tori burst through the door and in the blink of an eye, had taken out every one of them. It was a memory she tried to keep buried, but every so often, it reared its head. Like now. "It was before we were together, you know." She smiled. "We were on the *verge* of being together though. Anyway, she's great in the field. She doesn't hesitate."

"Has there been any news about John?"

"None."

"What about his family?"

"Malone was calling them. They don't live locally, so I have no idea when they'll be here."

"What about this girl he's been seeing?"

"John Sikes has a girl?" Sam laughed quietly. "I don't think he's ever dated anyone twice."

"Yeah. They've been teasing him. Apparently, he's in love."

"We'll need to find out who it is. She'll want to know."

They both looked up as Tori and Casey walked closer. Sam sent a silent thank you to Casey, then stood, moving into Tori's arms.

"I love you," she murmured into Tori's ear.

"I'm sorry. I lost it. And I didn't want you to see me that

way."

"I told you a long time ago that you can't be strong all the time. Let me be strong for you sometimes." She pulled out of her arms and looked at Casey. "But it's a sister thing, right?"

Tori smiled. "Yeah. If I had a sister, I'd want her to be like you, O'Connor."

Sam was surprised at the emotion that crossed Casey's face, surprised at the misting of tears in her eyes. She sometimes forgot that Casey had no family.

"Thanks, Hunter." She cleared her throat. "Make me cry in front of Leslie, why don't you?"

They laughed quietly. The kind of laugh to ease tensions, to lessen the strain of the situation of being in a hospital waiting room…waiting.

Chapter Forty-One

"So you weren't lying when you said you could cook."

Casey looked up from the wok she was hovering over. "I'm not a gourmet, don't get me wrong. But some nights, I just like to play in the kitchen with a glass of wine."

"So fried rice, huh?" She walked closer, refilling Casey's wineglass.

"Fried rice with chicken and shrimp. And a few veggies tossed in to make it semi-healthy." She took a sip of wine and smiled. "Thanks."

Leslie pulled out a chair at the small table and sat down, watching her. It had been an emotional few days, but they hadn't really had time to reconcile everything. Technically, their case was still open. Patrick was not in custody. But they'd been crawling all over the Deep Ellum area for three days and nights, and still no sign of Patrick. The few men on the street who would talk to them said they hadn't seen him in days. But it was only when they talked to Sammy that they feared Patrick had left town.

He ain't been around, the bastard. Poor John. I can't believe he's dead.

John Doe. As ironic as his name, that's how he'll be buried. There was no one to claim his body.

"Hey."

Leslie looked up.

"You ready to talk about it?"

Leslie shrugged. "It's just a tragic situation. I keep thinking, what if it had been me and you there instead of Tori and Sikes. I'd have taken the shot, yes. That's not a question. But could I live with myself? John was an innocent pawn in all this. Patrick used him at will, from wearing the dress, to dying his hair, to taking a knife to Sikes. He was innocent, all the way to the end. And now we have no hope of finding Patrick. He's slithered off to another city, no doubt."

"Most likely, yeah."

"So what did we accomplish? We have three women dead. An innocent, simple-minded boy dead. And John Sikes lying in a hospital bed, damn lucky to be alive. What did we accomplish?" Leslie stood. "And don't say he's off the streets here in Dallas. So what? So he moves on? There's now another city that's not safe."

"We did the best we could, Les. Like I said many times, he was like a damn ghost." Casey moved the wok to a cool burner and turned, facing her. "How do you think I feel? I had the bastard right in my hands, and I let him go. I should have known it wasn't John."

"They were playing a game. How could you know?"

"Because I *did* realize it," she said. "Before we heard the shots, I knew it wasn't John."

Leslie frowned.

"When I finally caught him, he kept saying *don't hurt me, don't hurt me*. And I'm like, I'm not going to hurt you. We've never hurt John. So I left him with one of the officers, told him to put John in the patrol car. And when I was going to go after you, it hit me. John never said *don't hurt me*." She tilted her head. "What did John always say to me?"

"*Don't tie me up, Miss Casey.*"

"Exactly. So I went running back. But he'd gotten out of the car and was gone. Then we heard the shots. And I knew it was too late."

Leslie walked closer and wrapped her arms around Casey's

233

shoulders, pulling her close. Casey was suffering too. She'd been too caught up in her own misgivings, too worried about Sikes, to realize that Casey felt partly to blame as well.

"There are so many variables in this case, aren't there?" She kissed her softly on the mouth. "Tori feels responsible because she sent Sikes in. She's taking the blame for killing John and not Patrick. You feel like it's your fault because you had Patrick and you didn't know it. And I feel like it's my fault too. We saw them together—one in a dress, one in pants. I was so sure that Patrick was the one in the dress. *So* sure." Her arms slipped away from Casey and she picked up her wineglass again. "The break this weekend comes at a good time. I think we all need it. Tori especially."

"Yeah. And you'll love being on the boat. Sleeping is wonderful. It's cool out. The motion of the water just relaxes you. It'll be great."

She smiled. "Sleeping, huh?"

Casey wiggled her eyebrows and grinned. "I think Sam is looking forward to you being there. She likes you. And Tori and I tend to get absorbed in fishing."

"I like her too. It'll be good to spend time with them. I'm looking forward to getting to know them as well as you do." She put her glass down. "I'm going to shower before dinner. Okay?"

"Sure, go ahead. I've got to warm the egg rolls yet."

She stopped at the door and turned back around. "Casey?"

"Hmm?"

"I…I really…like you a lot." She mentally rolled her eyes. *Like?* No, she was in love with her. But telling her in the kitchen while she cooked Chinese food didn't seem like the perfect moment.

Casey smiled and nodded. "Yeah. I like you too."

Leslie laughed. "Yeah."

But in the living room, her smile faded as she looked out the window to the lake and saw a face staring back at her. She gasped, unable to stop the startled scream. Then Casey was behind her.

"What is it?"

Leslie shook her head. "I thought …I thought I saw someone

outside," she said as she held her hand over her chest, embarrassed by her racing heart.

"Let me check it out."

Leslie grabbed her arm to stop her. "No, no. It was nothing. Just my imagination, I'm sure." *Wasn't it?* She made herself walk to the window, her eyes darting in every direction. There was no one out there.

"You sure?"

"Yeah. I'm sure." But her eyes bounced off every window, suddenly wishing Casey had drapes to hide the view of the lake.

Patrick? Was he out there?

Don't be silly.

But still.

"Casey?"

"Yeah?"

"Shower with me?"

Publications from
Bella Books, Inc.
The best in contemporary lesbian fiction

P.O. Box 10543, Tallahassee, FL 32302
Phone: 800-729-4992
www.bellabooks.com

WITHOUT WARNING: Book one in the Shaken series by KG MacGregor. *Without Warning* is the story of their courageous journey through adversity, and their promise of steadfast love.
ISBN: 978-1-59493-120-8
$13.95

THE CANDIDATE by Tracey Richardson. Presidential candidate Jane Kincaid had always expected the road to the White House would exact a high personal toll. She just never knew how high until forced to choose between her heart and her political destiny.
ISBN: 978-1-59493-133-8
$13.95

TALL IN THE SADDLE by Karin Kallmaker, Barbara Johnson, Therese Szymanski and Julia Watts. The playful quartet that penned the acclaimed *Once Upon A Dyke* and *Stake Through the Heart* are back and now turning to the Wild (and Very Hot) West to bring you another collection of erotically charged, action-packed, tales.
ISBN: 978-1-59493-106-2
$15.95

IN THE NAME OF THE FATHER by Gerri Hill. In this highly anticipated sequel to *Hunter's Way*, Dallas Homicide Detectives Tori Hunter and Samantha Kennedy investigate the murder of a Catholic priest who is found naked and strangled to death.
ISBN: 978-1-59493-108-6
$13.95

IT'S ALL SMOKE AND MIRRORS: The First Chronicles of Shawn Donnelly by Therese Szymanski. Join Therese Szymanski as she takes a walk on the sillier side of the gritty crime scene detective novel and introduces readers to her newest alternate personality—Shawn Donnelly.
ISBN: 978-1-59493-117-8
$13.95

THE ROAD HOME by Frankie J. Jones. As Lynn finds herself in one adventure after another, she discovers that true wealth may have very little to do with money after all.
ISBN: 978-1-59493-110-9
$13.95

IN DEEP WATERS: CRUISING THE SEAS by Karin Kallmaker and Radclyffe. Book passage on a deliciously sensual Mediterranean cruise with tour guides Radclyffe and Karin Kallmaker.
ISBN: 978-1-59493-111-6
$15.95

ALL THAT GLITTERS by Peggy J. Herring. Life is good for retired army colonel Marcel Robicheaux. Marcel is unprepared for the turn her life will take. She soon finds herself in the pursuit of a lifetime—searching for her missing mother and lover.
 ISBN: 978-1-59493-107-9
$13.95

OUT OF LOVE by KG MacGregor. For Carmen Delallo and Judith O'Shea, falling in love proves to be the easy part.
ISBN: 978-1-59493-105-5
$13.95

BORDERLINE by Terri Breneman. Assistant Prosecuting attorney Toni Barston returns in the sequel to *Anticipation*.
ISBN: 978-1-59493-99-7
$13.95

PAST REMEMBERING by Lyn Denison. What would it take to melt Peri's cool exterior? Any involvement on Asha's part would be simply asking for trouble and heartache...wouldn't it?
ISBN: 978-1-59493-103-1
$13.95

ASPEN'S EMBERS by Diane Tremain Braund. Will Aspen choose the woman she loves...or the forest she hopes to preserve...
ISBN: 978-1-59493-102-4
$14.95

THE COTTAGE by Gerri Hill. The Cottage is the heartbreaking story of two women who meet by chance . . . or did they? A love so destined it couldn't be denied . . . stolen moments to be cherished forever.
ISBN: 978-1-59493-096-6
$13.95

FANTASY: Untrue Stories of Lesbian Passion edited by Barbara Johnson and Therese Szymanski. Lie back and let Bella's bad girls take you on an erotic journey through the greatest bedtime stories never told.
ISBN: 978-1-59493-101-7
$15.95

SISTERS' FLIGHT by Jeanne G'Fellers. *Sisters' Flight* is the highly anticipated sequel to *No Sister of Mine* and *Sister Lost Sister Found*.
ISBN: 978-1-59493-116-1
$13.95

BRAGGIN' RIGHTS by Kenna White. Taylor Fleming is a thirty-six-year-old Texas rancher who covets her independence. She finds her cowgirl independence tested by neighboring rancher Jen Holland.
ISBN: 978-1-59493-095-9
$13.95

BRILLIANT by Ann Roberts. Respected sociology professor, Diane Cole finds her views on love challenged by her own heart, as she fights the attraction she feels for a woman half her age.
ISBN: 978-1-59493-115-4
$13.95

THE EDUCATION OF ELLIE by Jackie Calhoun. When Ellie sees her childhood friend for the first time in thirty years she is tempted to resume their long lost friendship. But with the years come a lot of baggage and the two women struggle with who they are now while fighting the painful memories of their first parting. Will they be able to move past their history to start again?
ISBN 978-1-59493-092-8
$13.95

DATE NIGHT CLUB by Saxon Bennett. *Date Night Club* is a dark romantic comedy about the pitfalls of dating in your thirties...
ISBN 978-1-59493-094-2
$13.95

PLEASE FORGIVE ME by Megan Carter. Laurel Becker is on the verge of losing the two most important things in her life—her current lover, Elaine Alexander, and the Lavender Page bookstore. Will Elaine and Laurel manage to work through their misunderstandings and rebuild their life together?
ISBN 978-1-59493-091-1
$13.95

WHISKEY AND OAK LEAVES by Jaime Clevenger. Meg meets June, a single woman running a horse ranch in the California Sierra foothills. The two become quick friends and it isn't long before Meg is looking for more than just a friendship. But June has no interest in developing a deeper relationship with Meg. She is, after all, not the least bit interested in women...or is she? Neither of these two women is prepared for what lies ahead...
ISBN 978-1-59493-093-5
$13.95

SUMTER POINT by KG MacGregor. As Audie surrenders her heart to Beth, she begins to distance herself from the reckless habits of her youth. Just as they're ready to meet in the middle, their future is thrown into doubt by a duty Beth can't ignore. It all comes to a head on the river at Sumter Point.
ISBN 978-1-59493-089-8
$13.95

THE TARGET by Gerri Hill. Sara Michaels is the daughter of a prominent senator who has been receiving death threats against his family. In an effort to protect Sara, the FBI recruits homicide detective Jaime Hutchinson to secretly provide the protection they are so certain Sara will need. Will Sara finally figure out who is behind the death threats? And will Jaime realize the truth—and be able to save Sara before it's too late?
ISBN 978-1-59493-082-9
$13.95

REALITY BYTES by Jane Frances. In this sequel to *Reunion*, follow the lives of four friends in a romantic tale that spans the globe and proves that you can cross the whole of cyberspace only to find love a few suburbs away...
ISBN 978-1-59493-079-9
$13.95

MURDER CAME SECOND by Jessica Thomas Broadway's bad-boy genius, Paul Carlucci, has chosen *Hamlet* for his latest production. To the delight of some and despair of others, he has selected Provincetown's amphitheatre for his opening gala. But suddenly Alex Peres realizes that the wrong people are falling down. And the moaning is all to realistic. Someone must not be shooting blanks...
ISBN 978-1-59493-081-2
$13.95

SKIN DEEP by Kenna White. Jordan Griffin has been given a new assignment: Track down and interview one-time nationally renowned broadcast journalist Reece McAllister. Much to her surprise, Jordan comes away with far more than just a story...
ISBN: 978-1-59493-78-2
$13.95

FINDERS KEEPERS by Karin Kallmaker. *Finders Keepers*, the quest for the perfect mate in the 21st Century, joins Karin Kallmaker's *Just Like That* and her other incomparable novels about lesbian love, lust and laughter.
ISBN: 1-59493-072-4
$13.95

OUT OF THE FIRE by Beth Moore. Author Ann Covington feels at the top of the world when told her book is being made into a movie. Then in walks Casey Duncan the actress who is playing the lead in her movie. Will Casey turn Ann's world upside down?
ISBN: 1-59493-088-0
$13.95

STAKE THROUGH THE HEART by Karin Kallmaker, Julia Watts, Barbara Johnson and Therese Szymanski. The playful quartet that penned the acclaimed *Once Upon A Dyke* are dimming the lights for journeys into worlds of breathless seduction.
ISBN: 1-59493-071-6
$15.95

THE HOUSE ON SANDSTONE by KG MacGregor. Carly Griffin returns home to Leland and finds that her old high school friend Justine is awakening more than just old memories.
ISBN: 1-59493-076-7
$13.95

THE FEEL OF FOREVER by Lyn Denison. Felicity Devon soon discovers that she isn't quite sure what she fears the most—that Bailey, the woman who broke her heart and who is back in town will want to pick up where they left off...or that she won't...
ISBN: 978-1-59493-073-7
$13.95

WILD NIGHTS (Mostly True Stories of Women Loving Women) Stories edited by Therese Szymanksi. Therese Szymanski is back, editing a collection of erotic short stories from your favorite authors...
ISBN: 1-59493-069-4
$15.95

COYOTE SKY by Gerri Hill. Sheriff Lee Foxx is trying to cope with the realization that she has fallen in love for the first time. And fallen for author Kate Winters, who is technically unavailable. Will Lee fight to keep Kate in Coyote?
ISBN: 1-59493-065-1
$13.95

VOICES OF THE HEART by Frankie J. Jones. A series of events force Erin to swear off love as she tries to break away from the woman of her dreams. Will Erin ever find the key to her future happiness?
ISBN: 1-59493-068-6
$13.95

SHELTER FROM THE STORM by Peggy J. Herring. *Shelter from the Storm* is a story about family and getting reacquainted with one's past. Sometimes you don't appreciate what you have until you almost lose it.
ISBN 1-59493-064-3
$13.95

BENEATH THE WILLOW by Kenna White. A torch that even after twenty-five years still burns brightly threatens to consume two childhood friends.
ISBN 1-59493-051-1
$13.95

THE WEEKEND VISITOR by Jessica Thomas. In this latest Alex Peres mystery, Alex is asked to investigate an assault on a local woman but finds that her client may have more secrets than she lets on.
ISBN 1-59493-054-6
$13.95

ANTICIPATON by Terri Breneman. Two women struggle to remain professional as they work together to find a serial killer.
ISBN 1-59493-055-4
$13.95

OBSESSION by Jackie Calhoun. Lindsey Stuart Brown's life is turned upside down when Sarah Gilbert comes into the family nursery in search of perennials.
ISBN 1-59493-058-9
$13.95

18th & CASTRO by Karin Kallmaker. First-time couplings and couples who know how to mix lust and love make *18th & Castro* the hottest address in the city by the bay.
ISBN 1-59493-066-X
$13.95

JUST THIS ONCE by KG MacGregor. Ever mindful of the obligations back home that she must honor, Wynne Connelly struggles to resist the fascination and allure that a particular woman she meets on her business trip represents...
ISBN 1-59493-087-2
$13.95

PAID IN FULL by Ann Roberts. Ari Adams will need to choose
between the debts of the past and the promise of a happy future.
ISBN 1-59493-059-7
$13.95

END OF WATCH by Clare Baxter. LAPD Lieutenant L.A. Franco
follows the lone clue down the unlit steps of memory to a final,
unthinkable resolution.
ISBN 1-59493-064-4
$13.95